Embers of Home

Janice Walker

Author: Janice Walker

First published in 2014 by Erin Rose Publishing

Design: Julie Anson

ISBN: 978-0-9928232-1-4

A CIP record for this book is available from the British Library.

An Erin Rose Publication

This novel is a work of fiction. Names and characters are the product of the author's imagination and any resemblance to actual persons, living or dead, is entirely coincidental.

Other books by Janice Walker

THE BIG SPRUCE SERIES

BOOK 1
The Lights of Home
ISBN: 978-0-9928232-0-7

BOOK 2
Embers of Home
ISBN: 978-0-9928232-1-4

BOOK 3
Forever Home
ISBN: 978-0-9928232-2-1

Dedication

For their love, support and constant enthusiasm, I dedicate this book to Elizabeth and Bobby. I'm forever grateful.

Acknowledgements

Thank you to 'the girls,' every single one of you.
A special thanks to the amazing Alison McNicol,
for being an inspiration and making the dream come true.

To Nancy, Joanne and Al, for years of friendship,
memories and especially the material! Thanks.

1

I'd been looking forward to this, but now I'm not sure I can rise. We lie with our heads touching like conjoined twins. I slide my hand toward him.

"Wouldn't you love to wake up like this every morning?" asks Shasta, slowly stirring beside me. I smile lazily back at him. Is he hinting that I move in? My slumbering commitment-phobia stirs. Old habits die hard.

"Come on. It's nearly sunrise."

"It can't be that time already," I groan, but the darkness in the airy bedroom of the lake house is subsiding. The sunrise is nearly here and there is a twist in the air today. The heady, bright, summer feel has given way to a nippy chill, and even the morning light has a yellow shade as late summer faces the approaching fall.

I pull my sweater closer to me and we wander to the lakeshore where light breaks through the eastern sky. Swathes of pink and orange stretch out above the horizon, reflecting in the still water of the lake. I used to dream of waking in the sanctuary of a place like this.

"Any regrets?"

"Yeah. That we didn't go to sleep earlier."

Shasta's dark eyes narrow and sparkle. "About leaving New York?"

"How could I regret being here?"

I'd wrestled with the decision to stay in Big Spruce or to return to the rat race of New York. Looking back now it seems inevitable that I would quit my job as a lawyer, but I didn't change direction without a fight. I'm so besotted with Shasta that he fills most of my thoughts; when I say he fills most of my thoughts, I'm thinking, now what do

I do? To make sure this works I need to decide what to do with my time here. I need a new job but I've no desire to return to law. I want something with more feel good factor.

After greeting the dawn, we wander back to the house to the comforting and invigorating aroma of fresh coffee. It reminds me how much I enjoy the ritual of coffee and chatter, and prompts me to think about Giselle's idea to take over a thriving local coffee shop, which doubles as a bookstore. It's a huge swing in direction, but the idea is becoming increasingly appealing.

Giselle is on the cusp of resigning from her job in New York and she's just waiting for the right excuse to jump ship. The irony is that Giselle once told me that she didn't think Big Spruce was enough for me. Now she has fallen under the same spell. There's something raw and dynamic about the mountain town which makes you feel like you can survive on love and beauty alone. The tranquillity is so soothing and uplifting that it strokes away the wrinkles in the soul. You almost don't want to leave.

That's not to say I don't think about my other life. I hadn't really had a chance to soften the parting ties, say formal goodbyes and officially leave – that chapter seemed to have closed naturally, albeit suddenly. I've settled into the mellow country way and adapted to the change of pace, but the contradiction is that I still catch myself trying to find top gear which I was permanently in back in NYC.

Fast pace had been a well worn groove, but staying in Big Spruce had been the right decision. If I need to, I could dip my toe back in my old life for a weekend, and knowing that I have choices, I don't feel backed into a corner. So, mentally that door is ajar, which is comforting, but my life is here now, with the man I'd fallen so deeply and irreversibly in love with. Life is good, but it would be better if my friends were closer. I miss their wisecracks, their boisterous banter and their solid union.

Simon is back in New York, while I'm happy to say that Giselle has been overturning every stone in Big Spruce, to try and come up with a new avenue to explore. She has completely fallen in love with the place.

It sounds selfish, but I want to help her settle here permanently and maybe in time we could persuade Simon to venture out too, although that could be a harder task. Giselle is much more of a risk taker. She has moved so many times that relocating is no obstacle, and it's just a fresh new challenge to her. Her family live in New York, but they're very much for living without attachments and expectations of each other – their motto is live free and dream big.

Giselle's dream had been to open a bookstore, but with huge rent and stiff competition in New York it had been out of reach. She used to talk of it when she was sick of work, which was pretty frequently, and she would ponder how she could raise the funds and put together a business plan, but no strategy seemed viable.

However here in the lakeside mountain town she already felt at home. She had met some of the locals and adapted to the vibe; for Giselle moving here was a promising and exciting option. Her dream could become a reality. The idea of opening a coffee shop-come-bookstore could really work for both of us. We get to be near each other and she gets her dream job. The only cloud on the horizon is that it could be a test of our friendship to be in business together, but I reckon we could pull it off. Giselle's enthusiasm is extreme, while I'm the one to think carefully and maybe overcook an idea – but I'm also prone to impetuous decisions when my instincts override my mind.

I've talked it through with Shasta; he's all for the venture, although he did put the ball back in my court and asked me what I wanted. He's knows I don't take kindly to being told what to do.

"You've got my support whatever you decide," he said last night. Actually, they were just the words I wanted to hear. Since the death of Aunt Rosa, who I found out too late was my biological mother, I'm financially secure, but her loss shook me to the roots. I feel her presence often and miss her even more. Having him quietly alongside gives me strength. I'd like to think I don't need him. I'd like to think I can do everything for myself, but despite being independent I sometimes feel like a green shoot, making my own way but needing something to support me.

"I've work to do," says Shasta as he strides through the kitchen, scooping me up towards him and we share a lingering kiss.

"I'm leaving now, too," I reply, relishing the feel of his hair against my cheek, wondering how the hell I managed to find and land him. I guess I did something great in a previous life.

"It's a good business and you want a new project."

"But what if-"

"Don't over-think it. She wants a quick sale. Someone else will bite her hand off."

"I love you."

"I know you do."

He grins and throws me over his shoulder before he carries me out to my car, laughing and shouting.

"See you tonight."

"Nothing could stop me," he replies with that broad, throwaway smile over his shoulder. He heads off to the corral where Penny, the blind palomino, is tethered and ready to be lunged. I watch for a few moments while he tenderly harnesses her. She is trusting and pliable – putty in his hands. Maybe he has that effect on all women. As I drive off, Shasta is already fully focused on what he's doing. I can't imagine anyone riding the sightless horse, but Shasta has a different idea. He thinks she wants more to her life than quietly living out her days in pasture.

Everything is coming together, and on the drive back to my house I make my decision. I walk in and I'm greeted by Hudson lolloping over, and the sound of Giselle singing at the top of her voice, and out of key, in the shower - she couldn't care less. *God, she makes me laugh.*

"Giselle!" I call, when I hear the water turn off.

"You're home." She throws open the bathroom door, appearing clad in a towel and a puff of steam.

"Let's do it!" I grin from ear to ear.

She only takes a couple of seconds to catch on. "The bookshop?"

"And coffeehouse."

Giselle starts to scream and we both jump up and down like a couple of teenage cheerleaders, hugging with excitement.

"Whoops!" says Giselle, scrambling to catch her falling towel before it hits the floor.

"I just hope no-one else beats us to it! I'll ring her now."

"Ha! It's just as well that I've already arranged to meet Elizabeth at the store this morning."

"That was quick off the mark."

"Tara, I want this so much. If I couldn't do it with you, I was going to try and raise the capital on my own."

"Now you won't have to."

"Oh God. This is amazing. You won't regret it. I'll just fling some clothes on," says Giselle, before disappearing into her bedroom. "We'll make a great team," she shouts as she clatters around while I go down to the kitchen.

I stuff my hand in a box of granola and chomp happily away, while perched on the edge of the Aga, warming my backside, thinking about what we can call the coffee shop. *Rosa's Kitchen* springs to mind. Nope. It needs to include the bookshop somehow. The radio is mumbling away in the background.

'The body of a man found at the foot of a ravine off the Fort Jarvis highway has not yet been formally identified, but it's understood he is not local. It's believed the body had been there for some time and was connected to the wildfire which started in a garage on the highway. Investigations are continuing. Anyone with any information is being urged to come forward.'

"Anthony's garage!" *Shit.* I lunge at the radio to turn it up, but the news bulletin continues onto something else instead.

"What?" Giselle appears. Her auburn hair is damp but she's fully dressed in a pair of jeans, white t-shirt and black waistcoat.

"A body has been found at the ravine near Anthony's garage."

"Whose?"

"They don't know – but it's connected with the fire."

"Maybe whoever it is started the fire. We now know your brother didn't set fire to his own garage."

"He was lucky that Shasta and James pulled him out when they did."

"Shasta and James didn't find anyone else there, did they?" asks Giselle.

I shake my head, as images of a charred decomposed body are conjured up – but who did it belong to? I remember the terror I had felt when I thought that Shasta had been caught up in the inferno and I shudder. It wasn't him, but sadly it had happened to someone else. Something else occurs to me.

"Maybe this person *did* start the fire?"

"Or maybe he was a hiker who just got caught up in it?"

"That's more likely."

"Don't let it piss on your chips," Giselle bounces back. "We've got a business to buy."

"Piss on your chips?"

"It's an English expression I picked up at boarding school. It means don't let it rain on your French fries, so to speak."

"No chance. By tonight we'll be celebrating."

We drive into town, exuberant with ideas, as though buying the coffeehouse is a done-deal because in our heads it is. Elizabeth, the current owner, wants to sell it as a going concern, and quickly. She wants to follow her husband down to Florida before he enjoys life without her too much.

From the outside it's difficult to tell what type of shop the wooden building is. The steps up from the street lead to a decked area, which would lend itself well to having small tables and chairs for the outdoor coffee drinkers. I have butterflies in my stomach as we walk in. I'm imagining this relaxing cosy nook with its heavenly smells as being ours, and with a glance at Giselle's glittering eyes I know she's thinking the same. We stifle grins behind serious faces, not wanting to seem too keen just yet.

The store is a good size and it's warm and inviting. There are rows of tall bookshelves on every wall, not hugely stocked; only a few books in each one, wooden tables nestled against the walls and a couple of comfy dark red sofas. When you sit down the book titles are at eye-level, which is an incentive to browse before you buy. Elizabeth is standing at a table laughing with a customer. She's well established and will be missed. Hopefully a fall-off in customers would only be temporary. I imagine myself and Giselle here instead. We could keep the atmosphere and give it our own flavor too.

Elizabeth leads us through to the quiet of the library room to discuss the details of the sale. We sit on the low couch at the window beside the fireplace. If the fire was lit, the cosiness would be even better. It's clear from the way she talks about her regulars, and the business, that she loves the place as though it was her own child, but she's also ready to go.

"It's time for me to leave the nest," Elizabeth points out. "I just want it in good hands to keep it ticking over. My old bones won't stand another harsh mountain winter," she says, rubbing her wrists.

"We could start mucking in today," I suggest. "It would make it a nice seamless handover."

Giselle's pretty green eyes are bulging - she can barely contain herself.

"You can show us the ropes and we'll blend in like part of the furniture," says Giselle.

"You aren't ever going to blend in," I laugh at my beautiful fiery friend.

"You two are what this place needs," says Elizabeth, eyeing Giselle and I carefully.

We go through the paperwork, the lease, what is included and arrange for the money to be transferred on handover at the end of the week.

"Are we all agreed?" I ask Giselle and Elizabeth. By now I'm fit to burst with happiness but I keep it business-like on the outside.

"Agreed," says Giselle eagerly, her already pink complexion is growing more ruddy.

"This is all happening so suddenly," mutters Elizabeth, nervously looking around. *Don't be having second thoughts now.* I'm willing her to sign on the dotted line. I have now set my heart on this place.

"Agreed," nods Elizabeth with a trace of sadness.

I breathe out through my teeth.

Giselle high-fives Elizabeth, who responds awkwardly. I shake hands with her to seal the deal, Giselle does a double take and shakes on it too. A crash from behind the counter signals a calamity and Elizabeth goes to see what has happened, leaving Giselle and I alone. We go temporarily insane with excitement, then become serious again as we follow Elizabeth into the main part of the shop.

"Grab an apron. I'll show you the ropes," says Elizabeth, not wasting any time as she puts us to work. She introduces us to Sophie, who does all the baking for the coffee shop and helps out behind the counter.

"Good job someone can cook," says Giselle to Sophie. "I didn't think about that," Giselle whispers to me.

"You muppet."

"Did you?"

"I've got all Aunt Rosa's old recipes."

Sophie looks at us in horror.

"Oh no. I don't mean...we need you of course." I reassure her.

"No, no. We wouldn't dream of doing the baking," says Giselle, who then turns away and pulls a face at me for being tactless. Sophie looks reassured and goes about serving the next customer a slab of Dutch apple cake with cream, promising the man that it'll put meat on his bones. Elizabeth shows us around the store room and we do a quick inventory. Giselle tugs open box after box of books which have never found a home on any shelf.

"You'll probably want to throw those away. They're just second hand books. They've no re-sale value, but they're of local interest. I didn't have the heart to get rid of them," says Elizabeth.

Giselle silently rifles through the box, clearly interested in the contents. "Some of these are really old," she mutters.

"Yep, and they smell really bad," says Elizabeth, contorting her face and holding her nose. "There's a couple about Big Spruce's history and gold fever."

"Gold fever?"

"In the olden days they believed there was more gold here than anywhere else in the U.S. I don't know how that one got started, but it was never found. It brought some families to their knees apparently."

Giselle snaps a book shut and a cloud of dust shoots out.

"I'll find a use for these," she replies, closing the lid before we head downstairs.

Back behind the counter, which is laid out with cakes and cookies, there is a lull in customers. Elizabeth helps herself to a slice of coffee and walnut cake and flicks the music over to the radio, but before she has the chance to have a proper break the door opens.

"Pastor Shimlow. I haven't seen you for a couple of days. The usual?" asks Elizabeth, swallowing a mouthful and wiping crumbs from her chin. I look up to see Cain Shimlow in a predatory, insect like stance.

"You know me so well, Elizabeth. I've not seen you at church recently,"

"No, nor will you. I'm migrating to sunny Florida."

"Oh. That's a surprise," he replies, counting out his coins and leaning in towards Elizabeth with a leer. "Are you closing the coffee shop?"

"You'll still get your caffeine fix. Tara and Giselle are taking over," announces Elizabeth, pointing to us. Cain Shimlow's eyes glaze over at the sight of me. His face fixes into an imperceptible concrete mask. Only his thin lips twist into a tight narrow slit on his face.

"You'll have a lot to live up to." His words suggest joviality; his voice is laced with contempt.

"We'll manage," I reply and give him a happy smile that equally lacks sincerity.

"I'll spit in his coffee," mutters Giselle from behind her hand. I nudge her leg and she waves over at him with a cheery smile. "We can all play that game," she mutters. The news comes on the radio and Cain lifts his finger to his lips, hushing Elizabeth to be quiet. He listens intently and for the second time today I hear about the body found in the ravine.

"Make that coffee to go," snaps Cain.

"You're not staying?" asks Elizabeth.

He looks over at us, skewering me with his steely stare. "I have business to attend to." His response is low and toneless. He grasps the paper cup and hastily leaves without another word, banging the door behind him. Elizabeth and Sophie raise their eyebrows at each other. I get the feeling that Cain Shimlow won't be one of the regulars when Giselle and I take over.

2

Giselle has a radiant glow about her when we close the store for the day, and we link arms as we make our way to the car, exhausted but thrilled to have found this little gem of a business.

"It's all been so easy," I remark.

"Don't you even think about what's going to go wrong," says Giselle pre-empting me with a waggling finger.

"It never crossed my mind." It did, but I pretend to be surprised by her accusation. I can't wait to see Shasta and share the news. Once back at the house Giselle checks her watch and picks up the phone.

"I have just one more thing to take care of."

"You're going to hand in your notice?"

She points to her nose. "You got it."

"You're calling Patricia? Wouldn't you be better putting it in writing?"

"I'm a temp. I don't have to give notice, but I do want to hear her voice when I tell her I'm not coming back."

"I can understand that, but don't expect her to cling to your coat and beg you to stay. Shasta will be here soon. I'll go open the bottle of fizz while you make the call." Shasta walks through the door just as the cork pops and hits the ceiling.

"You got it," he takes my hand and pulls me towards him. My heart thuds in double-quick time, his effect on me hasn't subsided in the least.

"How did you know? Was it that psychic connection?" I ask, thinking how tuned in we've become that he can throw thoughts into my mind and vice verse. Although I hope some of my thoughts don't get through.

"No. It was the grin and the champagne," he replies, and we kiss until Giselle comes in, looking slightly deflated.

"I didn't get to speak to Patricia, so I left a message with her underling," says Giselle. "She'll steal my thunder, but onwards and upwards."

"Here's to the coffeehouse and bookshop," I toast.

"To books," says Giselle

"And beans."

We take a swig of champagne, look at each other simultaneously and swallow it quickly before we choke.

"The name of the shop," says Giselle.

"That's it! To *The Book and Bean.*"

"God bless her, and all who sail in her," Giselle raises her glass.

"You'll be smashing that glass next," says Shasta.

"I must tell Simon," says Giselle, pressing buttons on her cell phone before putting it on speaker and placing it in the middle of the pine kitchen table. Simon picks up the phone in a professional but hushed voice. The shuffling noise suggests he's moving to somewhere that he can speak properly.

"That's better. I'm in the washroom. You could cut the tension here with a knife today. When are you coming back? I miss you," Simon asks.

"That's why I'm ringing. I've got some good news. I'm not!"

There is silence from Simon's end.

"I've just resigned. Tara and I have only gone and bought a business. Simon?"

There is a pause.

"Unfuckingbelievable!"

"Do you mean that in a good way?" I ask.

“In a ‘that is the last straw’ way!” Simon’s voice has risen. “You’re really not coming back?”

“Umm, no,” replies Giselle, and the realization of how it will affect him dawns.

“I’m not staying in this God forsaken hell hole on my own,” Simon rants.

In our excitement we didn’t even consider how Giselle’s leaving would affect him. He has gone from having his two best friends working alongside him, to both of them relocating to the other side of America.

“Simon, you know you are welcome here. I don’t even need to say that.” I put my head in my hands and try to appease him.

“Just as well – make a bed up for me. I’m leaving. I’ve had enough!” There is more shuffling and this time his voice is not as hushed.

“Simon what are you doing?” Giselle asks, her eyes growing round.

“Typing my resignation!”

“Don’t be ridiculous. Think this through,” I tell him, but I’m barely able to get the words out because I’m choking back laughter. Giselle has her hand clamped over her mouth.

“I need two hands to type!” he snaps, then abruptly rings off.

“Look what you started,” says Shasta, who is lounging casually with his back against the wall, looking subtly amused. I bite my lip and look at him, not sure what impression this is giving of me. We’ve not known each other that long and I like to think of myself as drama-free - I can’t say the same for my friends. Giselle is looking at me for a reaction, but I know that pensive look, and it means laughter is about to explode.

"What the hell. There's room for one more!" I reply, and throw my hands in the air. Giselle's repressed giggle escapes. She triggers me off. I couldn't be happier that Simon is coming – though at this point I'm not sure whether to believe it or not. Once Simon has cooled off it could be a different story.

"You seriously wouldn't mind?" asks Giselle.

"The house is plenty big enough, but there goes the neighborhood." I'm thinking of Errol and Pandora next door and Simon's divisive romantic intentions towards their son.

"To the three amigos," says Giselle, merrily swigging champagne.

"Did you hear that? Someone's at the door," says Shasta.

"I didn't hear anything."

Shasta goes to answer the door. I place my chin in my hands and watch, mesmerized at his lean graceful physique, and the way his soft, worn, jeans skim over his backside, creating a neat round shape as he walks. I could never get tired of that sight. Giselle carries on talking and a few seconds pass before I notice the feeling of uneasiness. I strain to hear the voices at the door. They sound too abrupt. Something is wrong. I jump up and run to the door; where there are two policemen. They are about to take Shasta away.

"You're too early for April Fool's, guys," says Shasta.

"This is no joke, Mr. King. We want to talk to you about a murder."

The blood runs cold in my veins, creeping icily around my temples, as I remember the discovery of a body today.

"What? Whose?" he asks, anchoring himself to the porch steps.

"That is what we are trying to establish, but Mr. Buchanan isn't in a position to formally identify himself."

"Buchanan? Jesus Christ. Tray Buchanan?" I can hardly breathe. One of the officers grabs Shasta's arm but he shakes it off as though it were a fly.

"Get your hands off me. I'm coming. I've nothing to hide." Shasta looks over his shoulder and flicks the hair from his face. "I'll be back in no time," he shouts, but I hear the doubt in his voice - I know he doesn't believe that.

Giselle rakes her hands through her hair while I stand frozen and motionless. I watch, horrified as they take him away. His raw power is diminished by his capture. I start running through the events and scenarios in my mind - it doesn't look good. Shasta pulled my brother from a suspicious fire. Now the body of someone who has been plotting to acquire native land from Shasta's people, and who had a bizarre, tenuous history with his girlfriend, turns up dead. Tray could easily be perceived as Shasta's enemy. In the eyes of the law it reeks.

3

I walk grimly into the Sheriff's office, looking for answers from the duty officer, but he gives me no information and advises me to go home instead. There's a lot of activity in the building: doors banging and whispered conversations. Through a glass partition I can see people moving around, but I can't see Shasta.

"There's James."

"They must be questioning him too?" replies Giselle. I nod, not wanting to say too much in front of the officer, but James was with Shasta at the time of the fire. James certainly had no vendetta, so that must go in their favor.

"I want to see Barnaby Whitelaw," I tell the duty officer, leaning in to emphasize my point.

"You and everyone else," he replies.

"I want to see my father." I repeat, my voice rising sharply.

"Your father?" he asks. A door squeaks open and I look up hoping it's him, but no-one appears.

"Barnaby Whitelaw IS my father. I need to see him now." I jab my words at him and he blinks unsurely. This is clearly news to him. A door squeaks and I feel like I'm being watched, then someone appears from a side room. I turn and meet the hard grey stare of Cain Shimlow, as he walks out of the interview room with Barnaby behind him. I instantly realize my mistake. Even though we hadn't intended to keep it a secret, the information wasn't supposed to come out like this. Cain looks back at Barnaby, then to me.

"Have you any more skeletons in your closet, Sheriff Whitelaw?" His top lip curls into a snide grin and he moves noiselessly past me. I'll swear that man's feet never touch the ground.

"Tara. Come in." Barnaby motions for me to come behind the desk and I signal to Giselle to wait in the reception. There's a difference in tone between Barnaby, the sheriff, and Barnaby, the man, especially in front of colleagues.

"What was Shimlow doing here?" I ask.

"He was helping with our enquiries. You know I can't give out details."

"But I'm helping you with your enquires. I know, or rather knew, Tray Buchanan. I can give you plenty of information on him, but I also know that Shasta had nothing to do with it."

"I know you mean well but we have to deal with the evidence."

"Why do you think he had something to do with it?"

"We have information that Shasta had a grievance against Tray."

"And that information came from Cain Shimlow?" I ask. Barnaby says nothing, but I know it's true. Shimlow was aware there was antagonism between the people on the Reservation and the syndicate Tray was involved in, and whom I suspect Shimlow was also in bed with.

"The grievance was against Shasta. He has been framed." I look Barnaby straight in the eye, imploring him to believe me.

"Look I understand that you're upset, but we will get to the bottom of this. If Shasta didn't do it then he has nothing to worry about," replies Barnaby.

"He didn't do it. You have to believe me!"

"OK. Then tell me what you know," says Barnaby

softening, but not giving anything away. I explain about being with Tray at the time of the hit-and-run accident in New York, which had been the catalyst for me returning to Big Spruce. I tell him about working for the Buchanan family when I was employed by Sheldon & Napier, and everything else I knew about their business interests in the area. I come clean that Tray had tried to pressurize me to close the deal for the Reservation land and about his links with Cain Shimlow.

"Were you romantically involved with Tray?" he asks.

"No."

Barnaby looks up from his notepad and raises his eyebrows. I can feel my neck start to flush and my eyes automatically drop. I don't want to even suggest there may have been romantic overtones to our business meetings, and I definitely don't want to admit that Tray thought he had feelings for me. It was total bullshit anyway – just an attempt to manipulate me.

"Tray had a reputation."

"I turned him down," I reply.

"Did Shasta know this?"

I hesitate. Lying is an option. "He knew it wasn't an issue and he was fine about it." I look my dad in the eye, daring him to see through me.

"We are waiting for a formal ID of the body. The initial ID suggests it's him, but we can't be sure until forensics have finished. The body is badly burned and it's not in a good state."

I can't help but wince at the visual horrors I get on that. This is the corpse of someone I knew, and although I wasn't his greatest fan I am human. It pales compared to the gut-wrenching nausea I have from the fear of Shasta facing prison. Fate couldn't be this cruel.

"Tara, go home. Please honey. Get some rest. I'll come and see you tomorrow when I get off duty. You look like hell," says Barnaby, standing up and stuffing his shirt into the top of his trousers.

"Thanks."

"I'll call you if there's any news."

"Can I see Shasta, just for a minute?" I ask, but Barnaby shakes his head and makes his way to the door, looking preoccupied.

"Were you aware Tray had a severe nut allergy? He was anaphylactic."

"No. Why?"

"His medical alert bracelet was almost undamaged," says Barnaby.

"I didn't know that," I reply, though that type of thing wasn't likely to come up in our conversations. I turn to give my dad a hug before he opens the door, unsure what the protocol is in the workplace of my recently discovered father, but I could really do with one. He awkwardly hugs me and tells me again to go home and that everything will work be fine. *Why do some people say crap like that when things clearly aren't fine?*

It's some comfort that James is with Shasta in this ordeal. They are straightforward, honest people and it must surely lend credibility that James is ex-military, although I've no idea what he did before he opened the outdoor adventure equipment store. I need to talk to Svetlana, James's partner before I go home.

We drive over to Svetlana's house, where all the lights are on. I'm glad she's still up, although if she's anything like me she's not likely to be sleeping while her man is being questioned for murder. She opens the door red eyed and void of any make-up. I've never seen her look so bare; she's always immaculately turned out. Without a word she throws her arms around Giselle and I. Her body is trembling but she doesn't shed a tear. Svetlana leads us through to the lounge, where a bunch of crumpled white tissues are tucked into the side of the chair. We talk for a while but there doesn't seem to be anything we can say to each other. It's the waiting and imagining all sorts of nasty scenarios which is the worst.

"James has never been in trouble in his life. This whole thing is ridiculous," says Svetlana, for about the fifth time.

"You know how quick they've been to pin things on the Native Americans. I just can't imagine Shasta getting a fair trial."

Svetlana shakes her head. "And after everything James did for his country," she says, angrily clenching her hands.

"Was it the army he was in?" asks Giselle.

She nods. "He was in Iraq for a time," she replies, biting on her fingernail. "He was also part of a controlled, remote-viewing experiment, but I probably shouldn't have told you that."

"Seriously?" asks Giselle, leaning forward on the edge of her seat.

"It was a 'black project', scientifically controlled. It's all been brushed under the carpet now. You aren't supposed to know it existed," says Svetlana, then she goes quiet. Giselle closes her hanging jaw and looks frustrated.

"Don't just stop. How did he get involved in that? Did James have an aptitude for it? Is he psychic?" asks Giselle.

"Perhaps, but he had three years training first," replies

Svetlana. "They were trained to retrieve information and perceptions using their minds. It was a powerful tool."

"James was a psychic spy, employed by the government?" says Giselle to herself, amply impressed.

"Ha. Well, maybe not exactly. Apparently they were employed by investigative agents, not a specific government branch. No-one wanted to risk their reputation. According to James other countries are still using the technique, which explains why they often have the element of surprise."

"Can he still do it?" I ask.

"He doesn't really talk about it. He thinks it unnerves people, even if they did believe him," replies Svetlana.

"That is so cool," says Giselle. "I wish I could do that."

My mind is running away with the possibilities a skill like that would have at the moment, when there is a sound at the front door and Svetlana jumps to her feet. "James?" she calls as she crosses the room.

"It's just me," returns his familiar voice.

"Is Shasta with you?" I'm shaking with expectation as Svetlana throws her arms around James's thickset frame.

"No. They've only released me," says James.

"And?" asks Svetlana desperately.

"Without any charge," replies James.

"So why haven't they released Shasta?" I ask.

"I don't know. I didn't get to speak to him," says James, looking relieved but there's still tension in his voice. "They questioned me briefly then someone came in, asked about the forces and afterwards they said I was free to go," says James dropping onto the sofa, looking pale and exhausted.

"What can we do?" I ask, but James shakes his head. Svetlana sits closely beside him and I take the hint - it's time to leave them. We make our way out to the car. I need time to think. I need to make a plan. Giselle talks but I'm removed from it, because I'm so caught up in my thoughts I'm not even aware of what she's saying.

"I don't like it when you're this quiet," says Giselle.

"I'm thinking."

"Can't you do that out loud?"

"I'm making a plan."

"What are you planning? A jail break?"

"I was thinking about asking Anthony to tell the police he remembers seeing someone hit him at the garage that day, and that it wasn't Shasta."

"But Anthony said that he doesn't remember anything," replies Giselle.

"He could say his memory has come back."

"And lie to the police? For a start you wouldn't get Anthony to agree to that. Jesus Christ, Tara you are desperate."

She's right. I am, but her words don't deter me. I have to find a solution, whatever it takes.

"I need to speak to Michael from the Reservation. Remember he told the police he saw someone leave?"

"You can't go over there tonight. It's far too late."

I check my watch. "I'll go over there first thing in the morning.

"Well, I guess if it makes you feel you're doing something."

As I turn the key in the door a sickening loneliness swells inside me as I come home to what was Rosa's house, compounding the longing for Shasta. It feels like whenever one love enters my life another one leaves. I hug Giselle goodnight and take Hudson up to bed with me.

It's a treat for the big Newfoundland, but I could really use his company right now. I lie in the darkness and lose my hand in the dog's thick black fur as I listen to his rhythmic breathing, racking my brains to think of something I've missed. *OK universe. What am I missing here? I'll do you a deal. (Well people have been known to deal with the devil, so why not?) Help Shasta out here, have him freed and I'll stick to following my destiny. I'll stick to my path, no complaints, no diversions – I'll develop my intuition. I'll do whatever I'm supposed to do here. Just say the word, but please have Shasta freed.*

I listen and wait but nothing comes to me. There is no profound, useful snippet of information which proves that Shasta is innocent. I give up and slowly drowsiness slips over me.

I'm lying awake, thinking, before I even realize I'm awake. It's 6:30 a.m. and it's getting light. I go over every meeting I ever had with Tray, analyzing and trying to remember every microscopic detail. I remember the hasty meeting in Seattle, where I was so late it ended up being a dinner meeting instead. In my mind I see him standing in the office and remember the Breitling watch on his right wrist catching my attention. I don't remember seeing a medical alert bracelet. We had gone to the hotel and had drinks at the bar: a couple of shots and some bar snacks before dinner. The bar snacks: wasabi peas, olives and peanuts. My mind freezes and backtracks over the details. *Peanuts.* Tray had eaten peanuts. They had no effect on him. He didn't have a nut allergy. Tray couldn't have been anaphylactic. I bounce out of bed, through the door and into Giselle's room in seconds.

"Wake up!"

Giselle is lying flat on her back with her mouth open. She stirs, smacks her dry lips and croaks back. "What?"

"Tray wasn't anaphylactic!"

"Verrrry good," she slurs.

"Come on. I've got to go to the Reservation. I've got to see Michael. That body can't be Tray's. On our first meeting he told me a story about how he and his twin brother had pranked girlfriends by pretending to be each other."

Giselle opens one eye at a time and sits up. "Are you sure he has a twin?"

"I'm positive."

I look up Tray Buchanan on my cell phone and press call. It goes straight to voicemail. I find a photograph of Tray and his brother Vaughan on Google and head out to Michael's house on the Reservation. He seems surprised to see me there without Shasta, although he is welcoming - especially when I tell him Shasta is being held for questioning and I need his help.

"You saw a man leaving the garage just before the fire – is this him?" I ask.

"That's him!" says Michael, his dark eyes becoming fiercely determined.

I bring out the second photograph, which is of Vaughan Buchanan: who is facially identical, although his hair longer and lighter.

"Which one?" I ask Michael.

He looks back and forward between the photographs and holds up his hands. "It's the same person."

I shake my head.

"No. They're brothers. But you would be forgiven for

thinking that. Will you come down to that station with us and tell them what you've just told us?"

"Let me put my shoes on," says Michael, his thin frame carries him swiftly onto the porch. The toothy grin above his strong, stubborn chin stretches happily around his face as we make our way to the car and set off for town. When we arrive at the Sheriff's Office a different officer is on duty.

"Can I see Barnaby Whitelaw?"

"You are?"

"Tara North," I reply, though I wonder if he already knows. It's likely that word that Barnaby has a daughter has spread. He calls through to the office.

"He's gone," replies the officer.

I sigh and tell him why we're here.

"Let me find someone else who can help you." He makes another call, and after a few minutes a burly man in uniform appears, looking brusque and efficient. If he's just done the nightshift, you would never know it. I start to introduce myself and he cuts me off.

"I remember you," he says flatly.

My stomach sinks and I stare at him warily.

"You do?" I haven't a clue who he is.

"Last time I saw you, you were considering breaking through a police cordon to get to your boyfriend in the wildfire." The officer's face is difficult to read, but it could be amusement or derision.

He's got me there. I remember the day well. This guy must be a mind reader. "Not me, Officer...?" I pause and wait for him to fill the gap.

"Newman."

"I'd never do such a thing," I tell him, averting my eyes.

"Come in," says Officer Newman, jerking his head to follow as he shows us into a room. "What's this about?" he asks.

Michael and I explain what we know. It transpires that the fact Tray has a twin is not news to them, but the fact that Tray didn't have a nut allergy is. It's definitive surely - the corpse they discovered was wearing a medical alert, which means it is clearly NOT Tray Buchanan.

"The body is being formally identified by a family member," says Newman.

"So Shasta can be released now?" asks Michael ambitiously.

"It improves his case, but we need to look at all the evidence," Newman replies.

"Oh come on," I hear myself argue.

"It doesn't work like that. I'm on your side. After all, you are trying to do my job for me," he replies dryly, but there is a gleam in his eye.

"When will we know?" I ask.

"Not long after I do." Officer Newman crosses the floor and opens the door, dismissing us. I look despondently at him as he turns and is already striding quickly away, leaving the duty officer to show us out. Giselle is waiting and her face slackens when she see's us.

"No?" she asks simply, getting up from her seat. I shake my head.

"We tried," says Michael with an audible sigh and we walk slowly to the door. I'm trying to think of anything else that can be done before we leave. Giselle's looks behind me and her face lights up. I turn around and see Shasta. My spirits soar. Officer Newman appears behind him, levelling the mood.

"The body has been formally identified as Vaughan Buchanan. He's free to go. Just don't leave the country," says Officer Newman giving a wry smile, and I'm not sure if he's joking but he vanishes once more. Shasta looks tired and drawn. I throw my arms around him, pressing against him to make sure he's not an illusion. Fine lines have appeared around his eyes and he's blanched pale behind his tawny skin. My heart contracts for him, but I'm utterly grateful for his freedom. Terrifyingly, I can no longer imagine my future without him.

4

With the warm water bubbling around us, I sit behind him in the hot tub and work my fingers through the knots in his sculpted shoulders. It's starting to get dark and the forest is stirring with a chorus of animals and several pale blue mystical lights dart through the trees. The pinch of the early autumn air is getting stronger and the arrival of winter is already echoing in the breeze. Soon, lounging lazily in the hot tub won't be so attractive. I shudder as the blast of wind from the lake snakes up my spine. I throw off my robe and submerge myself under the blissfully warm water.

"You're so tense. Are you tired?" I whisper, with my lips touching Shasta's ear as I stroke and soothe the taut muscle seam which runs to the base of his neck. The smooth, hollow niche near his clavicle is irresistible and I kiss it longingly because, well for one I can, but also, I can't help myself. I feel like a kid in a sweet shop; he's all mine. We haven't had enough time alone recently. I'd like to rip a couple of pages off the calendar just for us.

"I'm not ready for sleep," he replies, with a slow easy grin and that sideways look with those alert dark eyes, sparkling like black diamonds. I slither towards him. He is completely naked. A small gasp escapes from his throat and he pulls me onto his lap, wrapping his arms around my back – skin to skin only intruded upon by the swirling water between us.

He pulls my hair free and it drops into the water. Our noses touching, I reach slowly forward with my lips, closing my eyes and slowly stretching for contact with his mouth. His lips touch my mouth and the firm pressure takes me by surprise. In one mercurial movement he has me underneath him, against the side of the Jacuzzi without losing touch with his body.

He grabs both my hands and links his fingers through mine. I begin to sink in the water. He pushes and holds me in his needy grasp. I tilt myself back against the seat. His wet black hair clings to his cheek, flush with his strong, streamlined jaw as he reaches up and releases my bikini top. It drifts free. The top of my breasts break the surface of the water in response.

"I want you so much," he says softly.

My heart swells and I tingle all over. I arch myself towards him. I'm breaching that precipice where I would do anything to be in the same skin as him - to feel him on, around and in me.

"Here?" I murmur back as he gently bites my neck.

"Here."

"No one can see us?" I ask even though I know the lake house is cloaked by the forest and we're completely alone.

"There's only us. I can't wait." His rushed words are raw with impatience.

I run my hand down his chest, feeling every undulation in his toned torso on my way down then my hand reaches its goal: hard and defined, pushing towards me. He is already slipping off my bikini bottoms with one hand and I wrap my legs around him. He pushes into me and in synchronicity we gasp, deeply and appreciatively. Nose to nose and eyes wide open we keep momentum in the ebbing water, splashing around us, locked together as one – every rippling sensation more intense than the last.

"You make me crazy, Tara. You drive me so so crazy." His body begins to shudder. He clutches at my hair and pulls me even tighter to him as he breathes erratically. He makes a deep groan and we hold on tightly to each other.

"You are too much for me sometimes."

"You don't say."

"I'm going to make it up to you." He looks at me lovingly and grabs my hand as he rises from the water, pulling me with him. He wraps the robe around me and pulls the edges around himself so that we're both inside it.

"What are you doing?" I ask impatiently. He's normally such a generous, considerate lover.

"I'll keep my promise," he replies, and he sweeps me up and carries me dripping wet and giggling, upstairs to the bedroom, leaving tiny puddles and footprints on the stone and wooden floor. He lays me on the bed and when we make love again he keeps his word.

Afterwards, we lie blissed-out together with our bodies moulded to each other, fighting sleep and unwilling to let a second pass where we aren't fully aware of the other. I can't get enough of him. It's like a crazy addiction and the more I get the more I need. To move to the other side of the bed feels like another continent. Desperate for the bathroom I start to get up. He reaches his hand over to me and I squeeze it.

"Send me a postcard," he mumbles.

I smile at him. His eyes are heavy with sleep and he's curled in a near foetal position: naked, vulnerable and the most beautiful, humbly powerful, god of a man I have ever met. My mind takes a snapshot of him there and stores it to memory. I pull the duvet over him before I go to the bathroom, grabbing my toothbrush from my bag, complete with hygienic, portable holder. I wonder what he would say if my toothbrush took up residence in his bathroom? Isn't that like a universal symbol for 'I want to move in'? Do I want to move in? In my heart I want to be with him forever. The thing is taking steps towards something more permanent is great, but boarding that big, old boat with a one-way ticket to the great beyond is about the most scary thing in the world.

Giselle once had an astrology chart done for my birthday, and to her great amusement the astrologer said commitment was a dirty word for me. I laughed at the time but later I reflected on what a pain in the ass that was. He was spot on; but I believe in love and loyalty and take commitment seriously. I've never experienced forever – nobody has. Things are always changing. Yet I do want the commitment.

I have a vision of Julia Roberts in *Runaway Bride* and I imagine if it was my turn I physically couldn't get down the aisle without a general anaesthetic. Shasta doesn't know what he's got into with me; but I don't know his views. I can imagine myself taking a vow to be with him forever if he promised never to marry me. No shackles, no chains, no being pregnant and tied to the kitchen sink – just a promise to love and commit until we have completed our journey together. *Anyway why am I off on this thought train? Oh yes, the toothbrush.* I'm totally jumping the gun on this point.

I make my way to the kitchen to get a drink when I hear barking and whining from outside. *Scout.* We've forgotten she was out. The dog will have had an eyeful of Shasta and I; though I doubt she'll be needing canine therapy. I open the door.

"Scout?" I call out into the darkness.

The outside lights make it impossible to see beyond

their range but I can hear someone out there. The dog has stopped barking and I can hear her friendly whine and the whip of her tail against something.

"Hi!" a woman's voice calls out.

What the hell?

"Get down Scout. I'm happy to see you too," the voice says calmly.

I squint into the gloom as the woman approaches the door. What the hell is some woman doing out here alone at this time of night? Fuelled by millions of thoughts per second my curiosity builds as she approaches.

"I...am. I'm looking for Shasta?" she says hesitantly.

And who the hell would you be?

I finally get a good look at her. Now I wish I hadn't. She's absolutely stunning, an understated, natural beauty: late twenties, olive skinned, silky, black hair, delicate features and dark eyes, probably Native American. Scout is all over this girl.

"You are?" I ask, recognizing the need to be polite to Shasta's friends. My raging instinct alerts me that this girl signifies trouble. Big, big trouble. Visiting at this time of night surely means there must be only one thing on her mind.

"I'm Leonie. I'm a friend of Shasta's." The woman's doey brown eyes look wary and troubled. "I'm sorry. I should have called first," she says, trying to be light hearted. Woman to woman, I know she's hiding something.

"I'm Tara. Shasta's girlfriend," I offer out my hand. Leonie shakes it but looks uncomfortable.

"Hi." She fiddles with her perfect straight hair, tucking it behind her ear. "I didn't realize he had finished the house." She's bluffing that this is a casual visit.

"Would you like to come in?" I'll just check if he's awake," I ask, stepping back into the house. She checks me over with a glance.

"No, no. I've come at a bad time. I can come back some other day."

"Seriously, you don't want to come all this way for nothing." I don't want her to leave without finding out more about this girl and why she's here. "I'll wake him. Come inside a sec." I make my way inside, hoping Leonie will come in and I can find out more.

"No. Don't disturb him. Just tell him I called," she replies.

"Any message?"

"No. I was just going to catch up with him now that I'm back in town."

"Oh. You've moved back here?"

"Yes," she replies.

More information please. "Back to stay?" I ask in my friendliest tone, but I'm wondering if she can read me as well as I can read her.

She raises her eyebrows but there's a shadow of sadness in her eyes. "I think so," she replies. This girl has got to be an ex of Shasta's, and I'd gamble anything she's still holding a torch for him.

"Well, hopefully we can all get together sometime," I suggest. *God, I am transparently lying.*

"Sure. Do you live here too?" Leonie asks.

"No," I reply too hastily. *Wrong answer.* "Well, some of the time." *My damn toothbrush is still in transit.*

Leonie starts to make her way to the car. I follow her for a few steps in my bare feet – now more aware of my dishevelled appearance. I'm wearing an oversized t-shirt of Shasta's. My hair looks unruly: ruffled and obviously straight from the bedroom.

"I'll tell Shasta you called."

Leonie looks back with a forced smile. I imagine my foot on her skinny backside, pushing her onward. *Just keep on driving, right out of town.* I know that look - this is a heartbroken woman. My imagination treats me to a myriad of images of her and Shasta to antagonize me. The painful stab of jealousy tears through my ribs. I can understand someone feeling heartbroken over Shasta; I would feel exactly the same. I'm swirling with questions, but they will have to wait until the morning. I hone in on the hesitant, and perhaps conditional, reply from Leonie that she is here to stay.

5

The alarm goes rudely off in the middle of my dream. As the dream subsides I fumble to turn it off. I become aware of an uneasy feeling and remember last night's visitor. I reach round behind me to an empty bed. Shasta is not there. How did I miss him getting up? It's playing on my mind and I want to ask him about Leonie. There's a note on the bedside table in his sweeping writing.

I didn't want to wake you. Gone to Rez. Horse in foal. Love you. Xxxx

I'm disappointed he's not here, but a smile curves on my lips. It's not the first time Shasta has been called in the middle of the night for some drama or other. He seems to be everyone's go-to guy. His experience with horses isn't to a veterinary level but they trust him, and he is a damn sight cheaper than getting the vet out. Michael's horse had a still birth last year and is due to foal again any day now – I guess he's being cautious.

Today is a big day - it's the handover of the coffee shop and Elizabeth's last day, so it's our final chance to pick her brains over the running of the business. I drive over to Evergreen where Giselle is already sitting meditating in the back garden under the sequoia tree. I leave her to it while I shower and get dressed, planning what we need to know about the bookshop before we take the helm. The doorbell rings as I pass the front door. I open it and find Margy, my mom's friend from the garden centre, standing there.

"I was just passing and I wanted to run something past you," she says, pulling off her boots at the front door.

"Come in. I was just about to have breakfast. Do you

want some?" I ask, picking up a box of cereal as we walk into the kitchen. It's a far cry from what Rosa would have made; she would have set down something warm, stodgy and delicious.

She takes one look at the high fibre cereal. "Uh. No thanks."

"Not up to Aunt Rosa's standard. I mean, my mom. That still slips in there. I take it you know about that?" I ask, wanting to get it out in the open.

"Yep. Word got around. How are you?" asks Margy, in a motherly tone.

"Good," I reply. She gives me a meaningful look. "I miss her so much, Margy. Some days I can hardly bear it."

"I do too," she replies. "Oh love, they're only dead when we stop talking about them." She gives me a soft hug. *No sympathy, please.* I haven't cried for a while but if anything could trigger it that would.

"I have come up with an idea. I think it's great, but I want to see what you think?" says Margy.

"Fire away."

"I've been thinking about what you said about the tree planting and the new energy thing." Margy screws up her face, unsure how to describe it.

"About trees changing the energy? Raising the vibration?" I giggle. "I know it sounds a bit far-fetched," I reply, though I'm massively impressed Margy brought it up. I had talked to her about it after I had the visions of the tree energies. It's heartening to know she didn't think I was a basket-case.

"I've spoken to the undertaker and the florist about people buying a tree for a loved one when they pass over, instead of flowers."

“It would be like a living memorial. Some people do that already though.”

“Yes, but instead of flowers which just wilt away, what about a scheme where the money goes to buy a tree? They choose it, plant it themselves or I do it. I want to dedicate some land for that sole purpose. Eventually it’ll create a new forest, and if that goes well we could expand it even further. What do you think?” asks Margy hopefully.

“It’s a fantastic idea!”

“I thought so,” Margy grins. “Rosa would love it. I’ve spoken to my son about producing some literature and rolling it out to other outlets. I’ve got friends in the business who are also interested.”

“You are a revolutionary, Margy. It’s a great scheme and it’ll do so much good for the area. Do you want me to do anything?”

“I’ll let you know. Anyway I’m in a rush, I’ve got a meeting with the Mayor so I must dash,” she calls from the door as she tucks her trousers into her boots and she leaves. Margy is one of those busy people who seem to be able to do anything.

Giselle finishes her meditation and I tell her about Margy’s plan on the way over to the coffeehouse. I focus my mind on what needs to be done, but the thought of last night’s visitor still nudges at me uncomfortably. I mention it to Giselle. She gives me that down-played look which means ‘don’t be too concerned’ but actually translates as ‘you need to watch out’. I’ll ask Shasta about it when I see him later.

“It’s still hard to believe this is going to be ours…” says Giselle, when we arrive at the coffeehouse.

“I’ve checked and the funds have been transferred. It

already is," I tell her with mounting excitement. On the way up the steps to the shop Giselle is nearly foaming at the mouth with anticipation.

"Those shelves need filling up and re-stocking. We want them full to capacity with books at eye level to catch the customers' attention when they're sitting," says Giselle, getting ahead of herself.

"I can't wait for us to put our stamp on it, but we need to keep the original flavor. We can have an official handover to reassure the old customers things are *only* improving. It'll also give the part-timers a moral boost too."

As we walk in Elizabeth initiates a massive three way hug.

"I can't believe I'm going after all these years," she squeaks. Her eyes become dewy and she blinks fast to dry the brimming tears. It takes a while to run through the final list of explanations of how things work but once everything is in order she passes us the keys.

"Keep your phone on," says Giselle, as Elizabeth takes one last look around, swipes a finger over a half empty dusty bookshelf and looks at her grey finger.

"I never did get round to that. Oh well. It's not my problem now. Good luck girls," says Elizabeth and she gives us one final hug, dabs her eyes and with a sniff closes the door behind her. Giselle and I stay calm, walk through to the back kitchen and quietly squeal.

"Eh hem! Can I get some attention here please?" shouts an authoritative voice from the front of the store and it makes me smile. We break up the childish antics and peer around the door at Shasta.

"What can I get you, sir?" I wink and try to sound suggestive.

He smiles that enigmatic half-smile that masks a multitude of emotions, hiding a stilled, passionate, depth. "I'll just have a coffee – for now." The changes on his face are only miniscule. I don't know what my face says, but my heart clenches with happiness and his smile spreads. He knows the effect he has on me, but I suspect there is someone else he has this effect on too. That thought is sobering.

"Shasta, can I interest you in some passion cake?" asks Giselle playfully from behind the counter, lifting the lid on the sweet treat.

"Maybe later," he replies, and Giselle replaces the lid feigning offence.

"Come on. I'll show you around," I tug on his arm.

"Oh, show him the nook. That's what we're going to call the library room from now on," says Giselle, but we go to the upstairs office and she follows us up, to bring down a box of books which haven't seen the daylight for generations, dragging them out and dusting them off at the same time. As she sorts through them she discovers some are new and some are second hand, but she thinks some could be collector's items.

"I think we should have a couple of these local history books out on display but not to be removed. They're useful for reference. They may be of interest to tourists, as well as locals." She flicks through a yellowing hard back book. "I'm going to have a good read of this one. It's about the gold rush in Big Spruce," she thumbs through it and goes quiet.

I want to ask Shasta about Leonie and grab the opportunity while the coffee shop is quiet. I take him through to the nook so we won't be disturbed for a few minutes, but we are interrupted when the door opens and I call to Giselle to ask if she can see to them.

"Shop!" shouts the voice impatiently.

"I'll be right with you," I call, as I sigh and go to see to them. Giselle beats me to it and from the exuberant gushing and hugging she is pleased to see someone. Under the cloud of wavy auburn hair Simon's flushed face pops out.

"You're here already!" I shout.

"There's no point hanging around once you've made a decision," Simon replies.

"She didn't make you work your notice?" asks Giselle.

"No. Patricia put me on gardening leave instead, which suits me!" he says defiantly.

"You're here to stay?" I grin, hugging him.

"If you'll have me?" he asks, making puppy dog eyes.

"Sure, Hudson's kennel is free; he's outgrown it!"

"Charming. I've only just arrived and I'm in the dog house already."

We have a quick catch up but customers wander in and Giselle and I go to serve them. Giselle grins at Simon from behind the counter and mimics a kid playing shop.

"Cut it out. They are paying customers," I mutter to her.

"OK," she pulls a serious face and plates up generous portions of the pumpkin and pecan pie, while Shasta and Simon sit and talk.

"Can you give me five minutes to talk to Shasta?" I ask her.

She eyes me and nods, knowing that I want to ask him about Leonie. I need to know, but truthfully, I'm not so sure that I want to. As I walk towards him he watches me then stands up. "I have to go, darling. I've got work to do."

"How was the foal?"

"Alive. She was breach so it's a good job we were there," his tone is measured because he takes his horses very seriously.

"Don't go just yet," I say quickly, sounding a bit needy. Shasta eyebrows line up quizzically. "You had a visitor last night."

"When?" he asks, looking bemused.

"It was after you went to sleep."

He nods imperceptibly. "Who was it?"

"Leonie."

Shasta's face ripples as though a minor earthquake has just passed through him and he draws back ever so slightly, removing his eyes from me and he looks into the distance.

"What did she want?" he asks, re-connecting his eyes with me again.

"She came to see you. She said she's back in town and that she wanted to meet up." I reply, trying to sound casual but I'm fluffing it.

"Oh." Shasta's eyes shift from left to right. *What does that mean?*

"Why was she calling at that time of night?"

"Didn't you ask her?" he asks, with a flash of annoyance in his voice.

"Who is she Shasta?"

"Leonie and I go way back." I'm already hating that link between them. "Our families are friends and we've known each other a long time."

"Was she your girlfriend?" I ask, feeling the thrust of bravery.

"She was my fiancée."

I feel my knees give way as though the floor is crumbling below me. "You were engaged?" I ask in a low whisper.

"I was until she left town and went to California," he replies vaguely.

"You could have mentioned this before!" Of course he has a past, but I'm illogical with shock. I don't know what to say. I want to ask how he feels about her now, but the answer may not be one I want to hear.

"Does she still have a thing for you?" I ask the less pertinent question, not wanting to ask if he still has a flame lit for her. I don't want him thinking I have so little trust in our relationship.

"I doubt it. It's been a long time."

"Maybe you should go and see her, find out what she wants," I reply. *That's a girl Tara, show trust in your man; give him permission to see her knowing he'll come back to you.*

"I'll probably bump into her. You've nothing to worry about," he picks up on my signals and kisses me on the head. Shasta suddenly stares behind me and looks bewildered. I turn to where the chest freezer which holds the ice cream deserts and sits against the back wall. Giselle is stood beside it with the lid of the freezer open and Simon's legs are dangling out of it, thrashing wildly. He's hanging inside the freezer. Giselle lifts his legs and tips him – he slides further in then she closes the lid on top of him; all I can hear is hysterical laughter from her and muffled squawks from inside the freezer.

"Christ. It's like having children," I mutter, for the first time having second thoughts about going into business with Giselle.

"One day," says Shasta, embellishing those two words with an unblinking stare.

"Don't joke."

"I'm not."

My heart flips again. I don't know whether to laugh or cry but my heart is doing somersaults of joy – my head is raging; *commitment is dangerous. Save yourself.* In my experience men fall in love quickly and fall out of love even faster, just about when you're catching up. I'd wondered if there is actually a heart connection or if it's just the idea of love they fall for – in my case, time will tell.

"This isn't the place," I reply, looking around at the scene in the coffeehouse where customers are contentedly browsing and chilling out.

Shasta leans in to me, his mouth touching my ear, sending tingles shooting out of me in every direction. "Wouldn't you like to make a baby with me?"

A tremor of something primal runs through me. I say nothing. *Don't be deluded, Tara. Some men want to get you pregnant so they get a hold on you* a little voice coaches inside my skull. Shasta isn't like that – I shut the voice down. His eyes are smiling as he relishes in my fluster.

"Imagine what he or she would look like. Your green eyes–"

"Your lips." I add, but stop before the idea catches light.

He puts his hand on the small of my back and looks at me with unblinking intensity and no trace of humor.

"I can't tell what you're thinking?" I look away from him.

"I'm happy. It makes me happy to think about that."

"You don't look happy."

"I'm smiling here," Shasta points to his chest and draws

the shape of a smile on it. "This is where I keep it," he replies, his voice low and warm. I melt like hot butter.

A customer looks up from his cappuccino and I give Shasta a chaste kiss as he leaves, looking back over his shoulder. I draw a smile on my heart and his dark eyes glitter.

"Right, I need somewhere to get changed. I've got an interview," says Simon.

"You've got an interview already? But you've only just arrived. Where?" I ask, turning my attention to Simon, still feeling hot under the collar and everywhere else.

"The Hot Springs Spa," replies Simon as though we are first graders.

"Doing what? Oh no, wait. Don't tell me. Lifeguard... no, speedo inspector?"

Simon rolls his eyes, beseechingly.

"Massage therapist dopey. Did you forget I did night classes? I'm a natural."

"How could we forget?" replies Giselle. He had practiced on our willing bodies for months. You can't knock a free massage and he really had an instinctive flair and a great touch.

"You don't hang around. You can use the staff bathroom over there," I point out.

Once Simon has left for his interview, Giselle and I finally get stuck into work: some well overdue cleaning, shifting tables, chairs and sofas around to make the place more welcoming. The idea is: the coffeehouse is my domain, the book store is Giselle's, although we're both flexible. There's a serious need to de-clutter. I start that task while Giselle goes through the little cash desk for the bookstore, making space and setting out the extra stock, making an inventory of what we have and what she needs to order.

"I'm ordering the best-selling metaphysical stuff, and angels - you can't have too many angel stories," says Giselle talking to herself.

I've just cleared a wooden table of all the old magazines and outdated leaflets. "You can lay some local history books on here."

Giselle marks them up with 'not to be removed – for reference only' labels and lays them out, spending most of her time flicking through them while I see to the steady stream of customers. It's not quite as I imagined. I had a wanton vision of a long breaks, coffee by the fire and good conversation with the regulars. Right now my feet are aching and I need a sit down. I grab five minutes and two cookies, passing one to Giselle as I perch on the arm of the red leather sofa, looking over her shoulder at what she finds so fascinating.

The books describe how when the white settlers moved here they heard that the Native Americans had vast gold stores, because they overheard an old Chief talking about the secret gold in the mountains and how not everyone could find it, because they didn't know what they were looking for. There was talk of it being shrouded by a veil. The settlers believed it was Indian speak for the fact they were hiding it from them.

It must have been well hidden. Apart from prospectors finding a few traces of gold in the river beds there was never much evidence of a large haul. Many families had moved here, staked a claim and gambled what they had in the belief that they would find riches beyond their wildest imaginings. They invested money in the mining company to locate the gold, but many lost everything. Shootings and murders were an everyday occurrence when gold fever was at its peak and there were constant disputes over claims.

"Shasta was saying geologists still think there are large amounts of gold here, which could be why there's so much interest in the Reservation land. Apparently there could be more gold here than anywhere else in America."

"I wouldn't mind a piece of it," replies Giselle.

"Look who I found!" calls Simon, his staccato voice interrupting us. We turn around to see Roger Walsh standing next to Simon who is looking very flushed.

"Have you had a makeover?" asks Giselle, looking him over.

"No!" replies Roger laughing.

"You do look...different, Roger," I remark, noting that is the first time I've seen him in jeans as opposed to sensible trousers. His hair has lost that neatly scooped tidiness and instead it looks casually tousled. I make everyone a drink and watch my friends closely, looking for any sign of Roger's one-sided attraction to Giselle, which had been so obvious a short while ago. There is nothing to suggest it: no second glance, no lingering looks, no stuttering. He talks confidently and seems more self assured. He's over her. Maybe there is a new girlfriend on the scene. Giselle is giving Roger more attention though. I join them when Giselle starts telling them about the gold legends.

Roger moves to the edge of his seat. "I can't believe you're bringing this up," he says, looking at the book Giselle is talking about. "My parents were just talking about this. Apparently Pastor Shimlow talks about how his family were involved with the prospectors when they had a mining business. They found some gold, just not enough. They lost virtually everything they owned when the mine folded. Apparently Grandaddy Shimlow took everything of value and hid it when he knew his home was going to be raided by marauding investors, who were looking for things to scavenge and sell when there was a public lynching one night. Cain says that gold is his by birth."

"Sounds like he's passionate about it," says Giselle.

"Passionate?! I'd say obsessed. He thinks pagan worshipers stole his family's gold and melted it down. I think he's coming unstuck at the seams," replies Roger.

"Ha. Maybe they melted it down and made it into powerful amulets," jokes Giselle, looking at me.

"That would explain a few things," I reply, thinking of Blanche Whitelaw, who I now know was my grandmother, and her rare amulet which I inherited. Cain Shimlow despised her and everything she stood for.

Simon is totally riveted on every syllable Roger utters, and carries on gazing at him, long after he has stopped talking completely rapt in his presence. This boy has it bad, but without a miracle he has no chance - although stranger things have happened. Maybe Roger is going through a delayed adolescence. He's intriguingly more handsome and confident than he was, it's as though he's finally grown into himself.

6

"Your cell is ringing," I shout to Shasta who is showering.

There is no answer above the sound of running water. Should I let it go to voicemail? There is no caller ID showing. It could be anyone. *It could be Leonie.* I'll answer it.

"Hello."

"Who is that?" the man's voice is curt but at least it isn't Leonie.

"This is Shasta's phone."

"Is he there?" the voice is quickly spoken and I can't place the fast lilting accent.

"He can't come to the phone right now. Can I take a message?"

"Tell him it's Will. Will Quinn. Tell him I've got a job for him."

"OK. Is it urgent?"

"Aye. Aye it is," says the man with a short burst of laughter. "It's in Ireland!" His direct manner suggests he's someone who is used to issuing instructions.

"Ah. I guess it won't be today then."

"Why not?" asks Will, sharply. "I'm only joking. But when can he come? He knows me, so he does."

"I'll ask him to call you."

"Are you his missus?"

"No–"

"Are ya single? Ya sound very nice. I like a girl who rolls her Rs," he chuckles at his own joke.

"I'm Tara, Shasta's girlfriend."

"Now there's a good Irish name, Tara. Shasta's picked from good stock I'd say. So what's the craic?"

What's the craic? I'm dumbfounded. There's a pause.

"You've never heard that expression? Aren't your family Irish?"

"Nope. I've never set foot in the place."

"You'll have to change that, Tara. Och, once you've had an Irishman you'll never look back! "

"Well if they've all got your charm I don't doubt it." I hold the phone away from my ear and roll my eyes at it.

"Ah, bloody hell. What does she want now? The wife's calling me! Get the big man to phone me back will ya?" Will Quinn rings off abruptly.

"Jeez, talk about kissed by the Blarney!"

"Who kissed the Blarney?" asks Shasta, walking out of the bathroom with wet hair and a towel wrapped around his hips.

"I picked up your phone for you. It was Will Quinn."

"What did he want?"

"You. He's got a job for you in Ireland!"

"Oh. It's been a while." He looks curious, although underwhelmed.

"Are you going to take it?" I ask.

"I can't leave the country, remember?"

"Right," I reply, not wanting to part with him for more than a few hours.

Shasta shakes his head. "I'll give him a call and see if I can stall it. Will Quinn is a racehorse owner with more money than he knows what to do with," replies Shasta.

"How long would you be away for?"

"Usually a week or two, maybe more."

"Great," I say sarcastically. "You better leave room in your suitcase for me."

"No chance," he replies. I pull a face. "But you could take a seat next to mine on the plane?"

"Now you're talking."

"I've got something that'll put a smile on your face."

"I know," I smile as I watch him pull on his faded jeans.

"It's a surprise. Come with me. He grabs my hand and we head downstairs

"Argh. Yes, sir. You know I can't stand suspense!"

"That's why it's a surprise. I didn't want you to know until I was sure."

"Shasta. Don't wind me up. You've made me breakfast? It's Spanish omelette?"

He snorts a laugh. "You don't think I can do better than that?"

"You know I love omelette and anything to do with Spain."

"Give me a few minutes," says Shasta, dashing out the door.

Peering out the kitchen window to see what is going on reveals nothing. Shasta disappears to the stables behind the old lodge. I throw back a cup of green tea then hear him shout to me from the corral. I go outside where Scout is running back and forward and Penny, the blind Palomino horse, is tied to a post. Shasta is stood in front of her grinning and watching me with eagle eyes. I don't get the surprise. There's no neatly wrapped box. Shasta stands to the side, revealing Penny saddled and bridled.

"Why is she tacked up? Are you going to ride her?" I ask, confused.

"No, but you are!"

I draw back and look at him like he's lost his mind. I

haven't ridden in a long time, and to top it off this horse is virtually blind.

"You are off your rocker if you think I can ride her!"

"She needs you to be her eyes. She's desperate to be ridden and you need to trust your instincts; you'll be a perfect match. You'll just have to trust each other. This horse has so much spirit – she would rather die than live out her days as a disabled pet."

"That is blackmail, Shasta! Emotional blackmail! You know I adore her." I complain although I've always felt like Penny and I are inextricably linked. "Have you tried to ride her?"

He nods. "Yes. But you're more her size."

"But she's blind, Shasta!?"

"Not fully, she has some sight in her right eye. You'll have to train together and teach each other. She's willing if you are."

My heart melts. "But I have to get to the coffeehouse."

"Quit stalling. Just a few minutes a day and build it up."

I approach Penny, talking softly so that she knows it's me approaching. Her ears twitch forward and she whinnies to me. I'm dying to give it a go but I don't know if she'll respond to my rusty riding skills.

"Keep talking to her, tell her what you're going to do," says Shasta, as he begins coaching me. I follow his instructions, touching her flank and keeping contact so she knows where I am. I slowly step into the stirrup and draw myself gently over her back and into the saddle. She whinnies and steps restlessly back and forward, making me nervous that she wants to throw me off.

"It's OK, Penny. I'm just here."

"She's ready to go, Tara. Are you?"

“Dear God-“

“Stay calm. She’ll feel that you’re tense. I’ve got the lead rein.”

I take the reins and Penny steps forward without encouragement from me. *She’s keen.* I ride her tentatively around the yard once with Shasta leading, then he releases his tether and I guide her around by the reins and shifting my weight.

“She’s so sensitive. Eager too.” I can feel my smile spreading to my ears

“I know,” says Shasta, and I can hear by his voice he’s smiling. ”Once you’ve learned to ride her, riding anything else will be like driving a hand cart.”

Together Penny and I do another couple of laps before we wrap it up for the morning. I dismount onto wobbly legs which are unaccustomed to being on a horse.

“That was a lovely thing to do. You are fabulous.”

“And I’m taking you out for dinner tonight.”

“You spoil me,” I say, as I lead Penny back to the stable. “But keep it up. I’d better go, darling. Lunch?” I kiss him before heading to my car.

He shakes his head. “I’ve got too much work on, but I’ll stop by.”

It feels like it’s going to be a long day without him, but I’ve the coffeehouse to look forward to. On the way over I marvel at how much my life has changed. It’s not so long ago that I used to wake alone in my apartment in New York, take the subway to work, endure legal battles and fight with my paperwork until late, then I’d meet my friends for a flurry of cocktails, before going to bed and doing it all again the next day.

When I arrive at the store, Giselle has beaten me to

it. She's opened up and is in full swing. I launch myself into it and the morning passes in a flash. I look out the coffeehouse window at the man up a ladder. "The sign writer is putting up the new sign."

"Mmmmmmnn. Nice buns," says Giselle staring up at the guy. "Damn. He's wearing a wedding ring. I'm beginning to think it's true - all the best ones *are* taken."

"There will be one for you somewhere, but let's face it; he's not going to be normal is he? He's going to have to be a unique catch for you."

"I'll take that as a compliment."

"So, Roger? The new version is a big improvement, don't you think?"

"Hmm. Definite improvement. I don't know how that happened. Lovely guy, but too safe. How are things with you and Shasta?"

"That girl, Leonie?"

"Yeah?"

Ex-fiancée.

"Shit!"

"Giselle. I'm looking for some reassurance here!"

"What's she like? Downtrodden? Plain? Looks like the wrong end of a camel?"

"Gorgeous."

Giselle shakes her head. "At least you know he has standards. You have nothing to worry about. You and Shasta are good together. He'd never find another one like you."

"There is no flame like an old flame," says a grey haired lady who is sitting alone at a table, sipping tea and evidently sharing our conversation.

"You think so?" I ask, and smile to include her.

"I know so. I was that girl. Not that you'd know it to look at me now. I stole my dear old Stanley back from right under his new girlfriend's nose."

"I'll bet you were a bit of a goddess," replies Giselle encouragingly.

"Sorry," she mouths to me. "Keep your enemies close. Isn't that what they say? Take it from me, you keep your eye on that girl," she says sagely. "My name is Sarah by the way."

"I'm Tara, that's Giselle."

Sarah stands up slowly, taking in the world around her as she collects her walking stick as she stands near the door. "My Stanley was an amateur archaeologist. I hardly saw him because he spent so much time in his shed tinkering with his metal detector. He was lucky that he married me - no other woman would have put up with him."

Customers come in and push impatiently past her, with irritable expressions and a hurried manner. Sarah is oblivious that she's holding them up.

"I've not been out for months. It's the chemotherapy, but I may just see another winter." She smiles to herself. "I'm off to put flowers on Stanley's grave. I used to visit him every week, but I can't now - I'll be going to see him for good soon," she looks wanly out of the window. She seems detached and vulnerable as she smiles innocently to herself and starts to shuffle to the door, then she remembers her check and fumbles for some money.

Giselle and I look at each other through glassy eyes.

"This one is on the house, Sarah," I tell her.

"Ah. Bless you." She shuffles out while Giselle holds the door.

"Come back tomorrow. There's a slice of wicked

blueberry pie with your name on it," Giselle calls after her.

Sarah leaves the coffeehouse, having made an indelible impression.

"Wasn't that a swift kick up the ass to change your perspective?" says Giselle, leaning back against the wall and looking around while I blink furiously to fan the moisture off my eyes.

Just before closing time my dad arrives in - the novelty and comfort of being able to say that is amazing. Having been without parents since I was seventeen, it takes a little getting used to.

" *The Book and Bean.* I like it," he says, referring to the newly erected sign outside.

"Pull up a chair Barnaby. We're just about to close," Giselle tells him as she sweeps around the counter, piling leftovers onto a plate for him with a large mug of coffee.

"I'm sure you'll want to know," he looks at me seriously, "there are no charges hanging over Shasta. I just wanted to clear that up."

I breathe out through my teeth. "That is good news."

"They're recording a verdict of accidental death on Vaughan Buchanan," says Barnaby, forking in a mouthful of cake. "If you call setting fire to yourself while you're trying to torch a building an accident."

"And Tray? Michael thought he saw him."

"There is nothing to show Tray was there. It could have been Vaughan that Michael saw outside the building."

"Shasta will be relieved," I reply. However Shasta hadn't called in today. In fact, apart from a text this morning, I hadn't heard from him all day, which was unusual

We lock up and head for home, happy that business is ticking along really nicely and the handover had been smooth. I try calling Shasta but his cell goes straight to voicemail. I get dressed ready to go out to dinner, still unsure if I'm supposed to meet him at his house or mine. I've the unsettling feeling that he's bumped into Leonie, or more likely, that she has tracked him down.

It's after 9:00 p.m. when he turns up at the house, dressed in a black shirt and khaki trousers; looking windswept but delicious, with his glossy black hair looking more groomed than usual.

"Did you think I wasn't coming?" he asks.

"I didn't know what to think when I couldn't get hold of you."

"I've so much work on. I won't bore you with it," he collects me in his arms and looks down at me appreciatively.

"I was trying to let you know something important. The forensic results on Vaughan Buchanan are in. It was accidental death. You're completely in the clear."

His face lifts. "I knew I would be, once they got their facts straight," he replies, but I can see the relief on his face.

"I've missed you," I reply and reach up for a kiss, but needing more when our mouths connect.

"Let's go," he says, moving towards the door with his arm around my waist.

We drive over to the Spanish restaurant in town and I'm already salivating at the thought of their tapas. Shasta seems quiet and there is an odd atmosphere in the car. I'm unsure how to breach the gap between us, but it feels like there is something unsaid hanging in the air. As we walk in I smile at him, but his gaze doesn't stay on me for long. I should be reassured, but I'm not. Something isn't right. And he thinks I'm the one to hold back my feelings. The waitress shows us to our table and I'm marginally disappointed it's a table for four. I'd have preferred a small table for two in the corner, for greater intimacy.

"Is everything OK?" I ask, not wanting to crowd him.

He nods, smiles and holds my gaze for a long time. All my energy seems to collect in my heart and drift towards him.

"I love you," he says, still keeping his keen dark eyes intently on me.

"I love you."

"I saw Leonie today," says Shasta. The unspoken is revealed and my stomach flips over when my heart clenches. "What happened?"

"Nothing. She was at the Rez. I told you I'd bump into her."

"She still wants you, doesn't she?"

"I don't think so. It was just two old friends meeting."

Doesn't he get it? Men can be so naively unassuming about female nature sometimes. Women are a devious bunch. I should know.

"I saw how she looked when she met me. Trust me, she still wants you."

"She broke off the engagement. She wanted to go to California and 'find herself'," he explains.

To me that's the worst scenario. She left in a position of control and he was effectively dumped. Would he want to pick up where they left off, to discover what might have been?

"How do you feel now that you've seen her?" I pluck up the courage to ask

"Fine," he says quickly and picks up his napkin.

"Just fine? There's got to be more to it than that?"

"No. It's history. I like long relationships, Tara. I'm not a player. I wouldn't mess with someone's feelings. If I'm feeling something then it's real."

"You were engaged to this girl. Would you have married her?" I ask, hoping for an answer that soothes my concerns.

"Yes, but in hindsight it would have been a mistake. There was not enough depth to the relationship. She's was into making a name for herself in radio. I wanted a simpler life."

"But the commitment was important to you?"

"I didn't enter into it lightly if that's what you're asking."

"I just wanted to know how you feel," I reply, glad to have aired my questions. He gazes at me while toying with my finger.

"Tara, when she left I didn't feel for her the way I did the first time I met you."

I suck air through my teeth as I feel myself fall even deeper in love with him – as though I wasn't in deep enough already. The waiter brings our food but I've no appetite for it. Shasta tucks in as though he hasn't eaten all day. The waiter re-appears with a couple of drinks and he places them on the table.

"We didn't order those," says Shasta, barely looking up.

"They are from that gentleman over there." The waiter points to the bar where three men are sat with their backs to us.

"Who is that?"

"I've no idea," says Shasta cautiously. His angular jaw tilts upwards. The man in the middle turns and looks over his shoulder, he puts his hand up as he places an olive on a cocktail stick in his mouth then he wanders over, picking his teeth with it. He's a tall, broad, distinguished looking man in his late fifties, well built and expensively dressed. He slicks down his dark, greying, combed-back hair with his hand as he approaches, then pulls out a chair.

"Why the drinks, buddy?" asks Shasta, sounding unusually sharp.

The man drops into the chair without looking at either of us. "You're Shasta King, right?" he asks, though his lips barely move.

Shasta is watchful and motionless, apart from a subtle flexing in his jaw.

"I wanted to introduce myself – and to thank you."

"What for?

"Drink up," he says, picking up his glass and raising it.

I pick up the drink the man sent over, not really sure what is going on but it would be impolite not too. Shasta's hand shoots over it and he stops me.

"I wanted to thank you for letting me see the face of the man responsible for the death of my son," replies the man, with a cool menacing tone.

Shasta's eyes flash like daggers in flight. "You don't know what you're talking about!" he fires back.

"It'll make it easy for me to visualize your corpse when I'm stood at your graveside," the stranger's words are silken, but laced with poison.

"Bastard!" I seethe through gritted teeth.

"I'm Marshall Buchanan, father of Vaughan. I'm glad I've met you, though it won't be a long acquaintance," he whispers as he leans in with a cunning leer.

"Your son was an arsonist, among other things," says

Shasta, jutting his chin stubbornly towards Marshall, his eyes narrowed to slits of burning charcoal.

"My son was a businessman of great integrity and drive. I'm taking over where he left off. The only difference..." He smacks his teeth through pared-back lips. "Is that now it's personal."

"Your idle threats are wasted on me, but just for the record, if I had known your son was in that fire, I would have dragged him out – just as I would anyone. I wasn't responsible for what happened to him."

"Ahhhh. Mr. King, you see there is always somebody responsible. This time it's you," says Marshall in a sing-song voice, enunciating every word individually, suddenly skewering the cocktail stick into Shasta's meal.

"You need to get your facts straight," I spit, the words at him. "Your family have played outside the rules, and in my opinion your son got what he deserved."

"Let me guess. Tara North? Hmmm. I've heard about your naive little crusades. How are you since the accident? That was such a shame. I trust there is lasting damage?" he asks, twitching his head to the side.

Shasta shudders violently and knocks over a wine glass.

"Waiter, he'll need a cloth please," says Marshall, lifting his hand as he signals; the two goons on the stool are watching us closely. The waiter is with us in a second and Marshall gets up to leave.

"It's good to meet you both. I'll be looking out for you," says Marshall, then he leans over close to Shasta's head, bringing his mouth to his ear. "Just remember, it won't be me who pulls the trigger, but before that, I want to watch you run."

Shasta is as still as a rock: unmoving, poised and

seemingly impervious to Marshall Buchanan. The three men re-group and stalk out like they own the place.

"I'm sorry about that. Are you OK?" asks Shasta.

"Are you?" I snap. "You're the one he threatened."

"He's sore. He's looking for a scapegoat."

"I'm calling Barnaby!"

"Don't. It's a storm in a tea cup. I'll handle it."

"How can you be so calm?"

"Let's not inflame things," replies Shasta, putting his hands on the table. We wait for a while before leaving the restaurant and the street outside is quiet. Shasta looks around at the cars parked up. They're all empty. We agree it's better to stay at my house tonight rather than go back to the lake house in the dark, where someone could be waiting. We will need to be on our guard. I can think of nothing more unnerving than being the target of a vendetta by a notoriously powerful figurehead.

7

I can't lie - the fear of something happening to Shasta is playing havoc with my mind. I don't want the universe to play that card again because to lose another loved one would be unthinkable. I'm going to have to take action, despite what Shasta said. I'll keep it to myself; it's the only way I can think of to protect him.

It's just starting to rain as I pull up beside my dad's house, but his car is gone and he doesn't answer the door - not that there's much to report: a man turns up, buys you a drink, expresses his wish to see your boyfriend dead, then leaves. Its flimsy I know. There is one other thing I could try. Flicking through my cell phone I call up Tray's Buchanan's number. It's worth a shot. He picks up after several rings.

"I wasn't expecting you to call," says Tray smoothly.

"I thought it was about time we spoke."

"How are things in the country?"

"Never dull, but Tray I didn't call to make small talk. I'm so sorry to hear about your brother, it's a tragedy, what happened."

"Shouldn't play with matches," Tray replies but his tone is dark. "Sooner or later someone is going to get burned."

"Do you know what happened?"

"Tara, go ahead. Ask what you really want to know."

I bite my lip but decide to risk it. "Were you with Vaughan?"

"No, my brother had his own mind. He had his own way of taking care of business." His tone has changed and I know I'm treading on eggshells.

"I'm sorry. Not that I'd tell anyone anyway. You do know that Shasta wasn't responsible?"

Tray sniggers and there is a clattering noise from his end. A woman's airy giggle can be heard in the background, asking whom he's talking to. He's got company.

"Well, if you will play with the big boys..."

"Your father is holding Shasta responsible. It isn't right. I was hoping you would make him see sense."

"Because you and I are old friends?" he asks in a snide tone. This is a bad time to talk to him.

"We've both been through stuff, Tray. We are friends."

"Did your boyfriend put you up to calling me?"

"No. No way. He'd never ask me to do that."

"Your boyfriend should fight his own battles. My father is a stubborn man and once he sets his mind on something it's there for life."

"There must be something you can do, Tray?" I'm about ready to beg.

There is more giggling in the background and Tray laughs quietly then gasps. "Sorry. I'm busy." The phone goes dead.

Tray knows Shasta had nothing to do with Vaughan's death but he's right - the chances of changing his father's bitter, vengeful attitude are slim to none. I can catch Barnaby later. I've got my own business to attend to. I head back to the coffeehouse where I've left Simon with Giselle running things.

At least the place is still standing when I get back. Actually, Simon is a great asset to the business - the customers love him and his witty exchanges. We've given him a part-time job to keep him ticking over, but now we don't want to lose him. We've got a few part-time staff who know the ropes but they don't have his vivacious eccentricity.

"Take a break Giselle. Sophie will be here shortly. We've plenty of cover," I tell her.

"I think I will," she replies without her usual sparkle.

"You OK?"

"Yeah. I didn't think this would be so tiring."

"And that's all?" I ask.

She smiles and sighs. "You're not buying it?"

I shake my head.

"I guess I'm still adjusting. I don't know what I was expecting."

"I hope you're not having second thoughts on moving here?"

"I guess it's just different. In New York there were plenty of people like me. Here, I'm a rare breed."

"Yes, you are, but we wouldn't want it any other way."

"I just don't know if there is a special someone out there made for me. If there is, am I likely to find him here?" Giselle shrugs and grimaces.

"It'll turn up when you're not looking. I met Shasta in the gas station."

"I guess it's brought it home to me, watching you two together. No offense. I'm ready now. No more fooling around. It's weird but...I've been thinking of Roger. "

"No! You completely dismissed him before? You're clutching at straws."

"There's something about him."

"Safe, dependable Roger."

"Did I hear you mention Roger?" asks Simon, whose head pops up like a periscope.

"I was just saying I like his new look," bluffs Giselle.

Simon blushes red and falls silent. He looks awkward, like he's not sure what to say.

"I love him," says Simon in a weak voice and he gulps. His face reddens as his eyes grow moist.

"Oh my God! You're serious?" I reply, trying to soften my voice at Simon's sudden vulnerability. This is big, and surprising, news. Simon puts his hand over his eyes and lowers his head. It's followed by an almighty sob and he clasps his chin in his hand. Giselle's mouth falls open. Simon starts to cry and we put our arms around him, exchanging looks of surprise.

"I don't know what's wrong with me. I don't do this. I'm an idiot falling for a straight guy," Simon sobs.

"We thought you were kidding about him."

"You don't think I've got feelings? I know I'm a joke, but I've never felt like this. He gets me right here," says Simon, putting his hand on his heart.

"You really like him?" asks Giselle, still taken back.

"No." Simon shakes his head. "I love him Giselle. He's an amazing guy."

"But you hardly know him."

"I know all I need to know. I don't care about the details."

"But Simon, he likes girls."

"I know," he snaps irritably, dabbing his eyes with a serviette. "I'm not giving up on him. Maybe I should tell him how I feel."

"That would be a hell of a shock. You'd risk losing his friendship," says Giselle, as she tries to discourage him.

Simon has no idea of Giselle's surge of interest - this could get complicated if they both become infatuated with the same guy. The image of sale shoppers fighting over the last Gucci handbag comes to mind.

"Look you two, take a break. We're getting some curious looks," I tell them, noticing the continual glances from a sandy haired guy browsing the bookshelves; he stops at the reference section, which has been pretty popular. It seems there's no shortage of interest in the local history of Big Spruce.

Giselle and Simon disappear into the kitchen. I'm shocked that Simon really does have it bad for Roger, but what can he do? Meanwhile Sophie and her daughter Lucy arrive, carrying a large container of home bakes. I'm going to have to curb this continual picking if I want to keep wearing these jeans. The diet can wait - I need to sample the new stock.

"Leave some for the rest of us!"

I wasn't expecting to hear my dad's warm voice. It's a blessing to now live in a town where I can just bump into my family.

"Caught," I splutter, wiping away the crumbs sticking to my lip." You shouldn't creep up on people."

"Barnaby, leave her alone. She looks like she could do with a good meal," chides Margy, now appearing from behind my father.

"She doesn't take after me," he replies, patting his paunch.

"You kept that one secret, didn't you?" she teases, patting him on the back, referring to our recent discovery of my paternity.

"It was a secret even from me. Look how she turned out. Who'd have thought it?"

"Don't mind me," I say, contributing to the conversation about me.

"I've got something I want to show you," says Barnaby.

"What have you got there?"

"Photograph albums. Thought you might want to meet the family," he says, running his hand over their dusty covers.

"Oh no. There are more like us," I reply, pretending to be horrified.

"Oh yes," says Margy. "Let's have a look. I've not seen your Fen for years."

We flick through the album while Barnaby and Margy reminisce about the good old days. It feels good to know my roots and be part of something. Eventually Margy makes a comment about the time and gets up to leave.

"Tara, before I go, I've been thinking about this tree planting scheme and I think we need more land. The more we can get the better. I reckon there's great scope for this. We could look at is re-foresting from an environmental point of view, not just the memorial trees or the hocus pocus thing."

"Really? How much more land do you think we need?" I ask, thinking of the neat, green lawn at Evergreen that might be suitable.

"Acres, or miles possibly."

"That much?! You dream big."

"Well, why not? What do you think about some of the land at the Reservation? I could have a word with Shasta. There's a good deal of space out there."

"I don't know. Shasta's out of town working all day. It's probably better to talk to Michael about it," I reply, knowing Michael has the clout to influence those kinds of decisions on the Reservation.

"Would you mind having a word?"

"Leave it with me. I'll see what I can do," I reply, hoping

my rapport with Michael is still good. In a whirlwind of enthusiasm Margy makes a hasty exit.

"What a woman," says Barnaby, rolling his eyes which follow her.

"I'm glad you came in. I wanted to talk to you about something."

He sits back and listens while I explain about the visit from Marshall Buchanan and his threat to Shasta. His mood perceptibly shifts and his face takes on that austere professional look as he changes into Sheriff mode.

"There's just one thing. Shasta doesn't know I'm talking to you about it. You can't mention it to him. He thinks it's a fuss about nothing, but I don't."

"He had better not take things into his own hands," says Barnaby, pinning me with a look.

"He wouldn't!" I reply, knowing that he's referring to the alleged in-fighting on the Reservation and a community blamed for creating their own trouble.

"He's probably just sounding off, but don't worry - I'll keep my eyes open," he replies, with an upswing in his level tone, indicating everything will be just fine. I'm relieved to have given him the heads up. He then changes the subject and flicks through the photo albums, pointing out old photographs: some black and white and some grainy faded pictures from the 60s and 70s. It's funny to think of myself as belonging in his family album. There are a few photographs of my grandmother Blanche with her three children: Barnaby, Robert and Fenella. Robert lives a few miles away but Fenella had moved to Ireland many years ago; although she comes back regularly.

"I've told Fen all about you and she said it's open house if you want to visit."

"Sounds great, but I could be the niece from hell for all she knows," I reply, thinking how trusting that sounds but I'm keen to get to know my family having spent so much time without any.

"You can keep hold of the albums. Stick your mug shot in here," he says, with a wink as he passes them to me.

"Shasta's been asked to go to Ireland for work. Do you really think Fenella wouldn't mind me coming over?"

"I'm sure she wouldn't. She's pretty straight talking and she wouldn't say it unless she meant it."

"Hmm. I don't want to leave Giselle with the business just yet. Speaking of which, I've got work to do."

"Me too," he says, walking to the door, looking at me unsurely. I give him a quick hug with one arm around his waist and his face flinches.

"Cut it out. I'm a Sheriff. I don't want people thinking I'm soft," he drops his hand on my shoulder, the equivalent of a pat on the back and wrings out a smile.

A trip to Ireland sounds very tempting at the minute, but I wouldn't want Giselle to feel like I've just bailed out on her so early in taking over the business. There's also the possibility Shasta will think I'm clinging to his coat tails, like a kid on their first day at kindergarten. My mind flits back to what Margy said about finding some extra land for re-foresting. It's probably wise to wait until Shasta finishes work so he can come along for extra credibility when I speak to Michael.

"I got the job at the spa," shouts Simon as he comes running into the room and stuffs his phone back in his pocket. "Just part-time until we see how it works out."

"So you'll still be able to work here part-time too? We'd miss you."

"I'll still be here to keep you entertained. Life is good," he says, then gazes into space with a wistful look in his eye. I'd hazard a guess he's thinking of Roger.

"Get you, two jobs Miller. We'll have to celebrate with a nice hot mineral spa tonight. Who fancies it?" asks Giselle.

"Another time," replies Simon. "I want to see Hudson and have an early night."

"What?" She shakes her head in disbelief. "How about you?" she asks me.

"Sorry, not tonight. I need to see Shasta and visit Michael."

"You two are no fun anymore. It looks like I've got a date with the sofa."

My cell phone rings and its Shasta. I lower my voice to talk to him.

"That's got to be Shasta. Your voice always goes soppy when you talk to him," calls Giselle, as I walk into the kitchen to take the call and she stands with her hands on her hips pulling a smoochey face at me. I explain to Shasta about Margy wanting more land to plant up, and that I would suss out the possibility of tree planting on the Reservation.

"I'm working late, sorry. You go ahead without me. I've no idea what time I'll get finished here. I can meet you there if I get sorted sooner," he replies.

I can't hide the disappointment in my voice. Anyway it's an opportunity to get to know Michael and Shasta's culture better and strengthen those ties. I still haven't met his parents; not that it has come up at any point. At this stage we're still getting to know each other and we're being selfish with our time together. I have a niggling feeling they may not be too delighted that their son has taken up with me; although I've nothing to base it on, other than the distinct 'them and us' vibe which is lurking just below the surface of the community.

It's dark by the time I drive over to Michael's house and there's no sign of Shasta. When I arrive the door to Michael's house is wide open, although he isn't expecting me. I call out but there's no reply. I feel around the doorframe. The house is in darkness, but the kitchen door is ajar and light is spilling into the silent hallway. I call out again, but there is still no answer. *Is something wrong?* I tentatively look into the lighted room, half expecting to see someone in a pool of blood on the kitchen floor. Surely no-one would go out and leave their door open and the light on? The room is empty.

"Michael?"

Something soundlessly touches my shoulder. I scream and lurch backwards, knocking into something behind me.

"Looking for me?" asks Michael, his face half in shadow, only highlighted by the brash unflattering light from the kitchen. His tiny dark, penetrating eyes are indistinct.

I clutch my chest and heave a sigh of relief. "You scared me! I thought you might be dead or something."

"I popped in with my neighbor for dinner. My wife has gone to stay with relatives and I can't cook to save myself. My friend's daughter has just come back to live so there's a lot of catching up to do. What are you doing here?"

"I won't keep you," I reply, feeling like I'm intruding.

"Something important?" he asks, sitting down in an armchair.

"I know this might seem a bit random, but hear me out."

Michael sits staring forward while I explain to him about Margy's idea for memorial trees with the aim to re-forest barren areas as much as possible. There is no sign that he is listening to me as he sits there passively. I'm unsure whether to tell him about the visions, the earthwork Shasta did and the role the trees were playing in lifting the energies to a new vibration. I remember the promise I made to the universe that I would fulfil my destiny, in whatever form that took, in return for Shasta's freedom. I bite the bullet and explain to Michael about the light codes, including the portals, and how the new energy is being conducted in through the tree tops, through to the roots and communicated along a network. Michael's black eyes swivel towards me followed by the rest of his face. He stares at me for a few moments - neither of us saying anything. It's uncomfortable

"You're like your grandmother. That's the kind of thing she would have said," he says eventually, void of emotion; but I see respect in his old eyes.

I beam at him, feeling like he's just paid me a huge compliment. "Really?"

He nods. "Who is this woman, Margy? Why does she want to do it on this land?"

"She owns the garden centre and she was a great friend of my mom's. She's dedicating part of her land and she wants to take it a step further and create more forest."

"So she's not part of a big syndicate? Nor any big business?"

"Definitely not, Michael. She's on the level."

Michael eyes me suspiciously and leans his head to the side. "I'd like to believe you."

"I'd already thought of that. It doesn't surprise me that

you don't take people's word at face value, when what you've experienced is deceit and dishonor. I can only give you my word. I have nothing else to offer," I explain then sit back silently, letting my words filter through to him. We both sit, staring into the distance.

"Since when do people do something for nothing?"

"Since it's for the collective good. Since now. Like I said, I can only give you my word. If I'm wrong about this you can kill me!"

Michael's brown crinkly face ripples into a gummy laugh displaying his remaining tombstone teeth.

"You've been watching too many movies," he laughs.

"Yeah. That was overdoing it a bit."

"I can't speak for others, but I don't think anyone will buy it."

"But what if Shasta was supporting it? Would that make a difference?"

Michael eyes me carefully, pondering what I've said but his response is more silence.

"Just have a think about it. You know where to find me."

Michael looks up and nods as I cross the room to the door.

"Tara. Thanks. I know you mean well."

I nod back and take my leave as Michael flicks on the television to the sports channel, which noisily fills the room.

Shasta didn't make it, although I'm not sure the outcome would have been any different if he had been here. I like spending time with Michael. His energy is so different - he effervesces in a unique, uncouth way, which is intriguing and makes me feel like I'm crossing some invisible boundary. I run through the twists in our conversation and a red flag rises. He said his friend's daughter has just returned to live. I wonder if that is the lovely Leonie or if it's just a coincidence.

I turn out onto the main road and the black outline of Shasta's car, parked outside a square, wooden house on a hill comes into focus. My heart lurches and drops beats. He's on the Rez when he told me he was working. My head and my heart oppose each other. He's seeing Leonie, he didn't turn up because he's gone to see her; they're getting back together. *No, there must be a perfectly reasonable explanation:* Shasta's a confident, direct, guy. He would tell me if he was having second thoughts. I check my cell phone for a missed call but it's blank. I could go and call at the door, just say I was passing. *No chance.* What if I caught them up to something? It would torture me - as if the rampaging negative thoughts aren't already doing that. I toss my cell on the opposite seat and head back to town.

8

You don't know, what you don't know. That thought is on an infinite loop and I try to avoid thinking about why I haven't heard from Shasta. I turn up the volume on the radio and drown it all out as I swipe a muesli bar from the cupboard, devour it and wash it down with a glass of apple juice. I'm not that upset that I would miss breakfast, but I do feel on edge.

"Whoa there," Simons stalks in: hunched, bleary eyed and covering his ears.

"Penny needs riding! You've reminded me."

"Are you teaching her to break dance as well? " Simon winces and turns the music down. "Any chance of a ride to work?"

"Now?"

"Give me ten minutes or so?"

"I need to open the store," I snap, then remember it's his first day in his new job at the Hot Springs Spa and feel guilty.

"What's eating you this morning?" He gives me a keen sideways look and pours himself a black coffee.

"Sorry."

"Well? What have you got for me?" he asks, dumping himself into a seat at the old pine table in front of the range. He gestures to the chair opposite him and runs his fingers through his flattened hair, pulling it up in tufts.

"Nothing," I reply.

"Nothing, my ass!"

"Nothing, but an over active imagination." I tell him about not having heard from Shasta but seeing his car on the Reservation.

"You're right. You've got nothing, but if you want my opinion, and I'm sure you do, otherwise you wouldn't be telling me this, you want to learn to start trusting that guy."

"But-"

"No ifs, no buts!" he waves his hand in the air.

I take a deep breath.

"Tara, it is as plain as day to me, and everyone else, that guy has you on a pedestal and if you start letting your past experiences with some of the Casanovas you've dated taint this relationship, then you're a fool and you'll only have yourself to blame."

"What about Leonie? She wants him, I can see that."

"Leonie baloney. She's irrelevant. You've got trust issues – big time," he points a finger like a full stop.

"Don't be holding back there, Simon."

"I won't! I'm your friend, and you need to straighten this out," he says, draining his coffee mug. "That's not as good as the coffeehouse."

"That's me told," I mutter to Hudson as Simon dashes upstairs to fix his hair. And with the amount of product he uses, I do mean fix. Hudson sweeps the floor with his tail.

"Do you think I've trust issues, Hudson? One woof for yes, two woofs for no."

He tips his snout in the air as he barks. I look around in disbelief hoping someone else saw it, but I'm alone at the kitchen table.

"I guess that's the majority then."

There is a quick knock before the front door opens. My heart skids to a stop. That could be Shasta. Hudson barks as he runs past to greet him.

Shasta looks at me carefully when he comes in.

"Morning beautiful."

"Morning," I reply. Despite what Simon said. My tone is tepid. *Don't think you can butter me up.*

"I'm sorry I didn't make it last night," he says, eyeing me like a hawk.

"Oh. It didn't really matter," I reply indifferently.

"You're upset with me."

I tilt my head and raise an eyebrow trying not to portray my doubts.

"You are. I'm sorry, but things happened."

"Oh. What?"

"I got a call to say my mom had taken ill. She's diabetic. She had a bad turn and I had to get emergency medicine. I couldn't call you because my phone died, then when I got home I fell dead asleep."

The quick thaw begins. All it took was a simple explanation, and as Shasta takes a step towards me, his close proximity warms me further.

"Is she OK?"

He tilts his mouth down to mine as his eyes flick over my face and the fizzing between us increases. He stills and raises one eyebrow.

"Your mom?"

"She's fine. I've missed you. One night away from you and I need rehab. What have you done to me Mahasani? You've put a spell on me."

"I'm glad to hear that," I smile and reach up with my lips still parted to kiss him. "And what is Mahasani?"

He grins revealing all his square white teeth. "It's an affectionate term my mom uses. It's Lakota Sioux. It means 'my other skin' – inside our palms is a medicine wheel and when we hold hands the energy flows and mingles, as we journey together we are one."

"Oh my God. That's so beautiful," I tell him, melting at his words; I think he'll have to hold me up. He leans forward and presses me against the wall. I reach up and touch his lean jaw as we kiss.

"Mwah." Simon makes a smacking noise with his lips. "Put that girl down Shasta. You don't know where she's been."

Shasta grins. I want to feel those beautiful teeth on my tongue, and I snatch a kiss.

"Can I have that ride now?" asks Simon petulantly as he stands and taps his watch.

I set off to the coffeehouse with a spring in my step, remembering every detail of his face and touching my neck where he touched me, oblivious to the rest of the world. I drift through the morning in a hazy bubble of contentedness, leaving Lucy and Sophie to it while I try to catch up on some paperwork in the upstairs office, trying not to be distracted by my constant thoughts of Shasta. I catch myself staring into space and looking at the cell phone on the desk, resisting the urge to call Shasta, when the cell phone springs to life with a familiar ringtone.

"You were missing me?" I ask, smiling.

"Maybe? Were you?"

"No. You hadn't crossed my mind," I reply, flippantly.

"Ice queen. I hope you can find it in your heart to love another."

"Another?"

"I can see another male coming into your life. He's tall, dark-"

He's clearly referring to himself.

"Modest."

"Stubborn. Barely ridden" he replies.

My mouth curls up and I giggle. "I don't know who that could be."

"He's another King."

"One night away from me and you're deprived or depraved?"

"He's trying to impress this blonde but she's playing hard to get."

Now he's lost me. "What are you talking about?"

"I've found a kindred stable mate for Penny. His name is Sultan. He's a nine year old dark bay gelding I've had my eye on. Right now he's getting better acquainted with Penny. I have a new career as a matchmaker."

"He's a gelding. I don't know that Penny would thank you for that choice."

"She looks impressed so far. I better go. I think he's about to mount her," he says and rings off.

Another horse would be a welcome addition, and it would be another pair of eyes for Penny. I've a feeling Shasta envisions us both riding, though putting me on a blind horse would not be wise. I return to the hum of activity downstairs in the store. Giselle has arrived and is talking to a couple of women about one of her favorite topics: metaphysics and energy medicine. They peruse books while Giselle chats in a gentle, non-persuasive way which is great for sales. The women chatter enthusiastically and end up buying several books. There has been a steady and increasing stream of people through the bookshop since we took over, and sales are improving.

Giselle looks up and points at something, mouthing

incoherent words and rolling her eyes. Whatever she is trying to bring my attention to is obscured behind the two women at the counter. The women move away, still talking animatedly about a healing circle Svetlana is running which they are going to. It's great that Giselle has found more people of similar interest; I know she was missing that. Giselle brings me in on the conversation, introducing me to the women and we briefly make small talk before they leave.

Now I see what Giselle was drawing my attention to. Cain Shimlow is hunched over the reference books with his hands either side of the table; drumming his fingers irritably as he scrutinizes something. His intense face has the purple hue of stagnant blood, which often comes with hypertension. He had overheard the conversation with Giselle and the women but it's hard to tell if he is annoyed by what he is reading or what he heard. I had been pretty damn sure he wouldn't want to be anywhere near the store once we took over, but I was wrong.

"He was here when I walked in," whispers Giselle as I approach him, curiosity getting the better of me.

"Cain. How are you?" I ask, after all courtesy is good for business.

He looks up over his glasses, hardly raising his eyelids to look at me.

"It's always fascinated me how history books are written with such heavy bias towards the writer's personal translation. I think I should record my own version of what really happened."

"I guess there's no one around to ask," I reply.

"People here have long memories. The truth gets passed from generation to generation. My family knew there was more gold there. They were betrayed by those trying to steal what was rightfully theirs. It still is."

"As I understand it, apart from a few flakes of gold in the riverbeds there was no big find."

"You need to research your facts, my dear. My great, great grandfather was no fool, but after business went bust there were no investors for the mine. Instead of finding true riches my family lost everything, despite that, my great grandfather never lost his faith in God. Until the day he died he sought the treasure which rightly belongs to us. It's still there," says Cain, his face twitching unnervingly.

"I'm curious, Cain. Why does it mean so much to you?"

"It's my birthright," he snaps, his trite face is emphatic. "My grandmother always said there was no greater treasure than the one you discover yourself. Her family had been happy and wealthy but that was lost, she knew great poverty and unhappiness. She saw her father lose his mind, trying to restore value to the family. She made me promise to carry on looking for what my ancestors lost. I will uphold that promise."

"Maybe it wasn't literally gold they were searching for."

"You don't know what you're talking about. My ancestors stashed what gold they still possessed in the valley to stop it being stolen, but when they returned they couldn't find it. It was of no value to those pagans; the Indians are known for taking what isn't theirs."

"You don't know that. Maybe your grandfather just forgot where he put it."

"With God on my side I will find it and restore my family honor to the glory it deserves."

"How humble of you!"

"What do you know about it? You're keeping alternative

company. Those Indians know where it is, but they don't have the sense to use it."

"Good luck in your search. I hope you find what you're looking for," I reply, unable to make my voice sound sincere. I walk casually out of the shop to clear an outside table on the covered sidewalk. Cain follows close behind me. I can feel his dark grey coat fluttering against my side as he keeps pace with me. There is a weird, throaty snort from him as he breathes rapidly. He seems out of breath.

"Does the phrase 'the sins of the father' mean anything to you? Have you ever been in a church long enough to find out?"

"I'm familiar with that phrase. I call it ancestral karma," I reply, trying to ignore him as I busy myself.

"Congratulations on establishing your parentage by the way. Wasn't your grandmother a pagan deviant? Perhaps you have some dues to pay?"

"You're a fruit, Cain! Stay away from me!"

"Renounce your sins, Tara. I could baptize you."

"God knows what you'd do to me if you got my head in the water," I laugh it off and smile at a couple of teenagers who give us a wary look on their way into the store.

"I'm sure you know more than you're letting on. You and your friends are promoting sorcery."

"If that were true I'd say the magic words and you would vanish!"

"You will get what is coming to you. As will I," shouts Cain. He stoops forward as he walks down the steps, mumbling insensibly.

"I don't doubt it," I mutter under my breath. That man makes my teeth itch. I can't abide being told what to do and his superiority complex makes it doubly irritating.

I've done well to avoid him since Rosa died, but he came onto my turf. I remember something Giselle had said - I should let it go, but...

"Oh Cain. Just one thing." He lifts his head up. "If gold was found, do you think it should be returned?" I ask, playfully lifting my gold and ruby amulet between my thumb and forefinger and pretending to think. "Finders keepers I reckon."

His face wrinkles with darkness and it's the last thing I see before I go back inside and close the door. *That was bad.* However the opportunity to bait Shimlow was irresistible. I have no idea if local gold was used to make the amulet, and I'm pretty sure that my grandmother and her family had nothing to do with prospector's disputes, but it put the cat amongst Cain Shimlow's pigeons. *You'll pay for that* - I see the letters of the warning spelled out in front of my mind.

"Tara? Tara North?" says a fairy-light, sing-song voice. Balancing a tray full of crockery I stop at a table where the voice came from. A blonde girl with blue eyes and cheerleader like beauty is looking up at me, resting a cerise pink fingernail against her cheek.

"Hi," I reply, not having a clue who she is.

"I knew it was you. Didn't I say that looks like Tara North?" she checks in with the other blonde who looks, smiles and politely looks away at nothing, vaguely annoyed at the interruption to their gossiping.

"I'm sorry. I don't know who you–"

"Verity. Verity Kessler," she says, holding her hand up and framing her face.

"Of course. Verity. I'd never have recognized you," I explain my docile response. Of course I'd have recognized that baby sweet face anywhere, but not having given her a second thought since high school, she wasn't in my line-up.

"You look amazing. Doesn't she?" she nods, rhetorically, to her friend.

"So do you," I reply. She always looked great. She had one of those faces that needed no decoration but got it anyway. As I put the tray down I glimpse Giselle deep in conversation. The woman she is talking to flicks her silky black hair off her smiling face. My heart knocks hard twice then goes silent. It's Leonie. What are they finding to talk about that's so interesting? It's a distraction to Verity Kessler's tuneful gushing which I revert back to.

"I didn't think it could be you though, Tara. Not working as a barista in a place like this. Not that there's anything wrong with it, but I wouldn't have put you down for this. You were so...smart. Weren't you going to be a lawyer or something?" asks Verity, curling up her cute button nose with utter disregard for diplomacy.

"It turned out that being a lawyer wasn't all it was cracked up to be," I reply, distractedly.

"Aw. That's a shame. Isn't it?" says Verity, once again including her vacant friend.

"No. It's fine, really. What are you doing now?" I ask.

"Oh, you know. Nothing. I've been married for eight years, kids are at school. I have to find ways to occupy myself. Drinking coffee is a great pastime. We must catch up soon." With wide eyes she embellishes her words with enthusiasm. I'm not sure why now isn't classed as a suitable catch up.

"You'll usually find me here," I reply.

"Aw. Do they work you hard?"

"No. I own the place."

Verity pouts and nods as though her neck is on elastic. "Ah, lovely," she says with a twisted smile which indicates she doesn't believe me.

At the shift in their attention my focus goes to what Leonie and Giselle are saying. Toying with the idea of going over there, but in light of my argument with Cain Shimlow - avoidance is probably better. Regardless I go over and hover.

"I can recommend this one because it really keeps you guessing," Giselle advises Leonie and smiles at me. "Have you read this?" she asks me, holding up some random novel. I lower my eyebrows and swivel my eyes towards Leonie trying to alert Giselle, but she isn't able to read my expression.

"No. It's on my reading list."

"It's racy, though maybe not enough for your tastes," Giselle jokes.

Leonie looks at me and her face is already fixed into a pleasant expression.

"Hi, again," I smile back.

"Nice place. I like what you've done with it," says Leonie, arching her graceful eyebrows. How does she know this is our business? I could be a customer for all she knows.

"Thanks. It's early days yet."

"Shasta's proud of you," she says softly, and blinks her long dark lashes.

I try to hold my smile but the muscles in my face have temporary paralysis. Giselle's keen eyes dart from me to Leonie. Her expression changes to restrained alarm when she catches up.

"He is?" I ask, in full control although inside I'm

demanding to know how she would be privileged to that information.

"He told me. I hope Sultan settles in quickly into his new home," she replies, laying upon me that fact she is current with what is going on in my life. She has the upper hand on me, but I not about to let her think she knows more about it than I do.

"He probably already has if Shasta has anything to do with it," I reply, leaning casually on the counter.

"I know, that's what I told him. He has such a gift with animals," replies Leonie, sounding so incredibly nice. If her intention is to make me feel excluded then she is succeeding. Just when did she tell him that? He only got Sultan today, and even I didn't know about it.

"Shasta said he bumped into you. I'm glad you two caught up," I say with impeccable and Oscar-winning sincerity.

Leonie flashes a smile but it dies on her face and she looks away.

"Thanks for the tips, Giselle." She picks up the books. "Now I've got some bedtime reading - unless I can find something else to do." She grins at Giselle as though she is her new best friend and glances my way with a demure smile as she leaves. This girl has Napoleonic tactics!

"Giselle, that is the lovely Leonie." I watch as a man coming into the store holds the door as she leaves and he lets his gaze follow her.

"I had no idea!" breathes Giselle once Leonie has gone. "She was really nice."

"And I have nothing to worry about?"

"You and Shasta have got to stick tight together. Do not let her get in the way," says Giselle adamantly.

"I don't intend to."

9

It's gentle at first. The feeling of being electrified increases and I'm wide awake. It powers through my body, through every nerve ending; it feels like I'm on fire. I feel like I'm being lifted. It increases to ten – just as much as I can take – then it shifts beyond that. I twitch and shake as though I'm being electrocuted by the extreme surging energy. *Enough*, I try to cry out but my voice is only a thought discharged. I can't take any more. I feel like I'm being held up by a spiking current, as though I'm being hit by continual lightening. It's some sort of quickening. Still the electrifying heightens. No more. *Stop*, I demand. The arcing energy levels off. *That was all it took?*

The trembling subsides and I lie peacefully still in the bed once more. *What the hell was that?*

I'm completely fine but that was bizarre. My eyes prick at the shadows around the familiar room. My senses feel sharper; I feel invigorated, as though I may never need to sleep again. I need to speak to Svetlana about this and text her just after 7:30 a.m. to see if she has an appointment today. She offers me a cancellation for later.

That's not the only peculiar thing that has happened this morning. Shasta had sent me a text asking me to come over to ride Penny because he had to go somewhere. Ride Penny? On my own?

Shasta and I went for a swim at the Hot Springs Spa last night. We were tactile, close and affectionate, within the bounds of good taste considering we were in public. Dreamily looking out through the steamy haze which hung over the outdoor pool, that overlooks the town, everything was fine; great even. We talked about the day. He told me all about Sultan's robust character and heritage, and his plans to keep him as his own horse and retrain him. The previous owner found him too much to handle as a stallion and as a last resort had him gelded.

I told him about Leonie's visit to *The Book and Bean* and my hunch that she was playing a game to win him back. I didn't make a big fuss about it. I just mentioned it in passing. But I didn't predict the effect it would have on him. He had been remote ever since. Not in a dramatic way, but I could feel it. Shasta said he had seen Leonie on his way to pick up Sultan, which is a reasonable explanation.

However, I think I've crossed a barrier of trust. I'm starting to feel like I'm the only one that can see what is going on here, although Giselle is usually astute, I wonder if she is being hoodwinked by Leonie too. Shasta seems completely oblivious but it's easier for the pursued, they are the one in the driving seat with the option of thumbs up or thumbs down.

When we parted last night, we seemed to dance around each other. He said he would go home to his, with some vague excuse about having an early start. He gets the birds up; he always has an early start. I accepted it, and joked that it was probably a good idea not to spend *every* night together, to keep the mystery, but I felt the sting of rejection regardless. That's one of the myths about being seen as a 'strong person' – you're judged to be resilient. I don't put on a brave face, it just seems to happen. When I felt down and broken, people said how tough I was. What was I supposed to do? Lie down and weep? I only did that in private.

I thought Shasta could see beyond that perception of

me. In fact, I had been sure of it. He saw my vulnerability, and that is what I had tried to let him see. I'm not the fearless, determined, warrior chick people think I am.

It's drizzling with rain by the time I get to Shasta's lake house, and his car is gone. The wind has picked up, driving the raindrops at a sideways angle. I pull my waterproof jacket tighter around me, draw back my hair and put on the wide-brimmed wax hat to keep the rain from my eyes. The whinnying from Penny's stable means she knows someone is here. I reassure her that it's me, calling to her as I open the adjoining stable door to check on Sultan. The tall dark horse swings round to face the half-door, throwing his head up and flicking his black mane; he looks intimidating and elite. The watchful flashing eyes and imposing height make it clear why he got his name. I turn my attention back to Penny, tacking her up and leading her out of the stable. She's reluctant and I suspect it's the bad weather. *Now why do you want me to do this, Shasta? Couldn't this have waited until it was at least dry?*

"You don't like the rain, Penny? That makes two of us," I talk reassuringly to her, telling her everything I'm doing. "Just a little bit of exercise in the corral. No biggie. It's just you and me today, girl."

Damp, and becoming more and more irascible because of the gusting wind, I'm about to have humor failure. What was it Shasta said? I need her as much as she needs me? To tune into each other – there were things neither of us could see. *Cryptic crap.* But I know deep down that there must be some reason for it. I lead her into the corral, place one foot in the stirrup and as I'm about to throw my leg over and mount, my cell phone alerts to an incoming text message. Penny side steps away from me. I hop, but lose my footing. I'm swiftly dumped on the wet, sandy earth on my back. Penny throws her head in the air looking wildly, but blindly around. I free my foot and stand up, mentally swearing. It was a schoolgirl error - I shouldn't have left the cell phone on. I turn it off, after I glimpse a text from Shasta saying he hoped the riding was going well.

"Ha! He wants to know if the riding is going well, Penny?" I shove the phone in my pocket. He had this planned. He knows Penny's temperament and mine. This was a way of testing us both. *I'll show you trust.*

I mount properly this time and set off around the corral in the circuit we have done before. Randomly a couple of hay bales and a bucket have found their way into the corral which is *always* empty of obstructions for Penny's benefit. The whole time I have the feeling I am being watched. The wind whispers through the forest; there is nothing there, but I can't shake the feeling. Penny's ears flicker back and forward.

Maybe Shasta is watching from a distance. I glance around and see nothing to warrant the edgy feeling. I've had enough for today. I apprehensively lead Penny back to the stables, keeping check on my peripheral vision. I remember the ruby amulet and ask for its protection. A mountain lion, a cougar or any number of things could be stalking us. The thought of Marshall Buchanan's vengeful threat against Shasta has not been far from my thoughts, but I've kept them quiet and not given them focus. Things had been quiet on that front, but I know how the Buchanans operate and if it's not going on above ground it certainly is underneath.

"I'm being ridiculous Penny. Aren't I?" I say to her as I

undo the girth and remove her saddle as steam rises from her warm damp body.

On the way over to Svetlana's I dry off in the car and arrive in a better mood. She hugs me and looks at me oddly, then stands back scrutinizing me. "You're different. It doesn't feel like you," she says, apparently perplexed but trying to clarify her strange greeting.

"Do you mean that as a good thing?"

"I don't know. You feel very raw and strong."

I explain to her about this morning's electrifying phenomenon, hoping she can shed some light on it.

"I can't explain it, but it sounds like you've had an energy upgrade which is shifting you to another level. You've never had anything like it before?"

"Nothing like this."

"I guess you wouldn't get it if you weren't ready for it. How do you feel?"

"Physically good, just a bit spooked by this morning. I'm not sure what to make of it," I don't tell her that I'm concerned about things with Shasta, because I don't want to divert her attention. Svetlana takes my wrist and goes quiet while she checks my pulses. I found this odd the first time - I could feel her gently pressing different areas on my wrist. I'd asked her about it and she said that in Chinese Medicine there are twelve pulses points, six on each wrist which correspond to different organs in the body. She uses it as her main diagnostic tool. I love that she can tell so much about what is going on inside me from it.

"Well?" I ask, curious about Svetlana's silence.

"Can I see your tongue?"

I swallow then stick it out. She gives my tongue a cursory glance.

"Your pulses are vastly different. Pulses are like a signature - very individual. Sometimes you could be blindfolded and still know whose energy it is. I can hardly recognize yours today."

"They're good?"

"Very strong. More balanced. I want some of what you've got. I'm not going to give you much acupuncture today. I've never said this to anyone before, but you don't need it, and your body is implementing something new. Just let it."

"Aw, none?" I enjoy my sessions with Svetlana. The needle phobia is long gone.

"OK, just a couple of needles in each wrist for anxiety, but I want to do something else with you."

My ears prick up. "What?"

She smiles and meets my eye. "I just want you to relax and tell me what you feel."

I lie down and close my eyes. Almost straight away I can feel the heat from her hands as she places them on me. She removes them but it feels like she's still there. I open my eyes slightly and see her wafting her hands around me as though she is gathering something invisible and spreading it out. I feel peaceful, as though internal knots are unwinding. Svetlana finishes and tells me to sit up on the edge of the bed while she continues with something else. I haven't seen her do this before.

She makes a circle with her finger and thumb, places one the top of my head, the other at the base of my spine. I feel myself rising up to full height, then beyond, lengthening through to my head. It's happening spontaneously. I giggle because I can't help it. Once I can't extend any higher I feel myself being drawn backwards towards Svetlana, who is standing behind me. It's bizarre to be lying back at this angle but it's oddly comfortable. She then shifts the same linked fingers to each shoulder, then to my hips and finishes off on the soles of each foot. I start to laugh uncontrollably and fill with tears.

"What was that?"

"Are you OK?"

"Fricking amazing," I laugh. "I feel taller. Not that I needed that!"

"It's ring-linking. Something I've been guided to do on some patients recently. It's not for everyone. Apparently it increases and connects you with the highest sphere and keeps balance in the vibration. It's like a reconnection to the One. Those I've done it on say they still feel it weeks later."

"You can do that again anytime, Svetlana!"

"I may not need to. It may not have the same effect either once you're better connected to source."

"How did you work out what to do?"

"I saw it. I saw gold lines connected by circles at their junctions. These gold lines connect the body to something greater: a golden grid network is what I saw. What I'm doing is just acting as a mediator."

"Have you looked into this?"

"Yep. I didn't find much. Just a picture in an old pack of angel cards that was almost identical to what I saw. It's to do with Archangel Metatron linking humanity with energy," says Svetlana. "It won't be on my website because I'd be gambling my credibility."

"You've really found something special there."

"Well, I don't fully understand it but it feels good. It's like faster ways of improving the energy flow are coming in."

"I know someone who will be down here in a flash."

Svetlana laughs. "And how is Giselle?" We chat for a while until her phone rings. She waves me out with a promise of getting our eclectic bunch of friends together.

10

When I get home, Shasta is sitting in the kitchen talking to Giselle and Simon. Simon is re-enacting an anecdote about something that had happened while Giselle rustles up French toast for everyone; setting fresh berries and maple syrup in the centre of the table. Shasta looks up and smiles at me, saying nothing but his eyes are questioning and starting a conversation of their own. He stands up and gives me his seat next to the range. "You're cold," he says squeezing my hand under the table. "Good ride?"

"Great." I nod and look back at Simon who is looking at us, mildly annoyed at the audience interruption.

"So, Shasta, I haven't finished yet," chides Simon, resting his hands on his hips.

Shasta re-focuses his attention and looks amused by Simon's need to be the centre of attention. A subtle knowing smile passes between us.

"And then, that's when it happened..." Simon says dramatically, as though we are supposed to guess what happened next."

Giselle looks at me and rolls her eyes. "Get on with it, Simon," she says, serving up the French toast onto the kitchen table.

"That's when I saw Cain Shimlow walk out into the traffic. He nearly caused a pile up! Not an easy thing to do around here either I might add."

"Why did he walk out in the traffic, Simon?" asks Giselle, not keeping the irritability out of her voice. She's probably been listening to the build up to this tale for the past fifteen minutes.

"Well, people were honking their horns at him, and

going around him. He was getting them to roll down their car windows so he could give them a leaflet, or he'd stick it on the windscreen of the car when they slowed down. Well you can imagine, that went down like a fart in a space suit."

Shasta looks stern. His eyes are darker and more ominous than the clouds rolling in over the mountain.

"He could have got himself killed, but he was oblivious. He fell over the bonnet of one poor woman's car as she tried to avoid him. Poor old thing was white with shock. She thought she'd killed him," Simon continues, using theatrical gestures.

"What did the leaflets say?" asks Shasta, ignoring the plate of banana fritters Giselle has put in front of him.

"Well that's what I had to find out. What could be so important that you would stop the traffic? I didn't have to go far. The flyers are all over the main street. It's a bit of a mess to be honest. Especially in that wind," he laughs distractedly. "I can just imagine tumble weeds blowing through like in one of those old Westerns. Dodle-a-dah, wah-wah-wah!" he mimics old Western music from something like *The Good, The Bad and The Ugly.* "Except it was leaflets instead of tumbleweeds," he meanders like a stream not reaching the point.

"Simon! What did the leaflets say?" asks Shasta simmering with impatience.

"OK. OK. I'm getting to it. It wasn't that interesting anyway. He's trying to rally support to put together a local group to start mining for gold. He's selling it as a huge commercial asset for the town and one that'll attract business. He's trying to get together a work party and he's looking for investors with deep pockets. Do you think there's gold out there?" Simon looks seriously at Shasta.

"No, but I think they could do a lot of damage trying to find it," he replies, tearing into his food.

"I have to say, Cain did seem a bit exuberant - Not that I'm one to judge," says Simon raising his eyebrows and cutting up his toast with a knife and fork.

"It sounds like he's desperate," adds Giselle.

"Who would trust him with their money when he's running around behaving like that?" says Simon, who then changes the subject back to work and the lively chatter continues over lunch before Giselle and Simon sprawl out in the lounge ready to watch a movie.

"You set me up this morning, didn't you?"

Shasta laughs with a wide smile that lights up his face. "No. But I knew it would be good for you to build on things with Penny."

"I thought you might be in the woods watching me?" I ask and watch for any trace of a smirk, knowing he won't be able to keep a straight face.

"Definitely not. I've been shoeing horses at the riding school in Fort Jarvis all morning."

"I think you're messing with me Shasta King. I've got the measure of you. You're trying to get me to trust, and use, my instincts. Aren't you?"

"You're too suspicious. Grab your coat. I'd like you to come over to the Rez with me. You've still not met my family."

I freeze on the spot and concern shows on my face.

"Relax, they'll love you. How could they not?" he says kissing me. "You look different today. You're glowing."

"Like I've been in a nuclear accident glowing or 'expectantly' glowing?"

"What?" asks Shasta and his brow furrows.

"Relax!" I reply, and leave him with the thought as I dive up the staircase. If meeting the family is inevitable I need to make a better impression. "I just need to change into something more suitable." I can't show up in the mud splattered jeans I wore riding.

"No need. It's not Monaco," he calls after me.

By the time I reappear I've changed into a black sweater and clean blue jeans. Shasta is standing beside the door holding it open. I'm glad I didn't have too much time to think about this. Meeting the in-laws is never usually a high point of a relationship, although most of my relationships never actually got to that point.

"What did you mean, expectantly glowing?" Shasta asks, immediately following up on the conversation.

"Now who doesn't like surprises?"

His mouth parts as he studies my face which gives up the game. "You had me going for a minute there."

"How much have you told them about me?" I ask, mentally preparing myself for the meet and greet as we arrive at his parents' house.

"Oh, just this and that," he replies vaguely. "It's cool, you've nothing to worry about."

"Are they expecting me?"

"Kind of. Mom wanted to make you lunch, but I put her off. I didn't think you'd want to have to endure that on your first meeting."

"Yeah, better keeping it brief the first time." When we arrive at the little house on the hill, Shasta opens the front door of his parents' home and I follow behind him feeling like a high school kid.

"Hey Dad," he tapers off his voice, trying not to startle the man with the salt and pepper hair sat upright in a chair, napping with his chin on his chest. His father suddenly looks up and stares straight ahead before realizing Shasta and I are standing there. They look uncannily similar, apart from his father's loosening skin, softening what had once been a strong, handsome face.

"Was I asleep?"

"Yes, Dad. This is Tara. Tara this is my dad, Carson."

"Hey," he stands up abruptly and shakes my hand. "Sorry. I must have dropped off. Luna, come in here! Shasta's brought Tara home to meet us."

A woman's swarthy lined face looks around the door, wide-eyed as her mouth forms an 'oh' shape when she sees us. She catches herself and smiles broadly, looking nervously behind her.

"I thought you were coming later," she explains quickly, stroking back wisps of hair.

"Sorry, is this a bad time? We can come back later?" I offer, looking to Shasta for a cue.

"No, it's fine. We were just chatting round the table. Carson couldn't stay awake. Could you?" Luna nudges him.

"Power naps keep me young," he protests.

"Mom, this is Tara," says Shasta.

Luna smiles then lightly touches my arm as someone else comes into the room. "Have a seat," she says.

"Hey. I'm Seb. Shasta's brother," says the well built, confident figure now filling the door frame. "You kept her under wraps, bro! Tara, I'm the one with the looks, and the charm."

"Hey Seb." I shake his hand and grin at his disarmingly charismatic presence and note that he's not as attractive as Shasta, but his rounded face is appealing nonetheless.

"I'll fix us a drink," says Luna, who jumps as though she just remembered something and makes towards the door of the kitchen. She stops before she reaches it as someone else comes into the room and I realize why Shasta's mother seems edgy. Luna snatches a glance at me then at Shasta, just before Leonie walks casually in; with a slow deliberate walk, as though she is one of the family. I'm utterly horrified and shocked by her arrival. Cracks of betrayal spread through me like veins in marble, and I feel like I'm crumbling. My face is the first thing to fall. Did Shasta know she would be here? My heart has just turned to dust. Unable to keep the hurt from my eyes I look at Shasta, but he looks ashen too and more importantly he looks angry. His dark eyes flash dangerously and his chin juts out. Clearly he didn't know she would be here. Is she stalking me? I cannot believe this - meet the in-laws and the ex! This is a nightmare. The atmosphere of the room takes on a Baltic chill.

"Leonie? When did you get here?" asks Carson, looking confused but unaffected by the temperature drop.

"She came in when you were asleep Carson," says Luna with bravado to try and cover the awkwardness. She knows it's inappropriate. Carson doesn't seem to be any the wiser.

"I tiptoed past. I didn't want to wake you," says Leonie, making it clear her presence is so accepted here she can come and go as she wishes. "I hope I'm not intruding?"

she looks at Shasta's stony face. Under her concerned voice is the shadow of mischief. Luna quickly exits the room, as though she's expecting a bomb to go off.

"So, Bro. What's the occasion? Are you getting married?" asks Seb, stirring the cauldron. "It's a bit soon, so must be true love!"

The tension can't be lost on Seb. He's using it to goad Shasta. He looks delightedly between Leonie, Shasta and I; ready to watch the sparks fly as Carson puts his feet up and looks on, apparently oblivious to the atmosphere.

"Oh, this is awkward," says Seb grinning, almost to the point of laughing.

"What are you doing here?" asks Shasta, unreservedly making his irritation clear.

"Just a social call, to see the family," replies Leonie.

"Whose family, Leonie?"

"Oh...you don't want me to call? I'm sorry. It's just...I think of them as my own family," she says, looking meek and apologetic.

"Leonie, would you give me a hand with this?" calls Luna from the kitchen. It could be her attempt to defuse the situation.

"I take it you were just leaving anyway?" suggests Shasta. He puts his arm around my shoulders and cements the fact that he and I are a unit. Leonie looks crestfallen. Whether it's genuine or she's trying to gain sympathy is unclear. She blinks fast, but probably not as fast as she can think.

"I didn't mean to upset anyone," she says, her eyes becoming round and hurt-looking. "I'll just help your mom in the kitchen and then I'll get out of your way." Leonie sniffs as though tears are threatening.

"Come on, I'll show you round," says Shasta, taking my hand and walking out of the room, followed by his brother, as we head to the backyard.

"That went well," says Seb, beaming sarcastically at his brother.

Shasta punches him on the arm. His brother responds by wrapping Shasta in a headlock. He breaks out of it and amid shouts of derision a playful tussle begins. They bump against the door frame of the kitchen. I'm not sure where to put myself and grin at Luna as we pass through; she smiles gently back. She has her hand on Leonie's back in a motherly, reassuring manner. Leonie is looking at the floor and whispering; milking the situation for all she's worth. I don't just feel like a new arrival to the family, I feel like an intruder. Seb and Shasta bump into the worktop and the glasses shake. Luna rolls her eyes and shouts at them to take it outside, telling them they haven't grown up.

"Playtime," I say awkwardly and follow the brothers outside, hoping Leonie will take the opportunity and leave. Shasta picks up an armful of crisp, dry, leaves from the ground and dumps them over Seb's head. Seb reaches around Shasta's waist and pushes him into a deep drift of leaves under a tree. I can relax more out here, and when the cold, biting air catches in my throat I can't help but chuckle, seeing Shasta in a new light. I'd not had that kind of relationship with my brother, and it looks to be getting rougher as they get carried away.

"Who wants to shoot some hoops with me?" I call to them, seeing the basketball net attached to a shed. I loved basketball at school; being one of the tallest in the class was a help. The brothers fight to get to the hoop, holding each other back and tripping one another up. I don't stand a chance against Seb and Shasta: one – because they are both well over 6' tall, and two – because they cheat.

Leonie is still in the house and I keep watching the back door for any sign of her leaving. Shasta grabs me round the waist when I try to run so I can only run in circles, meanwhile Seb grabs the ball from me. It's then that Leonie comes drifting out of the house. I stop trying to get away and look over. Shasta follows my gaze and lets me go. He's sensitive and wouldn't want to rub it in. My breath catches when she comes towards us. I glance nervously at Shasta, looking for a clue to what he's thinking.

"I'm sorry if it was inappropriate for me to be here," she says, shifting her gaze to Shasta.

Shasta lifts his chin in acknowledgement. "It's OK. No harm done."

"I just want you to know you have nothing to fear from me, Tara. I don't mean you any trouble. I'm no threat," says Leonie, and if it weren't for the vice like grip in my gut I'd be inclined to think she was being sincere.

Leonie turns and walks off across the grass, with one little look back over her shoulder and a glimmer of a smile. My foreboding deepens that this girl is so plausible she can take in most people. I have no doubt she has her eyes on my prize. I've met girls like her before. I know the type. She's a cat-like, stealth operator and just when she has your trust she'll steal from under your nose.

"I'm glad she apologized," says Shasta, taking my hand and pulling me towards him and we hug.

"Me too."

The breeze moves the scent of his hair around me and I breathe in the moment. I'm so lucky to have him in my life and I'm not going to let anyone take him from me. I don't tell him my doubts about Leonie - after all he has concerns about my lack of trust in him. For now I'll let him believe everything is well but keep my radar on high alert.

11

With fading day light and the cold, mid-fall temperatures the lake shore is no longer where we greet the morning together. The pale, lemon light streaming through the glass wall of the upstairs lounge is much more attractive and warm; the view of the forest and waterscape, and the indigo tree reflections on the still water which are constantly changing. The first snowfall of winter may not be far away, and then the ice will tamper with the fluid condition of the lake and all movement will cease.

From lounging by the window in my grey-marl sweatpants and white t-shirt I make my way to the shower. Shasta has taken an early phone call and I can hear him talking in his study. I don't disturb him. It's his man zone - the only untidy part of the house because of Shasta's dislike for paperwork.

Like the rest of the house, it is light and airy: not overly decorated, light-colored walls with a few large Native American prints on the walls. The real beauty comes from the natural materials of the house: the wide, stone chimney breast of the open fire which runs from floor to ceiling, the golden, timber, struts holding up the vaulted ceiling, the black and orange-streaked, stone floor covering the under-floor heating. The front of the house faces over Emerald Lake and is fully glazed. The wide glass panes allow the feel of the outdoors on the inside.

I clean my teeth and place the toothbrush in the holder next to Shasta's, intending to leave it there. I feel like I'm ready. I have no idea what Shasta's reaction will be, or if he will even notice. At times I still find him difficult to read, and rely more on what I glean from tuning into him. His cool, subtle facial expressions don't always convey the strength of emotion that lies behind them. A strange feeling like a lizard skittering up my abdomen makes me shiver as I step out of my clothes and step into the steaming hot shower in the wet room. A few minutes later I reach for the towel with my eyes screwed shut when soft fabric wipes the water from my eyes, before I find it. I open my eyes to see Shasta standing there looking intensely at me, not blinking, just taking everything in.

"How long have you been there?"

"You're beautiful," he whispers, appraising me all over. Feeling exposed, I begin to wrap the towel around myself as the colder air wafts in.

"So are you," I reply, keeping the deep prolonged eye contact, which is becoming the signature of our relationship in a way that I've never experienced with anyone else.

"Just one thing?" he asks.

I watch him move backwards, keeping his eyes on me while his hand reaches for the toothbrush next to his. He holds the item in his hand. His eyes are still.

"It doesn't have to mean anything..." I grin, caught in my own dilemma of whether he'll think I'm being pushy or maybe not pushy enough.

"It's a slippery slope. It all starts with the toothbrush," his eyes twinkle and his voice is mildly menacing and I can't help but laugh.

"Would it be so terrible to wake beside me every morning?" he asks, with a look so sexy and thrilling my stomach churns with a thousand butterflies.

"There would be nothing terrible about that," I reply, speaking from the boundary of my commitment comfort zone.

"Well maybe we could talk about that when we come back from Ireland."

"Come back from Ireland?" I ask in astonishment, watching the delight on his face at my reaction.

"Yep. That was Will Quinn on the phone. I've agreed to do some work for him, in preparation for some racing. I'll be working a lot, but I'm sure you can find something to do there."

"Seriously?" I squeak, excitement getting the better of me.

"We leave tomorrow."

"I can't go tomorrow! I can't leave Giselle in the store on her own!" Reality bites, but doesn't kill the buzz and my cheeks are burning.

"I thought you'd say that. I've already spoken to her and you have plenty of staff. She was nearly as excited as you."

"Oh my God! I love you Shasta King." I breathe affection and love for him from every pore on my body.

"I love you, Mahasani," he reaches over and touches the wet hair sticking to my face.

"I have so much to do. I have things to organize. I need to pack and-"

"Right now you're not going anywhere." He reaches over and pulls off my towel, throwing it across the room. He kicks off his sweat pants and steps seductively towards me, never taking his eyes off mine. He lowers his head to the side and presses his thick sensual lips to mine. I'm lost in the moment as he pushes me under the streaming shower again, drawing me to him.

I arrive at work in a dreamy haze. Sarah, the elderly lady with cancer, is sitting in her usual place beside the window. It's the same spot she sits at every day. Her daily visits have become such a ritual of our day, as well as hers, that I hope she proves the doctors wrong. How peacefully and innocently aware of everything she seems, like a new puppy in an old body. Every day she imparts a little more about her life. She's become a bit of an icon to us. We joked with her about writing a book, because really, you wouldn't believe one person could have experienced so much hardship and love.

"Oh my God," Giselle says excitedly. "You're going to Ireland!"

"Giselle. I am really sorry. I didn't want to leave you on your own. Not yet. If you're not comfortable with it, I won't go."

"Don't be ridiculous. Sophie and Lucy are on hand, Simon will be here too, and if we get short there are a couple of students looking for some hours. You won't be missed, but I do want you to bring me back an Irishman."

"I think you've already got an admirer over there." I aim my gaze in the direction of a guy I've seen here before. I've caught him watching Giselle several times. He's reading but his eyes keep shifting in her direction.

"I like," she says, glancing back from checking out the blonde-haired guy. Without moving her lips Giselle makes a throaty noise, keeping her eyes on me. "I keep getting caught looking at him," she says, risking another glance at the guy. He looks at her and she averts her eyes as she giggles and gets all googly eyed. Her face flushes deep red and it makes me laugh.

"Giselle, I've not seen you like this for a while."

"Oh, crap. I'm fine to talk if I'm not interested in

someone, but if it's someone I like - then it's a different matter."

"Make some excuse. He looks kind of bohemian and he's reading in your bookstore, what more ammo do you need?"

"Go on! Times a wastin'," comes Sarah's dry croaky voice into what we thought was a hushed conversation.

Oh God. Giselle grimaces. She's hoping blondie didn't hear that.

"You young ones think you've all the time in the world! Shall I ask him for you?"

"NO," we both echo in a shouted whisper.

Sarah looks around and chuckles to herself as Giselle and I move away.

Giselle heads behind the counter of the bookstore, casually surveying the shelves. I get on with planning what needs taken care of before I go. Running a quick stock check, phoning suppliers and running through things with Sophie, who reprimands me for thinking that she doesn't already know what she's doing when, in fact, she has worked here longer than me. She complains about the litter she picked up from outside the store this morning. Apparently leaflets were strewn everywhere as someone had tried to put them through the letter box, but most had fallen on the ground and blown around with the wet leaves. Sophie says she was tempted to join the working party to find the gold, but she had concerns about anything involving Cain Shimlow.

Giselle is watching the new object of her infatuation. He gets up and leafs through various books. He stops at the local history and second-hand section, flicking through a couple before putting them back on the shelf. A piece of paper flutters to the floor. It's not clear if it's fallen from the book he was carrying or from one of ours. The guy finishes the last of his drink and begins to walk away.

Predictably Giselle sees her opportunity. She calls after him, telling him he's dropped something. The man stops in his tracks and pauses before turning around. Giselle gets up from her crouching position on the floor and passes the loose sheet to him. Looking up at him she mists over. It warms my heart to see that beguiled expression on her face.

"Oh," he smiles at her. There is lull in their conversation and more is said in the pause than in their words.

"It is yours, isn't it?" she glances down at it. "It's handwritten."

"No. Not mine," he replies, as he glances over the sheet.

"It must have fallen out between the pages of one of those old books. I've not seen it before," says Giselle.

Standing side by side you can tell their energies match. They even look similar with their wiry physique, oval faces and light complexions.

"Can I have a look?" he asks, reading over her arm and leaning in.

Giselle is stock still. "Sure," she passes the paper to him and reads over his arm.

"I'm Cooper," he offers his hand.

"Giselle," she replies, and shakes it.

Shall we sit down? Then we can both read it," he asks.

Giselle acts nonchalant. "Sure." She smiles at the floor and bites her lip. They sit down at a table for two with the sheet of paper laid out between them. There's a rush of customers and I can't hear or see what's going on. When the flurry clears Giselle and Cooper are sat with their heads together, deep in conversation. I keep out of their way.

"Tara, you've got to see this," calls Giselle, waving me over. I wander over and introduce myself to Cooper and glimpse the paper they're studying. The paper is yellowing and appears old, yet the content is modern and relevant.

"Did you write this?" I ask, perplexed.

"I'm not that eloquent," Cooper replies, cocking his head. "Although I am a botanist, so it would seem poignant."

"Are you?" asks Giselle admiringly, and they continue their conversation while I read the unusual paper.

Trees bring joy to the hearts of many. Tunes can be heard, lilting through the valley. The consciousness closes the door. It speaks of great vastness, unifying with the Great Spirit of Oneness that flows through all. We are the same in totality. The heart resonates. A great anxiety sweeps the desert, fools only tread here. Yet look up, for beyond here lies what you are looking for. I communicate it to you. For centuries you sought, outlanders preparing for doom when all the time the connection was here, look skyward it's all there, heaven-sent vibration of oneness, for all to join.

Monoliths, great living monoliths of power and movement. Currents of light waves pulse through the Universe, lifting the heads of daisies, conducting heavenly signals from the sky. A massive down-thrust intends communication with you. You don't hear. The beat goes on, the drumming stops and you calibrate once more to what you know. Let go of what you know and let us show you.

Every tree has a beat, a solar expression of living beings, co-ordinating and winning light emissions from far beyond the sun. The synergy and the growing beat of communication, rises and falls, pulses and stalls. The sun's expression is harnessed in the light, forbidden by clouds, yet still codes enter our galaxy - they are meant to be sent. You are encoded. You are scripted Great Beings of Light. I know you. Anoint yourself with light connections. You are better together than one.

This is bizarre. Where had this come from, and who had written it? There is no signature or any indication of its origin. Perhaps it was someone's poetic musings? I'm sure Margy would be interested in seeing this too, in light of the forestry quest, and with Cooper being a botanist – it was too much of a coincidence. I'd always loved trees but looked at them with even greater awe and wonder after I'd seen the light they were holding.

"Cooper, there is someone I'd love you to meet." And I explain about Margy and what we had found out about the raising vibrations with trees. Cooper's blue eyes take it all in without a trace of disbelief. It turns out that he's no stranger to energy work. Giselle looks completely smitten, staring at him like she's watching a mirage that could disappear at any minute.

Because I leave for Ireland tomorrow, I give him Margy's contact number, hoping uniting them will somehow be beneficial. I'm not sure what my role is, or if I even have one, other than energy clearing I've done with Shasta. I still see the lights in the forest and my intuition is getting stronger all the time, but I feel less of a need to dwell on it and just accept it as a part of life. I know raising the vibration is important, but I've had the epiphany that everyone needs to do it for themselves: tackling their own issues, facing the stuff they've been trying to avoid.

There are ways of shifting things on further, and

lightening ourselves to a better vibration. If the vibration here changes, we have no choice but to change with it. The shift is already happening, what's not clear is where it's taking us. I get the feeling we can either ride it or resist it. I've read and heard talk of how the veils between worlds shift when the energy increases. We see into another world which is overlaid on this one, seeing those we thought no longer existed, glimpsing the immaterial world of living spirit existing alongside us. When I had the near-death experience I saw that realm, and I can remember the euphoria I felt there. To have that in a living experience would be incredible. I admit I also cling to a thread of hope that I would see Rosa living with me once again. I've accepted her death to a point, but it's tempered by knowing I'll see her again, one way or another.

I tactfully retreat from Giselle and Cooper sensing three is a crowd and make myself useful behind the counter, checking through the stock of speciality teas, when my dad walks in dressed in khaki clothing and a hunting hat.

"Barnaby, what can I get you?" asks Sophie.

"Nothing for me thanks. I need to see Tara," he says, breathlessly.

"Are you in disguise or are you off out hunting?" I ask.

"No. Have you got a minute?" he asks and I sense something is wrong.

"What's up?" I ask, moving away from prying ears in the store.

"He's a stubborn ass your boyfriend," says Barnaby and he levels me with a serious look.

"What's happened?"

"Someone shot him with a crossbow bolt," Barnaby

replies, quickly putting his hands up in a calming gesture. "But he's OK."

Panic seizes me. "Is he hurt?!"

"He has a wound on his arm."

"Who did it? Where was this?" My mind wobbles, knowing a crossbow injury could be lethal.

"He'll be fine, Tara. I've been keeping an eye on the place, after what you said. He was hit only moments before I got there. He was trying to stop the bleeding and didn't want to go to hospital, but I knew he needed stitches. I took him in and they've patched him up.

"How did this happen?"

"Reckless hunting perhaps. It could have been an accident-" replies Barnaby before I interrupt.

"-Or made to look like one. It's started hasn't it? Marshall Buchanan is keeping his word. He's going to kill him!" I can't believe this is happening or that I'm admitting my thoughts.

Barnaby shakes his head. "I was in that forest within minutes and there was no-one there. They were long gone. Let's not jump the gun just yet."

"I had a feeling there was someone watching me the other day," I tell Barnaby, though he's more into evidence than hunches. "Where's Shasta now?" I ask, needing to get out of the coffeehouse and be with him.

"He's at home, not wanting to make a fuss."

"We're supposed to be flying to Ireland tomorrow. He's got work there."

"That wound won't stop him. It'd be good for you guys to get away."

"I'm going to see him," I reply. I signal to Giselle that

I'm leaving and grab my coat from the rack while Barnaby scribbles something on paper.

"Here, if you're going all the way to Ireland, go and see my sister Fenella. This is her number. I don't know where you're going, but she's in the North, near the coast and the Mourne Mountains."

Only one ear is listening to what Barnaby is saying, there may not even be a trip to Ireland. Right now I just need to see Shasta, to set eyes on him and know that he's OK. I drop the phone number into my bag and hug Barnaby, thinking how I'm going to miss him even though I'll be back here in no time.

"Thanks for keeping an eye out. The stubborn ass could have bled to death if you hadn't turned up."

"Oh, about that. Just to warn you, Shasta wasn't pleased when he realized I was keeping an eye on things. I guess he still didn't know you'd told me."

"Aw great," I sigh.

Barnaby walks with me from the coffeehouse to the car.

"I won't see you before you go, but enjoy Ireland," he says as I climb into the car. He doesn't know about Leonie honing in on Shasta. Now we have two reasons to be putting distance between ourselves and Big Spruce. I thrust the car into drive as I set off for the Shasta's house, leaving Barnaby standing on the pavement.

"Don't break any speed limits!" he shouts after me.

I race back to the lake house hoping to find him resting up inside. However as I drive down the tree lined track road Scout comes to greet me and I see Shasta leaning on Sultan's stable door. I'm relieved to see him, but he looks serious as he watches me walk towards him, then his face slowly lifts into a smile. I throw my arms round him, feeling the bulky bandage on his arm underneath his sweater; I carefully avoid it.

"You're alright!"

"Why wouldn't I be?" he shrugs.

"It could have been so much worse. Did you see who did this?" I ask looking at his left arm. He looks away into the forest, presumably in the direction the crossbow arrow had come from.

"No. It was probably a stray from someone out hunting, although if they were within range, they'd have seen that I'm no elk."

"You know what I'm thinking don't you?" I ask levelly, staring at him as he meets my eyes. He grimaces. "You worry too much," he says dismissively but I know he's thinking the same thing as me. This could be Marshall Buchanan's misguided vendetta against him. He puts his arm around me and a flash of pain crosses his face.

"Can I do anything?"

"You've done plenty already. You're already in trouble with me," he says sternly but his eyes are alight. "You got Barnaby to keep tabs on me after I told you not to tell him."

"It didn't stop this from happening though!"

"Tara, I can look after things. I told you that, but you don't believe me. Promise me you'll let me sort things my way."

"You have no trust in authority, do you?"

He looks at me sideways with a keen eye then he looks away. "I've never found it helpful. Do you promise?"

I purse my lips and look into the distance resisting agreeing. He tilts my chin so that I look at him.

I nod. "OK. I promise." He slips his arm around my waist and kisses me as we make our way back to the house.

"Will you be OK to travel?" I ask. Shasta rolls his eyes to the sky. "Alright, I'll stop fussing,"

"Before you ask, Seb is going to house-sit and take care of the animals."

"You've thought of everything,"

"Nope. Not everything. We've packing to do" he kisses from my forehead down to my nose, as cold flakes of snow touch our faces. We both look up at the sky at hundreds of swirling snowflakes, heralding the first, light snowfall of winter.

12

We manage to get some sleep on the plane and as we begin our descent into Dublin Airport the plane tilts gently to the side. Shasta leans over me to look out of the window.

"You're not frightened of heights are you?" he asks.

"Well, I wouldn't say I'm a lover of them. Why?" I ask suspiciously, noting Shasta's playful grin beginning at the corners of his mouth.

"You'll see," he replies and settles himself into a sleeping position, closing his eyes.

"Shasta!" I laugh and prod him in the ribs.

"Will Quinn is sending his helicopter to pick us up," he replies.

"Great! I think... That's a bit extravagant."

"He's not a patient man and it's the fastest way to get to his from Dublin."

"So how many times have you been here?"

"Only a couple. The last time was a few years ago though. He's got one of the largest racehorse stables I've ever seen. There's plenty to do. Now his daughter has her heart set on competing in showjumping and Will likes to get his money's worth. "

"Does that mean I won't see much of you?"

"That's a possibility, but at least we're in the same country."

We'd already agreed that I would visit my new-found relative while in Ireland, after a day or two at Will Quinn's. It would make sense after traveling so far, and Fenella had offered for me to stay. We descend past the bright glare of the sun on the white clouds and land in fine, misty rain at Dublin Airport. It is heaving with a cross-flow of travelers getting in each other's paths. A driver picks us up outside the terminal building and takes us to a hangar a short distancc from where we landed.

I dig deep and put aside my reservations about traveling by helicopter. The pilot is a friendly guy in his mid-fifties who starts talking to us as though we are already friends. When the helicopter lifts in the air I catch myself making peculiar noises in my throat.

"It goes up quickly!" I tell him through the headset, like this is headline news. He shakes his head and smiles. We are only a few metres off the ground. My hand shoots up and grips the strap as though it's that which is kccping us from falling out. Shasta's fingers close over my free hand and he lightly squeezes. I grip it back.

Making our way northwards the mist clears and the view of the patchwork, green fields is outstanding. We fly over the east coast and get a first class view of the Antrim coast and the Giant's Causeway. I'm enjoying the rush but we're nearly at our destination. The pilot takes the helicopter down onto a discreet landing pad with grassy area adjacent to a huge, white, modern property, surrounded by outbuildings, stables and a small private racecourse. As the rotor blades slow down, a rotund man wearing a tweed jacket and hat ambles towards us.

"Will," says Shasta, climbing out of the helicopter.

"How's it going? Long time, no see," shouts Will, thrusting a shovel like hand at Shasta and they shake heartily.

"Will, this is Tara."

"Ah, you didn't tell me she was a looker, Shasta," says Will. "Are there any more like you at home, Tara?" he asks, coming in so close that I think he's going to kiss me on the cheek but he grins cheerily instead. I wonder if he's short-sighted as he proffers his hand.

"You're all charm, Will. Good to meet you," I reply, and he tips his head.

"Aye, you too," he replies, and turns his attention back to Shasta, throwing an arm around his back as he leads the way.

"I'll take you to the house then we can get started. Better hurry up, for it'll be dark soon," says Will, either oblivious or unconcerned that Shasta just crossed the Atlantic and had flown a further 200 kilometres by helicopter to get here. He takes us to the square, double-fronted house, which looks stark against the muted autumn tones of the country backdrop. He opens the front door to reveal a wide hallway, with a sweeping staircase that leads up from the black and white tiled floor. He introduces me to his wife, Maeve, who is a quietly spoken woman, and the total opposite to Will. She tells us that Shasta and I are staying in the gatehouse.

"Now we'll let the women do their thing. Scarlett said she was going to saddle up. Where's she gone, Maeve? Scarlett!" shouts Will at the top of his voice.

"There's no need for that, Will," says Maeve gently. "She's here."

Already halfway down the staircase is a curvy young woman dressed in jodhpurs, and a close fitting pink and white Joules t-shirt, with her pale, blonde hair piled up loosely on top of her head. She looks exquisite: manicured, poised and working her entrance to maximum effect.

"Hurry up girl," says Will. "We can't wait all day." Although by the look of things Scarlett is used to people waiting for her.

"I'm ready, Daddy," she says, lowering her eyelids and giving Shasta a keen glance. Shasta looks taken back for a moment.

"You're Scarlett?" She nods, taking great pleasure in his attention. "It's been a few years. I didn't recognize you. You're so...grown up."

"Thank you. You don't look any different. Daddy says you can sort this bad-tempered mare out. I don't know what's gotten into her, she's so badly behaved. Too closely bred or something I don't know. And I've got this important competition coming up."

"She's a bloody thoroughbred! There's nothing wrong with her breeding. It's your bloody riding!" shouts Will gruffly, making for the door.

"You come with me, Tara," says Maeve, taking one of our bags as she signals for me to follow her. Maeve takes me down to the gatehouse, which has a panoramic view of the silvery-green Irish Sea. I feel like a guest in a hotel rather than someone's house. She leaves, and I flop on the comfy sofa for a few minutes and feel my head start to nod. I can't fall asleep yet. I decide to make use of my time and call Fenella, feeling awkward that I'm calling up someone I've never met before, and then expecting to go and stay. I needn't have been concerned. Fenella sounds warm and friendly on the phone.

"If you're only in Ireland for a week, can't you come sooner?" she asks.

I explain about Shasta's work and Fenella suggests I come over straight away if Shasta is busy, that he would be welcome to join us when he can. It sounds tempting, but I stall by telling her I need to speak to him. This is my first trip away with Shasta, and apart from that I actually don't want to be parted from him. The more time I spend with him the more I want to be with him, to the exclusion of everything else.

It's starting to get dark outside. I shiver at how isolated we are here. I put on an extra layer under my coat and wrap a scarf around my neck. For once I'd been organized and remembered to bring everything. The biting wind coming off the sea penetrates my clothing. I cross my arms around myself as I fight the wind to stay on my feet and find the schooling area, which is covered over but exposed on one side. Will Quinn is sitting on a bench watching Shasta giving instructions to Scarlett.

"I've been told to shut up," says Will, leaning over and nodding in the direction of Shasta. "I know my stuff, but I'm at a loss as to what to do with her. She won't damn well do what she's asked. I've got other horses I want him to look at but it's getting late."

"It's been a long day," I reply, hoping he'll take the hint as I let the yawn I've been stifling escape.

"For Christ's sake, Scarlett! You're not listening to what Shasta's saying. That's enough for today. I need a whisky," shouts Will irritably and he stalks out without another word.

Scarlett trots over to Shasta and flirts outrageously now that her father is out of the way. I look on in amusement at the girl who is no more than eighteen, and who knows that I'm watching. Shasta doesn't flinch and carries on giving her a run down on what she needs to work on. Scarlett couldn't care less, and pushes her horse into a fast trot as she exits.

"You look frozen," says Shasta, and we run back to the gatehouse to get out of the rising wind and rain, banging the door closed, locking everyone everything else outside. Here we are: alone in a romantic Celtic cottage perched on a windswept hillside overlooking the tumultuous Irish sea - it's then I remember what I forget to pack. *My contraceptive pill! Of all the things to forget.*

"What's wrong?" asks Shasta.

"I forgot to bring my pill."

My mind goes off on a folly of its own, tracing when I last took the pill and when I had my period - it seems like a long time ago. I grab my cell phone and check the calendar for when my last period was. It was two weeks ago. He says nothing but sits down on the bed beside me. I look at him.

"I guess that curbs our fun tonight."

Shasta's face is completely still.

"Tara, whether now or later, I want a baby with you."

"I don't know whether to laugh or cry," I reply, barely able to meet his gaze and a sneaky tear makes its way to the surface and decides for me. Jetlag and emotional exhaustion get the better of me. I smile and brush it off then tell Shasta about my phone call with my aunt Fenella.

"Look. Why don't you go? You've seen what it's like here. You'll be bored. Will has a lot more work lined up for me than I thought. I don't like the thought of you having nothing to do and it's so cold and bleak out there."

"Bleak but beautiful. I can always find something to do." However we discuss it over dinner of homemade shepherd's pie which Maeve left in the fridge, along with apple pie and cream. It would seem a waste not to spend the time with Fenella when we're in the same country. Eventually we decide that I should go to Fenella's tomorrow and that Shasta will catch up as soon as he can.

I call her and make arrangements to go and stay with her tomorrow afternoon. It occurs to me that young Scarlett may not be sorry to see me go.

"I'll miss you," I whisper to him.

"I'll be with you before you know it," he says, and exhausted we fall into bed. Cosy and warm we give in to sleep as the howling wind, coming off the sea, beats against the cliff top cottage.

13

The battering, howling wind of last night has gone and the morning sunlight finds a way through the chinks in the pale, pink clouds and spills onto Shasta's face as I draw the curtains back. He sighs and rolls over. I slide back under the covers and kiss his chin. He opens his eyes and smiles.

"What are you thinking?" he asks, and props himself up on one arm.

"That it's a bit weird to meet *and* stay with your new aunt for the first time. And I don't want to leave you?"

He pulls me onto his chest, then there is a heavy banging on the door of the gatehouse and we exchange puzzled looks. It's only just after 7:00 a.m. Shasta's face hardens as he gets out of bed and goes to answer it. I lie there, straining to hear who it is, but there is no need.

"Morning Tara!" shouts Will's booming voice, echoing through the corridor. "Bejesus, were you still in bed?" he asks Shasta. "I've been up for hours!"

I sit upright and pull the duvet around myself, half expecting him to bluster in. After waiting a second I dive out of bed, throw some clothes on and wander into the lounge where Will and Shasta are going through a list of things he has planned for today.

I explain to Will that I'm going to visit family near Newcastle and he offers for one of the grooms to drive me to Belfast, as he has a pick up there anyway. I look over at Shasta, feeling so torn. I want to cancel going anywhere. Shasta leaves without breakfast and hurries off to the stable yard. I go for a bracing walk to explore and return to the cottage where I collect my things before I close the door on the gatehouse. I find the guy waiting to give me a lift to the city, but can't find Shasta to say goodbye.

"Please, just give me five minutes," I plead, dumping my bag in the car and running to the stable block, hoping Shasta will be there. Thankfully he is. So are Will, Scarlett and a handful of other people who I've not met, including a couple of elfin-like men who must be jockeys. I'm not sure whether to interrupt, but Shasta glances my way and walks over. I whisper goodbye in his ear, feeling conscious of the eyes on us. I don't want to embarrass him but I can't resist putting my arms around his neck and hugging him tightly. It induces wolf whistles from the others and I leave with one last look over my shoulder at the jovial assembly.

The groom who drives me to Belfast is the chatty sort and great company. He keeps my mind busy with his quick-witted banter and as he drops me outside the train station where I'm to meet Fenella I suddenly feel acutely alone in this unfamiliar place, unsure what the next few days will hold. After a few minutes of waiting I send Fenella a message to say I've arrived. I look up and down the road expecting a car to pull over, then I hear my name being called by a chestnut haired lady with a neat bob coming towards me.

"Fenella?"

"Tara! I knew it had to be you. You have cat's eyes like my mother," she says, stepping back to get a good look at me.

"You remind me of Barnaby," I tell her, taking in the open face and friendly brown eyes, before we hug.

"We have so much to talk about, and call me Fen," she says, leading the way to her car.

It's nonstop chattering during the journey and any doubts I had about staying with her vanish completely. She tells me about her husband, who works away, and her two grown up children. She has a dignified, ladylike air, but there is also an indefinable vibrancy about her. I get the impression she would be as at home with the aristocracy as she would be with a bunch of teenagers. Barnaby seems to have told her my life story and most of my speedy précis of my life she already knew.

"That ahead of you is the Mourne Mountains," says Fen, as we round a bend revealing magnificent purplish grey mountains which drop down to the rugged coast line. "That's where we're heading."

As we drive through the town of Newcastle: with its touristy shops, ice cream parlors and kids' amusements, she points out the school where she teaches part-time. We drive uphill for a few kilometres before she turns into a discreet driveway which sweeps through mature woodland to an elegant house with narrow columns either side of the front door.

"This is beautiful," I tell her, looking around at the established gardens which enhance the historical ambiance of the house.

"We've done a lot of work to it, but we're a bit limited because it's a listed building and I wouldn't want to change the character of the place," says Fen, playing down the appeal of the house. She shows me around and takes me to my room: which has a high ceiling, simple decor and overlooks a back garden which goes on forever.

"I have one rule in this house," says Fen seriously.

"Oh?" I ask, thinking she doesn't seem like the authoritative type, but then again she is a part time school teacher.

"You have to make yourself at home. If there's something you need, look until you find it."

"Well, right now I really need the bathroom," I reply, and she shows me across the hall; the first thing I notice in the room is the lovely roll top bath. Fen goes off to see to her animals and it gives me time to unwind. I lay down on the white linen sheets, feeling very at home. It's been a good start to our new relationship. Tonight it's just Fen and I for dinner, but apparently she has invited a few people over tomorrow. Despite having Fen for company I'm missing Shasta. He hasn't responded to the text I sent him earlier, but I expect he's busy. I wanted to see how his day was and tell him about mine. I wander downstairs and offer to help with dinner but she pours me a glass of red wine and we talk incessantly while she cooks.

"So how come you left the States?" I ask, wanting to find out all I can about my family.

"I met my husband and he's Irish. I followed him here. Now he's in England most of the time. Isn't that ironic? This was his family home. I traded one set of mountains for another," she says, glancing out of the window at the shield of trees with a misty, heather-covered mountain visible beyond.

"It's special here," I say, already feeling mellowed by the wine and the soothing ambience.

"You feel that?" asks Fen, giving me a sideways glance.

"It feels clear and magical"

"You are one of us aren't you? No doubt about it."

"Us?"

"You're a sensitive," says Fen.

"I pick up on things."

"You see and feel stuff that others don't see?"

I look at her warily, then grin.

"It's a good thing, although when I was young in Big Spruce, it was something that was better kept under wraps."

"Do you too?"

"Oh yeah," she says, her American accent coming through stronger. "I was born that way, thankfully my mother embraced it. Not like some poor buggers who have their gifts knocked out of them and have to relearn it."

"This is music to my ears. Tell me about Blanche."

"My mom was a gentle but powerful woman. She put up with a lot of abuse, but she stayed true to herself. She was a healer and guardian of light, and that is what she was sent here to do. She said there were people like her all over the world."

"Like beacons."

"Exactly. She said that some people didn't know what they were doing but did good work unconsciously: just by being there, or even in their sleep. She did healing and had 'the sight'. She knew how to move energy. To her it was about maintaining a certain level of clarity and purity to reach the highest potential. It was all about balance and finding the right way to find it."

"Did she teach you how to do that?"

"She taught me a lot – when I decided to listen. She used to say 'feel the vibration and visualize the sound that created the pattern', because it affects the brain and nervous system as sound travels along it. Everything physical or non-physical has a sound and that sound can transform. Everything has a sound, a shape and an image.

She used to feel it. She said the sound was beyond what she could physically replicate."

Fen and I talk for a while about Shasta's earth healing and clearing the energy network to energize the portals.

"It's amazing that you've been doing this first-hand with him."

"Yep, but I've a lot to learn."

"You don't need to learn anything. People say they are spiritual and use it as a fashion statement, they study diplomas but they don't get it. You don't need to wear purple and 'hippy' clothes to be understand."

"It sounds like you have the same gift as your mom?"

Fen shrugs nonchalantly. "I guess. It's just part of lifting your energy to a higher dimension,"

"What about Barnaby? Does he have it?"

"He's one of those people I was talking about. He just gets it, but he'd never think he does. He says he doesn't have intuition but he acts on it all the time; he's got a great energy and good intentions." Fen exudes palpable warmth as she talks about her brother. I get the feeling she misses him.

"So what's our purpose? Do we all do the same thing because it's in the family?"

"Well, for one, what I learned in Big Spruce, because come on, it's a magical place and the mountains are where energy is at its highest – well everything I learned I transported here. Now I use it to raise the energy here. There's me and a bunch of others. That's who you'll meet tomorrow night. Maybe we'll do some meditation or a little ceremony."

"I'm not sure how to contribute or if I'm clear enough to do it."

Fen smirks down at the saucepan of potatoes she is mashing and starts chuckling.

"You're so funny," she says giggling.

"I am? I think you need to ease off on the red wine."

"We didn't know you existed, but my mother somehow saw to it that you became the custodian of the amulet, how she orchestrated that I can only imagine," she laughs.

My hand goes to the amulet around my neck, which I never take off now. I feel tiny sparks traveling up through my fingers and it feels like an endorsement on what Fen is saying. I feel fully welcomed into a family lineage which I'm only beginning to understand.

"You've been through shit!" says Fen. I giggle appreciatively at her blunt acknowledgment of my darker days and that she's making a joke of it. I like to laugh about bad things too, and I'd moved on from most of it the debris from my past.

"Sorry Tara, but you have, haven't you? Changes, ordeals, trauma; and you have come out of it intact and radiant. And there you are...doubting that you're good enough...or that you don't hold enough light to contribute."

"Mrs Brightside. You can stop laughing. It would have helped if I'd grown up with this stuff, then it would all have been normal to me."

"You went through your shit without a highway code, which means you had to work it out for yourself. That's a steep learning curve, but it's the most valuable lesson you'll ever have."

"You know what I found weird? It's that I moved to Big Spruce on the day of Blanche's funeral - it felt like one in, one out?"

"So what does that tell you?"

"That I got there too late to learn from her?"

"Think about it. You arrived to take over from her. You were entrusted to do what she did, another custodian in the alliance."

"You make it sound so mysterious, but it is a bit of a coincidence."

"Have some more wine," says Fen, about to refill my glass.

"We're not exactly purifying ourselves." I nod to the wine bottle. "Cheers!"

Fen chinks her antique crystal glass against mine. "Bottoms up! It's all about balance. I hope you're hungry?"

"Starving. That smell from the oven is driving me mad," I reply, relieved dinner is ready because my stomach has been growling for an hour.

"When do you think Shasta will get here?" asks Fen.

"I don't know. But the sooner the better," I reply, noting that he still hasn't returned my text.

"How is that going?" she asks.

I don't quite know how to answer that, because I'm not used to discussing my love life with someone of a different generation.

"He's amazing." I feel myself redden to the tips of my ears.

"Is he the one?" she asks.

I grin from ear to ear. "I've never felt like this about anyone." And I find myself telling Fen about deciding to stay in Big Spruce to be with him, once I'd dealt with my reluctance to trade in my life in New York, summing myself up as being commitment phobic; that even something I dearly want can cause me an issue.

"It's not commitment phobic. Everything changes and

you know that. If you're taking in the light, which you are, you're always changing, so are the things around you. Nothing is permanent."

"I do know that. So when I think of something being forever and nailing myself to that, knowing it won't be, then I'm lying. It's fundamentally never going to happen and it's just a cute convention society came up with."

"But what if he could change and grow along with you? Is he open to change, Tara?" asks Fen, sounding firm.

I know what she's getting at. He's strongly implanted in the traditional beliefs passed down through his ancestry, yet he switched jobs, changed relationships, and was open-minded and keen to better himself.

"Yes. It was him who told me that truth and value were evolutionary." And with the arrival of that realization something in my head clicks into place.

Fen plates us huge helpings of a hearty rosemary and garlic roast lamb with root vegetable mash. It's the kind of warming food that lines your insides and makes you sleepy. Fen tells me about her husband Mark, who works in London but flies home at weekends. She also has two grown up children, Jake and Hannah, who are at university in England.

"How does that work for you? I've only not seen Shasta for a few hours and feel like a limb has been severed. I left him with an eighteen year-old setting her sights on him," I say flippantly, but only when the words come out do I realize it niggles me.

"I have a secret I'll let you in on," says Fenella, dabbing at the sides of her mouth with a white linen napkin. "I talk to angels. It's a big thing of mine."

I compress my lips, not entirely convinced that is much

more than fairy tale stuff; but not that it doesn't exist either, I just have no experience of it.

"Have you heard of Metatron?"

"Wasn't he in the *Transformers* movie?"

"Ahh. I don't think so," replies Fen diplomatically as her lips curls in amusement.

"Oh wait. Yes, my friend Svetlana mentioned that name. Something to do with the 'ring linking' she discovered."

"What?"

"That's something I can show you later," I reply, glad to be able to contribute. "Carry on," I encourage, slowly savoring the earthy nourishment of Fen's roast parsnips and gravy.

"I invoke Metatron to strengthen the divine connection. It keeps the link between yourself and the oneness strong. It works for everything, creating a bridge where you think there's separation. I feel closer to everything, including Mark, after I've done it. The distance is immaterial."

Fen regards me for second as I digest what she said. I pull a face.

"I'm not sure I get the angel thing - I've no experience of it."

"That makes sense," she says, pushing her plate away.

She clears away the dishes and runs through what her mother, had taught her about sensing and matching the energies.

"Come with me. Grab your coat," says Fen, rising from her seat and heading for the double doors which overlook the garden. It's dark outside apart from the crescent moon dangling in the sky. As I follow her into the darkness she grabs a lantern and strides confidently across the grass.

The scent from her waxed jacket helps me locate her as the light from the lantern is gloomy.

"Where are we going?" I ask, thinking maybe she has lost her marbles.

"Down into the glen."

"You have a glen?"

"Just a little one," she mutters, as she walks into the darkness.

I follow her, stepping tentatively over paving stones and worn grooves between tree roots until eventually I hear the rushing of a stream. I grasp hold of the fencing on the pathway high above the bubbling stream below, thankful to have my hand on something consistent. At the point where a bridge crosses over the stream there are solar lights shedding an eerie but welcome glow on the woodland setting.

Fen instructs me to stand there and connect with what is around as she does the same. She asks what I feel, but apart from the tingling and sparkling sensations going on in and around me, I don't get an impression of anything specific. She tells me to stay with it and we both fall silent. Gradually as I relax and blend with the surroundings I get a very real and solid image of a translucent pyramid made up of golden rays, connecting at the tip. At this apex the rays burn brighter at the top with the connection from the other directions. It's the point of power at the top: as blindingly bright as a solar flare.

"You got it?" asks Fen, softly.

I make a clucking sound with my throat, not wanting to speak and spoil the vision.

"Is it a pyramid?" she asks.

"Mmm huh."

"Blend with it."

I do as she asks. A sensation akin to pins and needles begins in my feet and calves, traveling upwards; I'm aware of rising energy coursing up my body, ascending to the tip of my crown. I lose awareness of my physical body and feel like I'm leaning to the left, twisted out of shape. I peep through my eyes but I'm vertical. Fen is stood alongside me facing the steep tree lined bank which rises from the rocky bluff beside the stream.

"That's the energy of this mountain," she says.

"A golden pyramid?" I ask, to check we are on the same page.

"Yep. And there are small ones all around in the power spots, but the really powerful one is at the top of the mountain. The highest point to the heavens. It's particularly clear here."

"It's not just unique to here, is it?"

"No, but we work to keep it clear. That's why I put lights out here so I can come out whenever I want. I like working in the dark. Sometimes I can see the light streaming all around. It's magical."

"And you look so normal."

Fen throws her head back and laughs a hearty self-effacing chuckle, which also reminds me of Barnaby.

"In my opinion that is what everyone is looking for, the top of the pyramid. Remember the American dollar shows the top of the pyramid being disconnected."

"Which is because they don't want you to access the pinnacle of power."

"Now, now Tara. So young and so cynical," replies Fen.

"That's what we all have inside us. We just spend lifetimes looking for it. What is on the outside is also on the inside.

We just need to clear the cloudiness. Imagine yourself as the pyramid made up of gold and white rays? It works for me. If I'm feeling off kilter, or if something has gotten to me, I purge myself with the energy and power it brings."

Fen is so matter of fact; it's as if she's teaching a bunch of teenagers French, the amount of confidence and conviction she radiates. She talks about the energy work with the same degree of no-nonsense acceptance of facts.

We return to the warmth of the house and the exhilaration of today catches up on me with sweeping exhaustion. I retire to bed and check my phone one last time - there are no missed calls. I call him and it goes straight to voicemail. I sit on the edge of the bed, pondering what Fen had said. I make a quiet invocation to the angels, then point out, and apologize for, the fact that I'm not a big believer in angels but I'm willing to give it a go. I let go of the thought and climb into bed. Despite being tired it takes some time before I fall asleep.

Later, though I don't know how much later, I'm woken knowing someone is standing beside my bed. From my frontal sleeping position I turn my head around. There seems to be a light on and I realize the light is emanating from a source beside my bed. It's gentle, but bright enough to light the room; it is without limits: beside me, between my bed and the chest of drawers, gently glowing. I try to jump up, but feel a firm and reassuring touch on my back – with it a sedating tranquillity pacifies me. I know it's an angel, but my mind is prevented from analyzing that and I can only surrender to the peacefulness. I succumb and close my eyes as I sink even further into the soft thick mattress.

14

The sound of the cell phone, ringing, shatters my deep sleep. Not remembering where I am, I fling my arms around looking for the invading noise, and find the phone lying on the floor.

"Are you OK?" asks Shasta, his voice sounding harsh.

"I've been trying to get hold of you since yesterday."

"So have I. The signal here is diabolical. You made it to Fenella's?"

"Yes. When are you coming?" I don't want to sound desperate.

"I don't know yet. When I can."

"How are things? How is Scarlett doing?"

"I think we're speaking different languages-"

There is a garbled noise from the cell as words get lost then the connection strengthens again.

"Before I get cut off. I had a call from James last night," says Shasta. I don't know how James got through and I didn't.

"Is everything OK back home?"

"Yeah, kind of. James didn't know I was away. Apparently it's been in the papers that there is a major gold deposit near Big Spruce. Journalists are flocking around the place. Cain Shimlow's campaign has made the national news!"

"Jeez. He must be pleased."

"He might be the only one who is. His syndicate won't be happy at the attention. They'll have wanted it hushed until they secured the land."

"And you're worried if prospectors go plundering they'll destroy place?"

"Right, but on the other hand if there are any attacks on the Rez it'll look suspicious."

"There's nothing you can do from here, but then what could you do even if you were there?"

"Try and talk my people out of giving away their land and culture for nothing. Look, I'd better go. I'll get to you when I can. Worst case scenario I'll meet you at the airport."

"The airport! You don't think you'll make it to Newcastle?"

"I'll do my best."

"I miss you," I say, unable to hold it back any longer.

"I miss you too," he replies in a low whisper. He must be around other people.

"I love you," I murmur into the phone but it's already breaking up.

My heart feels like an iron clad fist has wrapped around it. The thought of not seeing him for a few more days is devastating. A jagged urge to head back to the Quinns on the Antrim coast prods at me, but it would be an intrusion. It might suggest I don't trust Shasta to be away from me.

That night Fen's group of friends arrive in dribs and drabs; each one brings a different dish until a delicious looking buffet has been assembled. As each person arrives I begin to feel isolated in the group, although I'm sure no one will pick up on it. However Fen takes me to the side and asks me what the matter is. I tell her that, because of his work, Shasta may not be arriving after all.

"Call me selfish, but all the more time for you to spend

with me," she replies. "But, I do have to work tomorrow. The school has called me to stand in."

"I'm happy to occupy myself." I tell her, before we join the others. I would never have put these bunch of people together and expect them to get along. Their ages range from about twenty-seven to seventy-two. The pretty woman, who is fashionably dressed, exudes coolness and chats easily with two middle-aged men, one of whom looks to be of some authority with a cool, aloof presence. A well-spoken, older lady, who is comfortably dressed in cotton trousers and shirt, is telling Fen about her trip to South Africa, in a plane which was flown by her son. A flustered redhead arrives carrying a plate of desserts.

I seem to become the focus of their attention once I open my mouth - my accent sticks out a mile in their midst. Someone is fiddling with the door handle outside. Fen strides to the double doors from the lounge part of the kitchen. She throws the doors open.

"Why didn't you use the front door like everyone else!" Fen shakes her head as two guys walk in.

"I was showing Nathan the garden," says a tall, good-looking guy who I'd guess to be in his mid-thirties. We shake hands and he steps to the side as his friend come through the doorway, my hand is automatically outstretched to the newcomer before I see him. The instant our hands connect there's recognition. *Where do I know you from?*

I feel like I've had an electric shock and drop the handshake. *What the hell was that?* Nathan is stunning: like he's stepped out of a magazine. Even Millie, the older lady, looks startled. He has black hair, smoldering grey eyes and a stubbly chin. Now ordinarily I'd be in there like a shot, but not anymore. I can look but that's all. I move around the room avoiding his gaze. I tell myself I'm being ridiculous. The frisson between us was nothing more than static and if he can turn a pensioner's head then I wouldn't be immune either.

I'm put my glass down on the table, and I've just sat down when Nathan sits to my right, at the end of the table. *You're not imagining this, Tara.*

"Actually, Tara, can you move round to the other side and sit there?" asks Fen pointing opposite me.

Though I've no idea as to her reasoning, I oblige, grateful for the intervention. Nathan sits leisurely back. When they start talking about music and he picks up the conversation thread, his eyes spring to life. He glances towards me. I can feel the heat in my cheeks.

After dinner Millie suggests we go for a walk down into the glen. Fen interrupts and tells the motley bunch about the ring-linking that I'd shown her earlier today – as shown to me by Svetlana. Fen and I demonstrate, and before long the group are doing it on each other and erupting in giggles; the same way I had with Svetlana. They link their thumb and fingers, make a circle and connect golden lines through their bodies. Sure enough, they were experiencing various reactions and sensations just as I had.

Afterwards, Millie and the others head for the glen. I step outside, in just a sweater.

"You need a coat," says Nathan appearing beside me. Before I reply he drapes his coat over my shoulders. I recoil and try to refuse, but eventually accept. The smell of sandalwood from his coat wafts around me. I put some distance between myself and Nathan on the walk through the glen, taking care what signals I give out. All the time I'm wondering why temptation is being put in my way.

Am I being tested? There's no way I want to trade in what I've got with Shasta, but how can a stranger be so arousing? It backs up my point that things change and makes me wonder how much temptation one person can resist. It occurs to me that Shasta may be being tested in the same way. Resolutely I stride out, noticing the beauty of the travelling light orbs as we pass through a fern-covered gully. Everyone is quiet, absorbing the magic.

We come to the well-lit crossing point on the bridge and Fen suggests we connect with other power points and feel the interconnection. During the meditation I don't get much because I'm distracted. When we arrive back at the house a few of the group leave and a hush falls on the room and I'm left alone with Nathan.

"I feel like I know you. Perhaps in another life," says Nathan.

"In this one I have a very real boyfriend," I reply. A puzzled expression ripples across his brow.

"Funny how we interpret magnetism as being sexual, like there's no other sort of connection. I'm married."

I flush from my neck feeling like a simplistic fool. "Sorry, I thought..."

"I recognized your energy instantly. I was drawn to you."

"You can see how that might look to me – you looking like a male model and all," I explain as light heartedly as I can, trying to laugh it off. He isn't wearing a ring so how was I to know? OK. Maybe it was a test. Regardless, it reinforces to me how things can quickly change, and if I can be so affected by someone else how can I reasonably say I'd commit to one person or thing for the rest of my life? Nathan gives me a sincere hug as he leaves. I hope if Shasta is having a similar challenge he overcomes it.

15

The days have slowly ticked past since I last saw Shasta. I've counted the hours in between phone calls and texts; which came all too infrequently. I've resorted to using Fen's phone to call him, because of the bad network coverage. Will Quinn has had him here, there and everywhere: searching for the best equestrian stock, attending a horse race and trying to get Scarlett and her mare to understand each other better. I still don't know if he'll make it to Newcastle before we are due to fly home, or if I'll meet him at Dublin Airport. I feel homesick for Big Spruce. I miss Hudson and waking up beside Shasta in the lake house. I've spoken to Giselle a couple of times, but life across the pond seems so far away.

Fen has been teaching for a couple of days while I've rattled around in her charming, old house and spent time reading, walking and meditating. Fen introduced me to Tollymore Forest Park and I've made that my stomping ground. I sat amongst the trees, feeling the pulsing and sensing the light coming through them the same way it does back home. I've covered every nature trail in the forest, crossed the stepping stones and lingered in the mossy, stone hermitage, surrounded by gnarly roots on a path overlooking the churning water. I'd borrowed Fen's boots, to keep dry in the leaf mulch. They've also been useful for another task which has been entertaining - looking after the chickens and ducks.

I've fed them and made sure they are locked up before nightfall. Yesterday I left the double doors to the lounge of the kitchen slightly ajar while I took a shower. I later came downstairs, wrapped in a robe with a towel around my head, to find six chickens perched on the back of the leather Chesterfield sofa, clucking softly and dozing. I ran around waving my arms, at the hens; creating mayhem amid squawks and flapping feathers. The shocked birds eventually ran outside and surprisingly no chicken poop could be found.

The noise from the front door tells me Fen is home, but there's another voice which I can't make out.

"Tara, look what I've found," calls Fen as she clatters through the tiled corridor that leads from the hall. Has a chicken escaped to the front garden? She appears, and behind her is a face I adore and have been missing with all my heart.

"Shasta!" I throw myself at him and wrap my arms around his neck. He must be in no illusion about my feelings for him and how they've grown in his absence. He looks exotic and out of place here: his indigenous looks, black, flowing hair setting him apart from the traditional, Irish, country setting. He picks me up and we fuse together in the long awaited contact. For the independent, freedom-loving, person I had been, I sure feel like I've been given back my limbs.

"I don't want to be parted from you ever again," he says, as though a telegraph had already wired him my thoughts.

"How did you get here? Were you trying to surprise me?" I give him a mock disapproving look.

"I didn't exactly plan things out. Fen picked me up from Belfast, after I couldn't get through to your phone."

"I'll give you two some space," says Fen as she vacates the room, clasping a cup of tea.

Shasta looks completely worn out: pale and drawn. We

flop onto the sofa, joined at the shoulder and thigh, as he wraps his arm around me.

"Are you're finished at Quinn's now?" I ask, and his mouth presses into a tight ironic smile, the type that portrays there's a story to that.

"I quit," he replies.

"Why? Something big must have happened for you to quit?"

"Not really," he says with a diffident shrug.

I scrutinize him when he falls silent, without filling the pause.

He takes a deep breath. "It was going fine most of the time, but Scarlett – she was a challenge. She refused to learn. I thought she was flirting to try to provoke her father. I thought nothing of it. She's like that with the guys around the stables - she's young."

I laugh, imagining the scene.

"You might not be laughing in a minute."

My smile falls away.

"This morning, I went in to check on her mare in the stable and Scarlett was sat on top of the horse with her back to me...and she was naked!"

"What! You are kidding me?!"

"She slid off and virtually landed in my arms," says Shasta, suppressing laughter. The visual I have on that is all too juicy and ripe.

"I told you that you'd stop laughing!"

"What the hell did you do?"

"I told her to grow up and chucked a horse blanket over her. I couldn't get out of that stable fast enough. If Will had seen it he would have had a heart attack."

"Did you tell him?"

"And risk being shot? Nah. I told him my job was done. Scarlett wasn't taking it seriously and he knew that. One of the grooms saw the whole thing –he nearly died laughing."

I knew she had been playing a game with him. My ire increases at the thought of Scarlett launching her naked body into Shasta's arms, but it's mitigated by the fact that he left and told me about it.

"You look like you're going to burst," he says, laughter erupting into every word.

"I told you that you're irresistible. I don't think I can top falling off a horse naked into your arms," I say, leaning closer to him, now feeling the fizzing friction between us.

"You don't have to," says Shasta. I straddle his legs and face him, touching his chest with my hands.

"I've missed you so much," I murmur against his cheek.

"I never stopped thinking of you - night and day – you haunt my dreams," he replies, caressing the back of my neck with his fingers.

"Do you think I don't feel the same?"

"I don't know, but I do know that you have to take away the feel of that woman. I want to feel your skin, so you can make your own mark on me."

"We have two days before we go home. Let's make it count."

I lean slowly in and as our lips touch with a lingering, sensual kiss it feels like it's our first. Later, when we are lying awake in bed holding each other, I lie with my cheek over his heart, hearing the rhythmic thud, and the swirling of his blood, aware of his every breath in my hair. I have this feeling we are joined - the same spirit living in two bodies.

16

On our last day in Ireland we packed in as much sightseeing as we could. After breakfast I took him to Tollymore. The forest was so alive, teeming with exquisite bright blue lights hovering and moving through the woodland. The trees radiated excitement. It felt like they knew us. We heard the whispering welcome and it was as though they spoke of wonderful secrets. We stood amongst the trees and immersed ourselves in their energy. This is a powerful meeting place for high energy. I was spellbound how connected to home and the rest of the world I felt, all at the same time. It was poignant to be on the other side of the Atlantic Ocean and still be connected to the same crystal clear vibration which funnels through the trees in Big Spruce.

Later, Fen took us for a drive through the mountains, stopping at Silent Valley Mountain Park and taking a detour to a friendly, local pub for dinner on the way home. The pub is packed with people celebrating the end of a folk music festival and warming up by having hot toddies while they're waiting for the firework display to begin. Fen seems to know everyone. As soon as we walked in someone called her over, and she's been introducing us to various charismatic locals all night.

I can't remember the names, only the faces and the dry, caustic wit of a few of the men who you might think didn't like each other. It's hard to believe Fen was from Big Spruce originally because she just fits right in here. I get coerced into trying the Guinness and wish I hadn't. It's an acquired taste and Shasta finishes mine.

Amongst the laughter I think of home and have a tinge

of sadness that we are leaving early tomorrow morning. I've become attached to Fen in the short while I've known her and I remind her for the tenth time that we want her to come over to Big Spruce soon. The first of the fireworks starts and everyone piles outside into the freezing November night to watch them. It's an appropriate send off. Like me, Fen can't stand the cold and we leave as soon as the fireworks have finished.

Back at Fen's house, Shasta and I throw our things into a suitcase, much more haphazardly than the packing for the outward journey. We need to leave here at 4 a.m. to drive to Dublin Airport. Fen calls me in to her bedroom where she's sitting on the bed with two ginger cats curled up, she's surrounded by boxes of photographs and keepsakes. She pats a space beside her for me to sit down.

"This is your grandmother on her wedding day," says Fen, holding up an old black and white photograph of a young couple being showered in confetti. "That's me with Barnaby, Robert and my mom. I must have been around five years old when that was taken."

"Do you remember much about your dad?" I ask.

"Hardly anything. He went away to work and never came back, so it's not like we missed him much, because he wasn't around anyway. I think my mom was in limbo for a long time, but she was a trooper. She did a great job of bringing us up on her own."

We go through the photographs together and she tells me stories about the family while she puts aside some photos for me to keep. She opens another box which is a mixture of diaries and newspaper cuttings. Fen looks quietly through them and becomes lost in her own nostalgic thoughts. She smiles to herself as she leafs through them.

"This one was my mom's bible," says Fen, stroking the front of a blue, leather book with the name Blanche Whitelaw on the front. I twist my head around to read the intriguing journal over Fen's shoulder as she looks through it then swiftly closes it with a tight smile. "This is yours now," she says decisively. I'm startled and watch as her hand lingers lovingly on her mother's book. I don't quite know what to say. I want to steep myself in family vibes and embrace my roots, but her memories mean a lot to Fen.

"Really? Fen, are you sure? I'd love it, but wouldn't you rather keep it?"

Fen looks blankly into the distance for a moment then curtly nods her head. "Yes. I'm sure. It feels right. I've been through that old book a million times, so what I don't know now I'm not likely to. It's your turn to have it," says Fen, and she pushes the journal towards me.

"Wow. This is very special. I'll take good care of it. It'll be in safe hands, I promise."

"I know. I wouldn't give it to you otherwise."

Fen and I hug tightly and I thank her, although it's one of those times when spoken gratitude doesn't really cover it. I glance through the journal while Fen tidies up. It's already nearly midnight.

"We'd better get some sleep," says Fen, "It's an early start and I don't like goodbyes, especially at the airport. So if I seem a bit stand offish in the morning, it's just to stop me making a fool of myself in public."

"How about we say our goodbyes now then we can just wave from a distance in the morning?" Fen and I put our arms around each other and I feel myself filling up. "You'll come and see us soon?" I ask, drawing back from her and looking at her through misty eyes.

"Stop it. You'll set me off." Fen tears up. "See what you've done." She grabs a tissue from the box.

"I'll see you in the morning – in like four hours." I smile at her as I head to bed. However the morning comes quickly and we set off in the dark, bound for Dublin. We say another emotional goodbye at the drop off point and apart from reticence at leaving Fen behind I'm eager to return to my own idyllic mountain home which has been calling me back.

17

We are flying back over the Atlantic towards home, and it's a luxury to have this time together before we get back to the everyday reality in Big Spruce. When Shasta drifts off to sleep I flick through the leather journal that Fen gave me last night. It contains all sorts of notes, sketchings and musings on everything from plants, herbs, energy medicine to theories she had arrived at. My grandmother's writing was sloping, curving and not the easiest to read, but beautiful to look at.

I felt humbled at accepting such a precious thing, but mostly honored that she felt it was my turn to have it. The journal contains recipes for concoctions to treat everything from influenza and menstrual cramps to worms. There are sketches of leaves with hand drawn maps of where plants can be found. Her instructions are so precise.

She even made footnotes on their effectiveness, and recommendations to use herbs from a different area. Blanche Whitelaw had written of the healings she had given, having abbreviated the names to initials, describing the impressions she got, the sensations the patient described and how she treated them.

"Excuse me, madam. Can you place your bag under the seat?" says the passing air hostess as we begin our descent into Seattle. *Madam? What happened to Miss? How very grown up.* I frown.

When we disembark in Seattle the biting cold stings my cheeks, but it's very different to the penetrating wind-chill and dampness in Ireland. It feels so good to be going home. One thing I like to do when I get off a plane is drive. I think it's a control thing, or something to do with needing to feel contact and movement with the earth again. We took Shasta's car to the airport, so I don't get the pleasure of driving today.

We head out along the highway, towards Big Spruce. I don't have that 'oh God, I don't want to go to work feeling'. I want to get back to my normal life. My mind wanders to thoughts of old Sarah, who has become a daily visitor at *The Book and Bean* and I'm troubled by the thought that she might not live out another winter.

Before we left for Ireland, Shasta had touched on the possibility of moving in together. My stomach somersaults. I don't want to be apart from him any longer than I have to, but it's tempered with that old unsettling feeling that I want to outrun myself. When I lived with my ex-boyfriend David in New York I'd always kept one foot in the door. That didn't end at all well, but this would be different. *Catch a grip, Tara.* He may not even want you in his home - but if this relationship is going anywhere that would be a natural progression. It's not on the agenda right now, so it's a moot point.

As we get closer to the familiar landscape of Big Spruce the homecoming feeling grows, it's like stepping into nature's fortress, cosseted from the rest of the world. However I'm shocked that the town has become this busy in a week, with such an influx of vehicles with registrations from out-of-state.

"This is all because of Shimlow's gold campaign," says Shasta, his jaw flexing stubbornly. I sense change in Shasta immediately. The gravity and weight of responsibilities he carries on the Reservation having a visible affect on him.

"James said they're running geology tests, but that'll

take a while. In the meantime people will gamble on the outcome and take things into their own hands."

"You mean people like Cain Shimlow," I reply.

"I think Shimlow has turned loose on this one. His syndicate would never want this much publicity. It's my bet they'll be running behind him fire-fighting and playing down why they want the land."

"On a positive, it'll be good for the store. Can we make that our first stop?" I ask, keen to get caught up on what's been happening.

From the street I can see plenty of heads sitting in the coffee shop. As we open the door the rich, nutty aroma of fresh coffee fills the room like a cosy, warm cloud. Sophia looks up from behind the counter with a startled look, clearly not expecting to see me. I silently put my finger to my lips and creep up on Giselle, placing my hand over her eyes.

"Whoever you are you've got cold hands," says Giselle. She spins around and I hug her. We spend the next half an hour catching up as Giselle rampantly delivers the news which is hot off the press. Apart from the swarm of visitors in town, Giselle has a new love interest in Cooper, the guy who found that piece of writing in the old books. Nothing had happened, just this tedious dancing around each other, but Giselle has an extra bright twinkle to her eye. Apparently Cooper and Margy have met with Michael on the Rez about the tree planting idea and it hadn't been totally rejected.

"Why don't you get off home and I'll lock up?" I offer, feeling guilty that I've been away while the others have been holding the fort.

Giselle's face falls and she looks at me in mild horror.

"No. Cooper might be popping in later," she replies. "You look like you need a sleep. Didn't you do much of that in Ireland?" She flashes Shasta a look over my shoulder. She falls close to the mark. After several nights apart, sleeping had felt like such a waste of precious time.

"OK. I'll swing by the house and see Hudson. I've missed the big old boy."

It's funny how relieved you feel after being away, knowing things aren't likely to change, but you're relieved to find everything is still as you left it. Giselle and Simon aren't wild party animals, but they do like a shindig. I feel like mother returning home, half expecting the teenage kids to have trashed the house.

Shasta and I drive over to Evergreen and, in actual fact, when we walk in the house is immaculate. I call out Simon's name but there's no reply. He mustn't be home. Hudson gallops in and launches himself at me. The Newfoundland stands on his back legs and lavishes us with slobbery kisses.

"Tara. Look," says Shasta, staring out the side window, overlooking the length of garden which separates my house from Pandora and Errol Walsh's.

I squint through the sunlight streaming in, trying to make out the jerky images. A man's head is bobbing behind the fence, then there's a quick whirl of arms and legs. Next thing we know Simon is scrabbling over the fence. Half-way over he tries to sit up. His mouth forms a tight round 'O' shape and it looks like he injured his tenders.

"What is he doing?" I ask.

"Pandora and Errol are coming back. He's trying to

escape," says Shasta. Roger's prim, starchy parents are walking up the steps to the house.

"Hurry up, Simon!" I shout, but there's no way he can hear me. If they look up now they will see him perched on the boundary fence, and with our already delicate relationship and tense history over my lifestyle, it could turn into a right royal battle.

Simon leans forward to swing his legs over and suddenly Roger pushes him. He falls down into the vegetable patch below, landing on one foot then he awkwardly tumbles skidding into the dirt on his chin. He gathers himself up and races in through the back door before slamming it behind him. He leans back against it and sighs. It becomes a scream when Shasta and I walk into the kitchen and make him jump.

"You're home!"

"That was close," says Shasta, with an amused smile lurking on his lips.

"What is going on, Simon? Are you seeing Roger?" I ask impatiently.

"What's with the inquisition?" He pouts and looks defensively away. "No. But I'm working on it. I like hanging out with him. Roger nearly blacked out when he saw their car arrive home. They don't think I'm good enough to be in their house," says Simon, using his palm to wipe away the earthy brown stains on his face.

"But, Simon. If Roger has got nothing to hide why is he scared of his parents finding out? Unless of course you're both on the same page?"

Simon does a double take of me. "Don't wind me up, Tara. But...do you think?" he asks with the unlikely timidity of a mouse.

"I'd say it's a step forward."

"Yes!" says Simon, punching the air and clenching his fist.

"Has somebody put something in the water while we've been gone? Giselle is love-struck too."

"Anyway, how was Ireland?" asks Simon, suddenly remembering he hasn't seen me for over a week. We give him the low down, but we don't stay for long before heading back to Shasta's. I don't want to stay in my own house tonight. I don't want to be without him, not just yet – if ever.

As we take the forest lined Fort Langley Highway towards the lake house a small group of people dressed in black are gathered at the roadside, close to where Anthony's garage was burned down. A middle aged woman who is immaculately dressed with blonde hair worn high on her head, kneels down and places a wreath of flowers near a tree just before the edge of the ravine beyond. Shasta's face forms an impenetrable mask and his intense dark eyes swivel to watch the group of mourners as we drive past. Suddenly two faces stand out and my heart lurches to a stop. They don't see us but we can see them very plainly. Tray and Marshall Buchanan are stood side by side. Marshall places his hand on the shoulder of the blonde woman. Shasta presses the car on faster.

"They're having a memorial for Vaughan," I hear myself saying, but Shasta hardly needs it explaining. I see the pain on his face, as he unblinkingly stares in front of him, heading for home. I try to erase a freshly conjured up image from my mind: an ulcerated, charred and decomposed body found amongst the undergrowth. In my mind the body moves its head and its eyes fly open accusingly. I shudder and rid myself of the gruesome vision. Approaching the familiar track road towards Shasta's house, we pass the sequoia grove and my spirits rise.

Scout is the first to greet Shasta, howling a welcome, making circles around him, hitting her own face with her tail as she arcs with excitement.

"Seb?" shouts Shasta, as he throws open the door.

"Hey!" Seb's head pops around the corner. "You came back?"

"Sorry about that," replies Shasta, patting his brother on the back.

"I've got my feet nicely under the table. Do you want a new housemate?"

"Not likely, Bro."

Seb shrugs and wanders back to the lounge. He slumps into the sofa in the middle of the room where he resumes watching TV and munching through the packet of cookies he's holding.

"Nice to have you back by the way," says Seb as an afterthought, turning to me and looking more like Shasta from this angle with his black, silky hair and the same short aquiline nose.

Shasta's cell phone rings. He's in demand already - we really are back to reality. A shadow crosses his face and he strides to the window while he takes the call. His voice is testy and the call doesn't last long.

"That was Leonie," he says, carefully, watching my reaction.

Mentally I flunk down in the chair at the mention of her name, but I keep my feelings to myself.

"What does she want?" I ask evenly.

"Cain Shimlow is out at the Rez. She was giving me the heads up. He'll be prying for information and coercing them. Since when has Shimlow had any genuine interest in the Reservation community?" Shasta swears under his breath.

"Are you going out there now?" I ask, although I already know the answer to that. Leonie calls and Shasta goes running. How come I'm the only one to see what's going on here? I'm not just paranoid, but that thought lingers with me and I start doubting myself. We've all got history. Mine just doesn't rear its head every other day.

Shasta nods. "Do you want to come?" he asks, though I get the feeling he doesn't want me to.

"No," I reply, and turn away from him.

"I'll be back soon," he says, putting his coat back on.

Though it's sorely tempting to go with him, I'm exhausted and can hardly even hold up my own weight. If he's bothered that I'm not coming it doesn't show in his voice. Whatever he needs to do, he needs to do it on his own. At least when Scarlett threw herself at him – literally – he firmly rejected her and put me in the picture. That meant a lot. He needs to work out for himself what's going on.

"Do you mind if I stay here again tonight, Bro?" asks Seb, upending the biscuit pack and filling his mouth with crumbs. "This is good," he points at the TV. "And I haven't got Mom talking over it."

"Sure. Have the horses been alright?"

Seb nods, only half listening, as Shasta stalks out without so much as a backward glance.

I go upstairs and change into a pair of sweatpants, feeling disappointed not to be carrying on the closeness

I've shared with Shasta, and simmering with anger that Leonie has edged up the ladder in his priorities. I hope, not for the first time, that she isn't staying around and that she's already booked to return to California now that she knows Shasta and I are a couple. I drag myself downstairs, thinking I should check on the horses.

"Aren't you coming to sit down?" asks Seb, placing a hand on the sofa next to him. "You look exhausted," he says with a sidelong double-take.

"Once I stop, I'll fall over," I reply, but I join him by staring at the television as he dips into a bag of potato chips and passes it to me. His glances at me and I suspect I'm giving off irritable vibes.

"I hope *I* didn't make you this angry?" Seb asks.

"You?" I screw up my nose, not having a foggy notion what he's talking about.

"That day when Leonie turned up when you met my parents. I love winding Shasta up, but sometimes I get a bit carried away."

"You didn't make me angry." I smile, feeling bad that he thought the irritable vibes were because of him.

"So what's up? I'm no scholar but I can read an atmosphere."

I've no intention of telling Seb about my paranoia over Leonie, not giving light to my dark thoughts...

"Leonie." I hear the word before I realize it came from my own mouth. It must be the jet lag. Seb's mouth narrows to a thin line as he eyes me carefully.

"I guess I was just looking forward to spending the night with Shasta," I try to light-heartedly sweep it away.

Seb puts down the bag of chips and fixes me with a serious look.

"Leonie made things very difficult for Shasta and I. She put herself between us and I was over the moon when she left."

I'm dying to ask how Shasta was after she left, but if you don't want to know the answer then don't ask the question.

"I suspect she's here to get him back." I bite my lip after I've confided. The softening look in Seb's eyes confirms that he thinks I'm right.

"Look, if she is, then she's bought herself a losing ticket. My brother doesn't believe in going over old ground. Shasta's hard like that. Once it's over, there's no going back. He's black and white," says Seb.

I smile at him, heartened to hear those words, hoping he's saying that because it's actually true, not because he thinks it's what I want to hear.

"She'll be moving on in no time, right? She'll go back to California and things will return to normal."

Seb drops his head and looks up at me with hooded eyes which aren't revealing something. His chest rises and he sighs.

"You don't know do you?" he asks.

My nerve endings start to tingle, anticipating danger. "What don't I know?"

"Leonie has landed herself a job at the radio station. She's here to stay," he says, his voice weakening as he tries to soften the blow. Seb is more insightful than I first thought.

I look towards the ceiling, wishing this wasn't true. I let my breath out before I suffocate.

"Tara, just don't give her any leeway. Stay on her tail. I'll look out for you," he says innocently, pulling a happy face; he looks ridiculously young. I feel like I'm talking to my little brother.

I rise from the edge of the sofa, pressing my feet into the floor, making sure my jangling legs can still hold me up.

"I'm going to check on the horses."

I pull on my sneakers and wander across the yard towards the stables. It's completely dark now and the hush of the surrounding forest is disturbed by the sound of Penny whinnying as she hears me approach. I turn on the stable lights and she is peacefully chewing on hay hanging from a net on the wall. The smell of leather, hay and horse is intoxicating. I bury my head in her neck as I whisper to her and put my palm over her lips, feeling her velvety mouth flickering on my skin. Sultan's low grunt from his deep chest vies for my attention.

I close the door on Penny and look in on Sultan, who is standing with his back to me in the middle of his stable with regal indifference. It's not that I don't trust Sultan, but he's so big and spirited you've got to give him respect. I make a clicking sound with my tongue on my teeth as I move around to his side, avoiding the powerfully muscled rump and sculpted back legs, knowing the damage one nervous kick could do. As I stroke Sultan's neck, a car drives into the yard. The headlights dim as the engine is cut. *Shasta is back early.* I duck out of the bright light of the stable and into the gloom. A figure disappears into the house, followed by a second shape.

I know immediately from the short stocky silhouette that it isn't Shasta. So who would just go into the house like that? My senses fire up and my eyes gain acuity as adrenaline kicks in. I run quietly across the yard, unable to see what kind of car it is. The door is swinging in the wind and I place one hand against it and slide my back against the wall, listening hard. I creep silently through the corridor as the sound of men's voices shouting becomes muffled. There is a crash as something gets knocked over then the sound of grunting and swearing as the commotion escalates. My heart is thundering in my ears. I grab a knife from the kitchen worktop, clutching it tight as I peer around the side of the wall into the glass fronted lounge.

Where Seb was sitting, two men in ski masks are wrestling with a brown sack. They've place it over Seb's head and shoulders. One man is holding his arms around the lumbering shape while the other throws punches into Seb's folding body. The man holding Seb looks up at the window and yells. He's spotted my reflection. The masked man charges towards me and I back up, pressing my back against the wall and thrusting the knife out in front of me. I slash across the man's passage, but he keeps coming forward. I slash again catching his hand as he lurches at me.

"Bitch!" he screams.

Every cell in my body is telling me to fight. The other man is dragging Seb towards the door and is now close behind the muscle-bound freak who is swearing at me and dripping blood on the tiled floor. I step backwards suddenly aware I'm making primal threatening noises.

The man lunges towards me and I keep moving backwards, aware that soon I will have nowhere else to go; he'll have me in a corner and I'll have no choice but to struggle against his superior strength and weight. I get back further still, taking a few short steps through the doorway to the kitchen. The man is taunting me with obscenities.

"You bastard," I spit. "Let him go!"

"Run, Tara!" yells Seb, just before another blow strikes him. He falls silent and his hooded shape crumples as the captor drags him forward.

"Seb!" I kick at the door with every ounce of strength I have, just as the man pounces towards me and crosses the threshold. The door ricochets off my foot and splays into his face. I run blindly into the darkness outside, unable to think of a reasonable place I can defend myself. I probably know the forest better than them, but in this darkness it would be dangerous. I career towards the lights of the stable, grabbing the pitchfork which is against the wall as I throw myself into Sultan's open stable door. I trip and fall onto the straw on the floor, then scrabble towards the furthest away wall as the curses of the masked man get closer. I hide the pitchfork under the hay, keeping the long blunt prongs upright, ready to thrust it at him if he gets close enough. I'm breathing rapidly, and blinded by sweat or tears, I wipe my brow on my sleeve as the man enters the stable. He sees me, apparently helplessly cornered, and screams with victorious rage. Sultan tramples nervously beside me.

"You little bitch. You're not going anywhere now."

"Come on." I hiss through gritted teeth, taunting him, knowing I need him to make a swift movement if I stand a chance. The man's menacing laugh erupts with hell bent fury. Sultan suddenly strikes out with his back legs. The sickening crack of hooves on flesh and bone reverberates with the agonized grunt from the man as he is thrown backwards out of the stable.

I jump up, still clutching the pitchfork; holding it in front of me, passing Sultan, who is rolling his eyes and snorting. There's shouting and scuffling as a car starts up and the man who was after me, staggers toward the vehicle.

"Seb!" He must be in the car. I race out just as the car screeches forward, with the passenger door open.

"It's not him!" I hear the other man shout. The injured man falls into the car as it drives off with the door banging against his trailing legs. The dogs' frenzied barking from their den in the utility room is the only noise I can hear in the house. *If only they'd been able to get to us.*

Breathing heavily, I stumble through the door and drop to my knees beside the crumpled outline of Seb, who is motionless on the floor, with the sack lying beside him. A small oval of blood has formed on the ground beside his face. I can't hear him breathing.

"No! Sebbie!" I tilt his chin back and put my fingers to his neck and feel what could be a weak pulse. "It's alright Sebbie. You're going to be alright."

I prop Seb on his side before the nausea which has been pulsing through my sternum rises further. My vision and the nausea swim together into one long wave. A black circle appears around my field of vision. It comes inwards and the weight pressing down on my shoulders becomes unbearable.

18

At the Kings' house, Luna fusses around Seb as though he is six years old and has just fallen off his bicycle. For the second time in twenty-four hours Seb recounts what happened. The first time was for Shasta's benefit when the hospital checked him over. Now Patrick from the Sheriff's Office is taking a statement from him and Barnaby is sitting in. Seb is enjoying repeating the tale - his version is from the inside of a hessian sack and mine is the full version - minus the descriptions of the attackers. I could only describe the physique of the two men, nothing more.

"That goon is going to have two large hoof prints tattooed on his body, so at least that's something to go on. And Tara...don't call me Sebbie again!"

"You should *not* have fought. You should have run! says Shasta, running his hands through his hair, before pausing with his head in his hands.

"I heard them say, 'it's not him'. That's the only other thing I can tell you," I say to Patrick, completing my statement.

Barnaby glowers at Shasta with his face puckered into unbecoming folds. Shasta is standing stiffly with his arms by his sides, with guilt written on every line which has appeared overnight. His proud jaw is angled to the floor as his eyes flick around the room, focusing on nothing, and it seems there is only room for whatever is going on in his head. For him there is no escape. Everyone wants a piece of him and he's caught in a trap, feeding on guilt and blame as penance for doing what started off as being the right thing. Shasta is blaming himself, and so is my father. The treacherous looks have been traded. I can't watch his torment any longer.

I tweak my head towards the door, signalling I want to talk to him in private. He follows me out of the room as Barnaby and Patrick get ready to leave without a shift in the angst between the two men I care about most.

"It's not your fault," I whisper beseechingly into his ear, placing my hand on his chest and imploring him with every fibre of my being.

"They came looking for me, Tara. How is that *not* my fault?" he snaps back, turning his solemn face away from me. Barnaby and Patrick walk past us on the way out. Then the door opens with another visitor.

Holy Hell! What does she want now?

"Seb, how are you?" Leonie says, rushing to his side. He looks at her with a sneer which turns into a tepid smile.

"Come to feed off my bones, Leonie?" he asks, folding a slice of hot buttered toast in half and stuffing it in his mouth.

I shake my head and march angrily outside, unable to stand another second of the tension and manipulation that is going on inside. Shasta walks out behind me at a slower pace. I turn to look at him and the wind whips my hair over my face. He tilts his head in a questioning gesture which, with a smile, would have been endearing, but his eyes are hard and he looks cold, angry and questioning.

I thrust my thumb in the direction of the house, indicating one of the sources of my irritation. I shake my head and hold my hands up, expecting the answer to fall into them as I implore from him why this is happening. Shasta puts an arm around me, smothering some of the flames of irritation beneath, but there is a distance, an unfathomable depth in him which I can't reach. I forget Leonie's latest intrusion and focus back on him.

"Are you going to tell me what is wrong?"

He looks beyond me over the open landscape and shakes his head, avoiding the lingering looks which are a special, integral part of who we are together.

"Too many people around me are getting hurt and it has to stop!"

"Leave it with the police. We don't even know who it was!"

Shasta looks at me blisteringly. "Marshall Buchanan? The syndicate? Shimlow?"

"Leonie called you out last night to talk with Shimlow, if Seb hadn't been there I'd have been on my own and-"

"Don't even follow up that train of thought!"

I have never seen Shasta so frightening angry. I'm on his side but I'm increasingly feeling like I'm the problem. Last night after the attack he had been so upset. I could see it in every whispered word and in his tight embrace, but now he's pulling back from me. I don't understand why he's changing. I don't understand what's happened to cause it.

"Where is it going to end?" he asks, keeping his eyes focused on the middle distance and looking at nothing.

"Look. We're both overwrought. Tonight we'll have dinner, just the two of us and we'll put all this behind us. Forget what is going on at the Rez, forget all about the gold rumors, the land acquisition, the Buchanans. Let's just focus on what matters. Us."

I pause, expecting a reaction from him - but there is nothing, not even a readable expression; just a mask of indifference. From the corner of my eye I see movement at the window of Luna and Carson's house, but it's Leonie's dark face I see at the window.

"Shasta, speak to me?"

He nods and gives me a half hearted smile. I tuck into his chest and put my hands on the flat of his stomach. His arm goes around my shoulders and I feel him kiss the top of my head. My heart is telling him I love him, but I'm not feeling it back from him. I keep it to myself, wishing he would tell me he cared. Wishing he would include me in whatever torturous thoughts are going on in his head. My ego is bruised and I'm edging onto the periphery of rejection. I can feel it from him, but there are no words of communication to give me something to rally against.

I remove myself from his arms and his penetrating eyes blanket any softness he is feeling. "Where are you going?" he asks sharply

"To work." I reply, not letting him see how upset I am. I realize I'm reflecting how he is with me - as though I care - but not that much. I gird myself to be stoic, strong and focused. No man will make a fool of me again. No man will ever again manipulate me into ending a relationship because he hasn't got the balls to. If there's a problem, then say there's a problem. I look up at him. His eyes connect with mine then with a squeeze of my fingers our hands release. I walk to the car as he watches me drive away.

I bury myself in work but memories of last night's attack push up through my thoughts like weeds. Simon is working with me at the coffeehouse today, but even he is off his stride. He's mooning over his unrequited love for Roger. Simon's slim boyish face hollows out when his jaw hangs open as I tell him about last night's break-in at Shasta's.

"I would have wet my pants and run. Why are you even in work?"

"That was yesterday."

"Honey, I like to think I'm brave, but I'm not. If a man comes in with hoof prints on his head he'll be looking for you. Don't call me for help. I'll be out the back door making a run for it."

Simon's melodramatic, feminine mannerisms make me giggle uncontrollably, a trace of delayed shock may also have something to do with the tears welling in my eyes as I laugh.

"You're such a tonic, my friend." I plop my arm affectionately around him, glad of his light-hearted support and ability to make a comedy from a drama. He's all talk - I know he'd be on my side.

The regulars come and go. Sarah comes in and sits at her usual spot. Simon makes a fuss of her, and in the quiet spells throughout the day Simon and I get to talk for longer than we have done for a while. James and Svetlana pop in for a take-out and a chat before going back to work. James mentions that he and Shasta had been out for a hike earlier but he doesn't elaborate. I presumed Shasta was working today, but perhaps he needed to clear his head first. He had mentioned fitting shoes for a couple of horses at Margy's. Maybe that had changed.

"Did you go anywhere interesting?" I ask, trying not to sound too curious.

"Just around," he replies, shaking his head dismissively.

"He and Shasta were trying to sniff out the gold, weren't you?" whispers Svetlana teasingly to me, within earshot of

James "Carson and a couple of others went too. He was using his special skills."

James frowns and gives Svetlana a look. She smirks and shuts up.

"Tell me about Ireland. I've got time if you have," she says, looking around the store. I explain about Fen's group of energy workers, the translucent pyramid in the mountains, and the visitation in my sleep. I feel awkward describing this stuff in front of James because he's so practical and masculine. He takes me by surprise and points out that all mountain peaks have a higher energy connection and it isn't news to him. He's a regular guy but there's more to him than meets the eye. He reminds me of the friends I made in Ireland: all regular people and not a hippy guru amongst them.

"You're an enigma, James."

He looks at me curiously with a smile lurking behind his blue eyes. "I live in the mountains because it's the clearest place to live: the closer to the top the higher the energy. I think more people will be drawn to live in the mountains, but I'd like to keep it quiet, just the way it is."

After they've gone I serve some customers, eye the chocolate cake winking at me from the display and distract myself from it by flicking through the notebook of my grandmother's, which I've been carrying in my bag. There may be useful remedies for bruising that will help Seb.

"Is that your spell book?" Simon asks, looking at the book with the name Blanche Whitelaw on the front. "Oh, I didn't see you there," he says suddenly in a peculiar tone.

I look up to see who he's talking to and Cain Shimlow is at the counter. He looks, thinner and more haggard.

The dark shadows under his sunken eyes accentuate his beak like nose. My chest tightens. I didn't think he'd be back after our tiff. I don't want to antagonize another argument, so I say hello to him, then let Simon see to him when I walk off.

Cain's eyes blatantly follow me around the room and he makes no attempt to disguise it. I haven't been privy to what was discussed on the Rez, I've been preoccupied by everything else that has been going on. Perhaps Cain, Shasta and some of the others on the Rez had found some neutral ground and relationships were being fostered, although in my heart I find it hard to believe. I walk to the book counter, and stand leafing through the book. Cain takes his drink and peruses the bookshelves; his eyes rove around without settling on anything in particular. That is until he sets eyes on Blanche's journal.

"What's that?" he asks.

Mind your own freaking business. "Private." I flick the book shut.

"Is it for sale?"

I wrinkle up my nose at the absurd and obscure question and reply as though it was a normal thing to say.

"No." I smile and put the book under the counter, confused by his attention and wanting to wrap up the conversation before causing another fractious outbreak. Cain's eyes look unfocused and vacant; hinting at depression or madness, or both. I look over at Simon who is also watching Cain and a flicker passes between us. Simon curls up his lips and pulls a repugnant face. Cain puts down his cup, having barely touched his drink and wavers out of the store.

All day I've been looking forward to seeing Shasta and now, as I shut up the store a twinge of nervousness settles over me, though I don't know why. I hope he's in a better mood than the one I left him in this morning. I'm about to leave and head for home when I get a text from Shasta. It says 'something has come up' and he won't be over for dinner tonight. My heart drops several beats. He offers no explanation as to what the 'something' is. I feel like I'm straddling a boat that's drifting from shore, with one foot on board, the other on land. Something is wrong and I'd rather know what it is. I didn't say anything to upset Shasta, and anyway he's not the type to easily take offense. Perhaps something *has* come up, perhaps I'm being over sensitive; but I can't shake the feeling.

I'm not as important to him as I thought.

A chill passes through me and I push aside an unwelcome thought. *Damn.* I have to face it. It's too much of a coincidence. The only other variable is Leonie. Her re-appearance is having an effect. Maybe their feelings haven't yet receded into history. The whirlpool starting in my head swirls downwards, pulling my spirits with it. I've got to stop this merry-go-round of worry. If I don't, what I'm wishing *not* to happen, could well materialize. I shove my fears into my boots and trudge out into the cold night air with Simon. As we're about to lock the door Sarah appears on the steps to the coffeehouse, which takes us both by surprise.

"It's OK, I'm not here for more coffee," says Sarah, reading the surprise on my face.

"It's freezing Sarah. What are you doing out on a night like this?"

"It won't take long but I wanted to do this tonight. There's something I want you to take care of for me."

"Sure. Come in," I reply.

Simon, Sarah and myself stand inside the doorway of the store. She takes out a small wooden box with a small padlock on it.

"I'm getting my affairs in order."

"Aren't you a cheery soul?" says Simon, putting his arm around her.

"This was my Stanley's and I didn't want to part with it, because it meant so much to him, but it doesn't belong with me. It needs to go back to someone else, but *only* after I'm gone - that's really important. And they say people round here take their secrets to the grave with them," she chuckles to herself.

"Ah, OK," I reply, looking at the box.

"I want you to see they get it. I don't trust my Executor to follow it through. Would you do it for me?"

"It's not stolen goods is it Sarah?" jokes Simon.

She grins and laughs.

"Why do you want us to do it? I mean we're happy to, right?" I ask turning to Simon. "But what about your family?"

She shakes her head. "I want you to keep it safe, then just hand it over anonymously. There's a note in the envelope with the key, it'll tell you who it's for."

"Are we allowed to know who?" I ask.

"No. Don't open it till I'm gone. Promise me you'll do that? It won't be too long." She smiles.

"I hate it when you talk like this Sarah. You could have years in you."

"No. I'm ready. Will you do it for me? It'll put my mind

at rest. I'll be able to make peace with something that's bugged me for years."

"Yes, we'll do it. I promise," I reply, feeling mystified and honored. Of all the people to be asked to keep a secret, Sarah is asking Simon and I. I'm concerned that she may not be in her sanest frame of mind. I can't stand suspense or surprises at any time. "I'll put it in the safe for now," I tell her.

"Thank you. Good night then," says Sarah, and she walks out into the night. Simon and I exchange puzzled looks then gaze at the old wooden box with an envelope taped to the top of it.

"What do you think it is?" I ask.

"Shall we open it?" asks Simon.

"No way!"

"I was kidding!"

"I'm choked."

"Why did she ask us?"

"Maybe because we're not family and we won't benefit from the Will."

"Oh. I just love Sarah. I don't want her to die," says Simon, getting tearful.

"Me too. She's a wonder. I better put this away," I say, pondering what's in the little box before stashing it in the safe.

Simon suggests going out for something to eat. I'm exhausted and don't feel like going anywhere. We call Giselle who fancies grabbing a take-out and inviting a few people over. That's a much better plan.

Once we get home Roger from next door arrives, which triggers an especially exuberant response from Simon. His cheeks flush red and his eyes flash with mischief. Svetlana and James turn up and I feel awkward that Shasta is missing; James and Shasta are like each other's wing men. I give the only excuse I have, that 'something came up', to explain why Shasta isn't here.

The hollow nagging feeling doesn't go away, and as the group's merry dynamic bubbles around me I feel like retreating from it. It's not long before Giselle and Svetlana get metaphysical and the conversation sways in that direction. Svetlana shows them the new 'ring linking', taking turns to go around and do it for each of them. She does it again for me, and once again I feel like I'm being fine tuned. Afterwards I feel more positive and my earlier concerns seem irrelevant.

Roger sits in between Giselle and Simon. I'm still not sure which one goes with which, but if Giselle has any design on him other than friendship it's not obvious - although they do complement each other. She's feisty and passionate; he cools her fire and is steady and reliable. On the other hand the same could be said of the Roger and Simon combination, that same fire and water balance would apply.

Svetlana and James leave and I get ready to head off to bed, leaving Roger, Simon and Giselle playing poker for candy.

"Whatever happened to Saturday night? New York's finest cocktail bars, a club, dinner and music?" moans Simon.

"It's called growing up, Simon," replies Giselle, in that sisterly tone.

"You could at least play strip poker. That'd liven things up," I say swiping a handful of jellybeans from the table.

Simon looks at me as though I've struck on an amazing

idea. His eyes open as wide as his mouth as he looks at the others, gleaning their reaction. Roger stares at his poker hand, Giselle gives him a disapproving look and he pouts and goes back to his cards.

"Night all," I call as I wander upstairs. The lonely feeling settles around my heart, building a defensive buttress. Tomorrow will be different. Shasta will have had a decent night's sleep and we'll be back to being that tight, loved up couple again.

Just after midnight a car alarm goes off in the street. From the window I can see lights flashing on my car below. I race downstairs, where the others are still up, grab my keys and run outside into the chill to turn it off. In bare feet I stop dead on the path as my eyes adjust. The windscreen is smashed to pieces. That didn't happen by accident. I open the door and a large rock is lying in the foot well of the driver's side. In horror I take a step back with my pulse racing and shaking with adrenaline, as I look around for who threw it. Scanning around the shadows there is no-one in sight. Under the street lights only curtains move as neighbors look out.

"It must have been kids," says Roger, who appears beside me. "It'll be a group of teenagers out looking for something to do."

"Probably," I reply and smile at him, grateful of his support and simple explanation, but I'm not buying it.

19

By breakfast time the following morning I still haven't heard from Shasta. He didn't send me the usual good-night message and I haven't sent him one either. This is ridiculous. We need to shift the dynamic. We're like two magnets pointing at each other, but pushing each other away. I call but his phone goes straight to voicemail, so I text.

Morning gorgeous. How do you want your eggs? Missing you xx

Rather than sit around waiting for a reply I take Hudson for a walk through the woods and down to the lakeshore, noticing how vivid the light orbs are today. It's a normal occurrence but one I've been taking for granted because it's as regular as the sunshine and the rain. The blue and violet lights flash around me and the occasional small starburst of sparks blazes against the low light of forest backdrop. I hold the amulet and tune into the pulse of the forest echoing the heartbeat of Big Spruce.

I know now that the sparkles are how some people see angels, which reminds me of Fen and how she told me about she keeps her relationship on track. Shasta and I could do with a boost to our communication right now. He's always been the one to speak from his heart and it's usually me who struggles. He had helped pull it out of me and build my trust. That's beginning to wrinkle, as the loving leverage he provides is missing, so I try not to retreat in fear of rejection. I keep my head up, and mentally start affirming positive messages, but the work I've done feels fragile and on the cusp of withering without nourishment. I start to head back to the house.

I've not discounted the possibility that Shasta is upset because he feels he put Seb and I in danger. If he's pulling back from me because of some guilty notion that he was responsible for what happened then he's misguided. If it were me I would do everything I could to protect someone. I'd keep them away from danger and I'd tell them why. I'm giving this too much head space. However the matter of my smashed windscreen does need sorting. It's a Sunday and the only option is to call Anthony for a suggestion. Things with him have improved of late, presumably because Shasta saved his life.

Once I'm back in the house I notice Shasta's black 4x4 parked up and he's sitting inside, staring straight ahead. My car is in the garage so I bet he thinks I'm not in. I open the front door and he comes walking up the path. I smile as he walks towards me, but it twists and distorts inside - Shasta looks stern and there is no soft, welcome twinkle. He sees my hesitancy and smiles briefly, but it vanishes like mist. All this business on the Rez has really taken such a toll on him. He looks pale behind his swarthy skin and his jaw is tensed forward, protruding his chin at a stubborn angle.

I go to put my arms around his neck, wanting to love away his troubles, but he catches both of my hands in his and holds them, restricting the embrace. My pout for a kiss vanishes. I draw my face back from him, mirroring his posture.

"What's wrong?" I ask, barely able to whisper the words because the tightening in my throat is strangling me.

Shasta looks around, avoiding my gaze. "Where is everyone?"

"Inside. Come in."

"No. I need to talk to you alone," he replies.

I step closer to him, hoping to create more intimacy. I'm only a few inches from his body, in that fizzing zone, but today the acute energetic tension is different, weaker.

"Why? What's going on?"

There's a pause as Shasta shifts his weight then he eventually lifts his eyes to look at me.

"I'm sorry, Tara. I can't see you anymore," he says.

He delivers the line on the end of a sharp sword which pierces my side. At first there is no pain, only numbness. The rest of the world fades out of focus. I'm scanning his every movement, flicker, tone and gesture trying to define what that means.

"What? Why? I...I don't get what you're saying, Shasta..." I feel divorced from my words. They are separate to me, everything is separate to me.

"I mean...it can't work between us. It's over," he replies, the severing words are delivered with the same cutting tone.

In the silence something snaps. My shoulders fold together as my body crumbles around my breaking heart. My legs buckle below me as I shake with the effort of being alive. The persistent trembling is the only constant.

"Why...why are you saying this? I don't understand. Everything was great between us. What's different?" I try not to sound pleading but it doesn't work.

"I can't give you what you want. What you need," he replies, making steady eye contact and I think I've got him back for a moment. Surely from here we can communicate. "Things have changed," he adds.

"Nothing has changed, Shasta. For me nothing has changed!" I want to tell him I love him more than life itself, but I can't. He's rejecting me, I just can't say it. If he doesn't feel the same about me then I'm not about to beg. Yet I hear the pleading in my voice. How can I be so weak?

"It's you I need. I'm not asking for anything else. I don't need anything else." I bite down hard on my lip, forcing myself to stop talking. I draw blood and lick the coppery tasting liquid from my mouth. He notices it, leans down and briefly kisses me. *How dare he play with me like that!* I grasp the fence rail around the porch. My body is betraying me as my legs are shaking uncontrollably with desire and love, against the pain of knowing it isn't reciprocated.

"You'll always be special to me. You know that." He looks away, and I've lost him again.

"I don't know that! How could I know that? You're telling me it's over with no good explanation. I thought we felt the same?" My anger surges to the fore, trailing hurt and destruction behind.

Shasta looks down and shakes his head.

"Look at me. Damn you!"

He looks at me coolly and defiantly. There is no trace of a lie in what he's saying now. That can only mean one thing – what he felt for me had not been real.

"I'm sorry. I don't want to hurt you, Tara. That's the last thing I want," he says and I recognize something familiar in his eyes now.

"You lied to me. I let you in. You let me believe we had a future and you lied to me."

Shasta shakes his head and his lips part to say something, no sound comes out and his words never leave his taut lips. That tells me all I need to know. He can't deny he led me wrong. I rile against the injustice of it. I'd given it everything. I'd left my life in NYC. For once in my life I had gambled everything for love, left myself wide open to him; he came in and plundered, took what he wanted and now he is leaving me.

The tears are pricking my eyes, making me more and more frustrated. I don't want him to see the effect he's having on me now. He doesn't care and I don't want him to take any power or pleasure from my hurt.

"Is it Leonie? Is that the real reason? Couldn't you find the courage just to tell me the truth, Shasta?"

"It's not Leonie. I only want what's best for you. That's why I'm doing this. It just won't work."

"This...you think this is good for me?" I spit, through blurred vision and tears. *Damn, I can't hold them back.*

He quickly pulls me to him and squeezes, before pushing me gently away from him, but I see the moist film in his eyes too. It gives me some kind of sick hope that he does feel something for me. We can work with that.

"Don't go, Shasta." I reach for his hand but it slips through my palm as he walks down the steps. I want to plead and throw myself at his feet but pride won't let me. He looks back at me and I see it again - his eyes are glassy.

"Shasta!" I stumble and grab the handrail, knocking over a plant pot. It crashes to the ground and smashes on the path below. It's only then I notice Pandora and Errol coming out of next door, taking in everything that is going on. They will take great delight in being witness to this...this break up with Shasta. I can't believe it, but that is what is happening. Shasta has unequivocally broken up with me.

I cannot comprehend why this is happening, when days

ago we were talking about our future together. I'd set my mind free and come up with ideas of moving in and the possibility of serious commitment. I'm aware of nothing, only the images of Shasta driving off; all around me is a blur. I drop to the floor, spent of all willpower to defend myself. I must be sobbing because my breathing comes in short inward bursts. There is a voice and then Giselle is beside me, pulling me towards her in a sympathetic embrace as she swears after Shasta.

"Come on. Get off the step. Come indoors," says Giselle, well aware that Errol and Pandora are intrigued by the scene and are probably thrilled that their neighborhood will no longer be blighted by an indigenous person.

20

I would never have chosen to feel like this. The worst of it is, I had made the choices that brought me to this. The effort of being with people yesterday was too much. There was too much blubbing for anyone to make sense of me, anyhow. I had no control over it, until the force of the weeping eased. I only rose from the bed when the nausea became too much: my head was slitting open and the idea of smashing it against the wall to release the blood and pain seemed like a way to escape it.

I called him. I texted him. There was no reply.

I had lain alone in my room, having mental conversations about all the things I wanted to say. If he knew how I felt, he wouldn't be doing this - but then he is a liar. He never did feel about me the way I did about him. The gaping wound of that unmistakable truth is festering with the toxic thoughts that keep lingering on that fact. *What a fool I've been.* I think of all the women around the world who've had heartbreak and still lived. The population didn't decline because of deaths from broken hearts.

It takes a mask and a lot of bravado to go out in the world when you're damaged - necessitating extra make-up and a free pass to deal with it in your own time, away from the scrutiny of the well-meaning. The pain is mine to deal with, and mine alone. Yet I don't feel I can face anyone without crying.

I can't accept that Shasta has broken up with me. I can't accept such a monstrous loss. Irrational thoughts abound: perhaps I should go back to New York, maybe relocate to Ireland, take time out and travel, or perhaps I should just stay here and face the fact that Shasta and I are over. The thought brings another wave of sadness and despair.

I shower, dress and apply some make-up, ready for work. I blow dry my hair so its length falls forward over my face, like a curtain, hiding as much of it as I can. My eyes stay dry long enough to put on the waterproof mascara. The concealer and eyeliner do a marginal job of reducing the bull frog appearance of my swollen lids.

Giselle and Simon had been in stunned silence yesterday, as much as they are ever quiet. Neither of them saw the breakup coming. The norm during a breakup is to denigrate your friend's choice of boyfriend, slather on sympathy that they were never good enough anyway, topping it off with clichés about the number of fish in the sea, and how they will 'never find anyone else as good as you'. In actual fact there is very little of that.

They had been fond of Shasta and thought he was authentic. He fooled everyone. Roger had come in, apparently just for a social visit, but in all likelihood he heard from his parents about the split. I didn't want to talk, but was glad to know they were there, but it didn't make me feel any less alone.

"Tara?" calls Simon through my bedroom door. "I'll cover at the coffeehouse today."

I throw the door open and grab my bag. "I'm going in," I mutter, smile and gulp.

"You don't have to."

"I want to." I hug him and stride past, putting on a brave face as I head out the door on my way to work, keeping silent about my intention to see Shasta first. I need to see him. We need to sort this out. I'm hoping there's still a chance we can patch things up. As I arrive at his house my heart sinks. His car isn't there and neither is he. The anticipation that I might see and touch him ends, and the depth of disappointment floors me. I don't know if I could see him without making a spectacle of myself and an image of me clutching his ankles as he walks away from me pops up. Desperation is so undignified. I leave quickly, thinking what a bad idea this was.

Work helps me take my mind off things, or rather gives me something to think about parallel to thinking about Shasta. I keep busy welcoming the steady stream of customers, and the reassuring hubbub of chatter and stability that work brings. It's easier to talk to those who don't know me, to make pleasant small talk and carry on as though everything is normal in my world. However every moment I get that takes me away from others, to the kitchen, the bathroom or the storeroom, the tears bubble up unbidden and I expertly tip my head forward and blink them away. I steel myself then go back to face others with a deep breath and a freshly appointed smile. Inside the excruciating ache in my heart is merciless.

"You're a stubborn ass," says Giselle, following me into the nook.

"It takes one to know one."

"Why don't you go and see Shasta? Maybe you can sort something out?"

"I did, this morning. He wasn't there. It's pointless anyway," I shake my head and carry on clearing the table.

"OK, well why don't you go and see Svetlana? Maybe she can give you some acupuncture.

"Maybe later." Right now I'm not feeling any faith in anything metaphysical.

With a gust of wind Cooper arrives through the door,

and he sweeps through the library with his gaze maybe looking for Giselle.

"Look who it is Giselle."

Giselle makes a high pitched squeaking noise behind me, bolsters herself and casually goes to greet him. Cooper is clutching a picture frame, which holds the hand written poetic piece about the forest which they had found together. Giselle's face lights up with the sentimentality of the gesture. She finds a place on the back wall of the library for it, then they sit down together and get lost in conversation. I can see they are into each other but no-one seems to be making a move. Giselle would usually be so up front with guys that it probably scares them off but it's funny how hesitant and unsure she looks around him. She's like fizz trapped in a bottle: all light, airy and contained. A little gentle nudge might be just what they need, but then I'm no expert. I can't help but wonder if a true friend would encourage romantic entanglement.

When Giselle goes to the bathroom I take my chance.

"Hey Cooper." I sit down on the leather sofa beside him. After a brief conversation about how the forestry project I get to my point. "When are you two going to get it together?" I ask quickly, knowing Giselle will be back at any moment. Cooper flushes from the neck upwards and is about to deny that he knows what I mean. He glances around.

"I don't think she's interested. She's so...cool."

"Take it from me...she likes you. One of you needs to make a move."

"Err, right," he replies, barely moving his lips as Giselle crosses the room back towards us.

"I was just saying how great it is that they've agreed to use

Rez land for the forestry project," I say lightly to Giselle, bluffing over the suspicious pause in the atmosphere.

"Really? Yeah, that is good news," replies Giselle, her direct gaze tells me she doesn't completely believe me.

"I'll get you a drink." I go behind the counter and Giselle follows me.

"What did you say to him?" she mutters, her face cloudy with suspicion.

"Nothing. Nothing he didn't need to hear."

"Tara!"

"I just mentioned that you might be interested."

"You did what? Christ, how high school!"

"You two needed an intervention. Now go, he's watching over. You've been dancing around each other long enough."

Giselle tucks her hair behind her ear; the redness of her cheeks is more vibrant than her flaming hair. She turns back towards Cooper with a faint but real smile tweaking her mouth. For a brief matchmaking minute I hadn't thought of Shasta. I take Giselle and Cooper peppermint teas plus a couple of pink heart cup cakes. Giselle clocks the cakes and scowls at me.

For the rest of the afternoon I can't take my eyes from the windows, hoping to catch a glimpse of Shasta in the town, but knowing full well that he's probably elsewhere. In the distance I see someone with shoulder length, black hair - my heart flips - but the man turns around it's not him.

I endlessly check my phone, for a returned message or a missed call but there isn't one. I keep going over his words and the times we had spent together, but nothing makes sense. His words don't match the feelings we had for each other. I'd gotten it so wrong. Against everything I know about positive thinking, I berate myself for being so naive, so stupid. And the worst thing is – I'd do it all again. I'd risk it all again just to be with him for even a moment.

Sophia is stood in the doorway of the kitchen, listening to the local radio station. A familiar voice comes across the airwaves. He sounds so smooth, articulate and charming. He also sounds like he has the female presenter eating out of his hand; if the timely pleasant tones of her voice are anything to go by. Tray always was able to read and capably seduce women. I only hear the end of the broadcast, but it is enough to glean that he is representing a company who are offering shares to Native Americans on the Rez. He says that whilst there is only a small chance there is gold, his company are willing to risk it in return for their cooperation, because they think they deserve to be 'better represented and taken care of'.

They wouldn't be interested if they didn't believe there was money to be made here. Shasta had been right. The syndicate do seem to be setting the record straight and distancing themselves from Cain Shimlow's public crusade. I didn't get to find out from Shasta what happened with Cain and the people on the Rez or what had gone down there.

"That's that new presenter," says Sophia "What was her name again? Lenore...Lennie–"

"Leonie."

"That's it."

Seb did tell me she landed a job on the radio. She just keeps popping up. I sigh, but can hardly allow myself to think about it - now the way is clear for her and Shasta to be together. It's a blunt knife that jabs at my heart and splices me open. The thought of her with my man is too much. He is still mine. There is no other way to look at it. Before I can get away from anyone the floodgates open up and a fresh round of unwelcome tears erupt. I dash into the bathroom. Outside the door Sophia is talking to Giselle, telling her one minute I was fine, the next I wasn't.

"I'm alright," I call through the barrier of the wooden bathroom door. I gulp a few deep breaths of air and my throat closes over as I open the door. Refusing to speak is the only way to stem the flow of tears.

Giselle is standing there: flushed and stern looking. She stares hard at me for a moment and I remove my gaze to the distance. She sees too much, this one. She places a hand on my arms then slips it around my neck I wrap my arms around her, and the tears run free.

"See what sympathy does!" I wave my finger at her and blow my nose into the scrunched up toilet roll. "I can do acquaintances and I can do alone time, but I can't be doing with people who want to talk about it."

"You should go home."

I shake my head. "Where's Cooper?" I divert her attention.

She breaks into a huge grin and goes a deep crimson as her expression changes. "He's gone. Although he is taking me out tonight," she tries to sound less enthusiastic than she actually is.

"Don't play it down on my account. Now you can thank me for interfering."

"Yes, Tara. Thank you for interfering."

"Go home. I'll finish off here," I retreat into the bathroom to splash water on my face and cool the mottled pink skin and wipe away smears of makeup. There is a knock on the door and Svetlana's even tone comes from outside. I open it to her and she brusquely comes in, catching me off guard.

"Giselle told me what happened. I'm so sorry."

"Oh dear God, no more sympathy, please."

Svetlana pouts and shakes her head then tells me to sit down on the seat. "I've something better than sympathy. Give me your wrist."

She tears a strip of paper from a sealed plastic wrapper and I see the acupuncture needle in her fingers.

"What? Now?"

"It's for shock."

I roll my eyes and flinch as she confidently takes my hand, and with a deft movement I feel the gentle sting of the needle in the crease of my wrist.

"Don't expect me to thank you." I rub away the ache. Svetlana smiles and after a bit of motherly advice she leaves to go back to the clinic.

As the coffeehouse empties and the afternoon draws to a close I realize I got through a day without him. With fist screwing frustration it grates me to realize how I'd gotten so used to being with him until I'd become virtually mentally dependent on him. I'd known it from the start how it could end, and yet I still did it.

At closing time I find solace in the empty store, giving me somewhere that I won't be disturbed. Only then do I realize that Sarah hadn't been in today and that is concerning. I take a chamomile tea into the nook and dim the lights, curling up in the corner away from the window where I can't be seen. I take out Blanche's journal and aimlessly flick through it, hoping by touching it some healing can take place. Exhausted and emotionally spent I rest my head on my arm for a few minutes.

Repetitive banging on glass wakes me and I glance at my watch, shocked to realize it's 1:00 a.m. - I've been sleeping in the coffeehouse. The banging comes again and I see two uniforms from the Sheriff's Office in the moonlight outside. The faces of my dad and Patrick appear at the door.

"We spotted the light on. I thought it was suspicious," says Patrick.

"No, everything is fine here. I just fell asleep." I blink the sleep from my eyes and turn my head to get rid of the crick in my neck.

"You young ones have no stamina," says my dad.

"They're not like us, eh Barnaby?" says Patrick.

I grab my coat and walk out with them, listening to their banter as we walk to my car. From a side street a shadow tumbles out and knocks into us. The dark figure grabs onto me as he falls and rolls onto his back. The street light shines on his face. The waxy pinched features of Cain Shimlow are smeared with blood from a wound on his head. He tries to stand but Patrick makes him sit on the pavement and radios for an ambulance while Barnaby runs off in the direction Cain came from. The blood is pouring down and covering his eye. I stem the blood flow with my scarf.

"There's no one there," says Barnaby, arriving back breathless and sweating from his head.

"Who did this Cain?" asks Patrick, but Cain just looks at him, dazed and confused. I remember his threat to me in the car park that night after my meeting Tray Buchanan, the nasty tone and acrid smell of his breath. It seems a long time ago now. This is a different man, sat here bleeding in the street. He looks his age of seventy years plus. He looks like someone's grandfather: vulnerable, fragile, and broken.

21

As the hours turn into days without hearing from Shasta, we drift further and further away from each other. There is nothing else I can try. I wish I could stop time. It's up to him now and by his conspicuous silence, it's clear he doesn't want me. I've phoned, messaged and prayed. Nothing has worked. The longing doesn't go away. If only we could talk we could find a way, but if he really doesn't care then it's pointless.

I saw Svetlana: we talked, I had acupuncture and healing - but I'm having a crisis of faith. After my trip to see Fen I'd felt only optimism: that somehow life would be sweet, that somehow just by being in Big Spruce and surrounded by bright positive people life would be great. However, I feel spent and stupid for feeling like this over the break-up with Shasta. As he would say 'we're all one', so it shouldn't matter that we're not together – but it does. It makes a mockery of what I had believed. If such a fundamental belief is wrong then the whole thing is a house of cards.

I had spoken to Svetlana about how I felt. She said that my challenge was to keep it together through this. It's another test and frankly I'm fed up with it. If it means being away from what I love then no reward would be worth it. I could be promised all the riches in the world and it would mean nothing compared to being with Shasta.

"Keep yourself shining through this. You're learning how to use the energy. Stay positive," said Svetlana.

"Right. I almost couldn't care less right now, whatever I'm supposed to do or, whatever I'm meant to achieve.

keeping the vibe up, clearing energy fields. I can't do it. I don't want to do it," I replied.

"It'll pass. Just be grateful that you've been in love." She speaks like it's all over, but for me it isn't. I don't want to be rude to Svetlana but it's all lost its lustre. The only thing that really helped was reciting Ho'oponopono endlessly - a repetitive affirmation, simple to do when my mind was too numb to do much else.

I wonder if owning the amulet is a poison chalice of spiritual responsibilities. A light bulb goes on. *Of course.* It's increasing the vibration and pushing my development too far. I've had things go wrong since it came to me: Rosa's death was so sudden. However I've also had good things happen: meeting Shasta, living by the lake, immersing myself in the wilderness, being happier in myself, but now I've lost those things too. Maybe the amulet needs to go, but to who, or where?

"Let me tell you something. I probably shouldn't..." she pauses, having second thoughts over what she wants to say.

"Don't bail on me now, Svetlana. Give it to me straight!"

"Shasta has gone."

I pulled myself upright, straining to understand. "What?"

"He went into the mountains a couple of days ago. James spent a bit of time with him, but he wasn't in good shape. He left James and went off alone."

"Why? Where did he go?"

"You know James, he doesn't give much away. He's protecting his friend's wishes and that's all I know. If you're thinking he doesn't care, I think you're wrong. He's hurting just as much as you. Don't do anything stupid, like going looking for him. He might be back by now for all I know. I shouldn't have said anything, but I don't like seeing you like this."

"OK. I won't. I'm glad you told me."

So naturally after my visit to Svetlana I went round to Shasta's. He wasn't there. I looked in on the horses and they've been fed and watered. If Shasta had gone, then Seb must have been here. I'd missed the whole of our little family, and visiting reinforces the brutal reality of what I've lost. I loathe self pity. I've got to shake it off. I take my mind off the ache in my chest by thinking about Simon's upcoming party, although my brain juggles the two issues simultaneously.

As it's Simon's 30th birthday tomorrow we've decided to organize a party for him. It was supposed to be a surprise, but he was so intent on organizing something for himself that he made a list of people he wanted to invite from work, so Giselle and I gave in and told him what we were doing. He went hyper with the organizing and is playing the party diva.

Sophie has baked a cake for it. I swing past the supermarket and stockpile party food, throwing myself into planning what we can do to make it more fun for Simon. Giselle had suggested a princess theme, Simon turned this idea down but suggested a Diamonds and Divas theme instead - which actually doesn't sound that much different. It just requires plenty of glass decorations (diamonds), and as Christmas things are now in the shops that's easy, plus black and white feather boas (divas). We found fine white muslin in Rosa's cupboard and silver colored chains, usually used on Christmas trees, to adorn the house.

I drive out to Margy's garden centre to pick up some

outdoor lanterns for the party. It triggers more memories of Shasta; I'd bumped into him at the stables in the field after Hudson ran off. It's a bitter sweet memory now. I have a brief chat with Margy about the memorial trees and reforestation project, then head back to town and the coffeehouse to let Giselle have the afternoon off. She had a great time with Cooper on their first date and since then there have been a few more, although there is still hesitancy between them and things haven't moved particularly fast.

Back in the coffeehouse I get a glimpse of Simon's birthday cake as prepared by Sophie's skilled hand. It's two tiered, black and white, with a black bow tie across the middle, strewn with black and white sugar feathers plus a few silver leaves. It's perfect, and as Simon walks in to meet Giselle, Sophie hides the cake in the kitchen

I have the sudden and strong feeling of Shasta, or I could be imagining it. I look out the window into the street and there is no-one there. Giselle opens the door to leave and I spot something from the corner of my eye. It's the familiar black 4x4. My heart flips over in my chest. Giselle stops and glances sharply at me then in the direction I'm facing.

"It's Shasta." I take a step forward then freeze. The car disappears from sight without stopping. For a brief second I thought he was parking up nearby, but he didn't. Giselle closes the door after an icy cold blast of air comes in, leaving Simon stood outside.

"What do you want to do?" she asks.

I can feel my nose wrinkle up questioningly and I shrug. Next to lying in front of the car and refusing to move until I can talk to him I can't think of anything.

"Nothing." I reply. "You go."

With that Giselle strides out into the street and I pace

around, looking for something to do to distract my attention from Shasta. Of course it doesn't work, but at least I feel like I'm doing something. So he's back in town, without the excuse there is no phone signal, and he still hasn't been in touch. I wonder if he's had my other messages. On impulse I text him three short words - *I miss you x* - and send it, just hoping to hear anything back. I slip the phone into my back pocket and try to forget I've sent it; like the others it will probably not be returned. Several minutes later my cell phone rings. I answer it, reading 'Shasta' on the display. My breathing gets erratic.

"Hi," he says quietly.

"Hi," I breathe back, unable to stop my lips trembling. After all this time thinking of him, all the things I wanted to say escape me. I hear him sigh. It could be boredom or a tinge of sadness.

"Are you OK?" he asks.

"Yes." No, I really mean no, but that's not what I want him to hear.

"I'm so sorry, Tara. It's just...things had to be this way."

"You once told me there were always choices."

There is a lengthy pause. "Not this time," replies Shasta, his voice sounding anguished.

"Why not? Explain it to me."

There is perpetual silence. He could have put the phone down.

"I miss you too," he replies, although his voice lacks intonation but it's enough to shine a ray of hope on my heart.

"Do you mean that?" *Don't ask him that he might change his mind.*

"Yes. I mean it."

"Well...shall we meet? We could talk," I ask tentatively.

"It won't change anything."

"I want to see you, Shasta." Saying his name makes me feel warm and the love I've been missing is even more apparent. "I love you, but if you don't feel the same...You know where I am."

A combination of anger and pride take over and I slowly hang up. I can't believe I've just done that! If this is some kind of power game he's playing with me I don't want to know. *You stubborn fool, Tara.* I want him, but I won't play a game. If it is a power struggle then he is not the man I thought he was. Arguing with myself about all the reasons not to like him don't matter – I can't help but love him - whatever his reasons or whoever he is. I wipe away tears that are dripping off my chin before going back into the store.

Bleary eyed after another sleepless night I wander out of my bedroom and onto the landing, which is still in semi-darkness. I blink twice at the shape of a fair haired figure in a lilac robe streaking from the bathroom to Giselle's bedroom. It's Cooper. He flashes me an embarrassed grin. *Someone got lucky last night.* I'm dying to talk to her but clearly now isn't a good time. It makes me smile but there's no-one to share it with.

I wander downstairs as the shifting, orangey light of morning starts to creep in from beyond the trees, silhouetting the sequoias in the back garden. Surprisingly, Simon is sat at the kitchen table staring out into the garden.

"It's not like you to be so reflective - or up so early."

"Peace and quiet, and thinking time."

"What did you do with the real Simon?"

Amusement registers in his face but his thoughts are far from here as he fumbles with Hudson's tufty ears while the dog buries his head in his lap.

"This is the new model. The triple decade version," says Simon.

"You've got the birthday blues? This'll cheer you up. Guess who I just saw running into Giselle's bedroom?"

"Well, let's think. It's been a while, so...the local basketball team?"

"Cooper!"

Simon clasps his hand to his mouth. "Go on! At flaming last," he beams.

"Happy Birthday." I hug his shoulders as he doesn't get up from his chair.

"Thanks."

"Spill. What's going on?"

I pour steaming hot water on a couple of green tea bags and place one in front of Simon.

"I'm always like this on my birthday. I'm feeling it pretty bad this year though."

"Because?"

"Because I've no one special in my life, Tara. I want my life partner, not just anyone I want the right one, but he's living next door and I don't think he'll ever feel the same about me."

"Roger thinks the world of you – just not in that way."

"It works though, him and I together, it just works."

"But he's straight."

"If I could only make him see it's not their gender, it's the person. I need a love potion. I don't suppose that journal of your grandmother's had a recipe for one?" he asks sarcastically.

"If it did I'd use it myself."

"You give off those 'I don't need anyone' vibes, so only the brave and the stupid would approach you."

"Simon, this time I let myself be much more vulnerable than I've ever been."

"Shasta probably thinks you've moved on already."

"That's not true. He knows how I feel, it's up to him."

"I'll bet you didn't invite him to the party?"

"No. He doesn't want to see me. He's made that very clear."

"Honey, he is my friend too. You could have invited him for me and put aside your differences," says Simon.

"Don't you try and guilt trip me."

"Just saying," replies Simon with a wobble of his head as he drinks from his mug.

"Fine."

"Well at least someone is loved up around here," says Simon, raising his eyes in the direction of upstairs, meaning Giselle.

"I could sound Roger out for you? It worked with Giselle and Cooper. I have matchmaking skills I didn't know I had."

"I'd be mortified. Roger would never speak to me again!"

"I'd be really subtle. I could just plant the seed."

"Argh! No," wails Simon, covering his eyes with his hand.

"Look, I'm not exactly the person to give advice at the minute but I still believe love exists. I'm just not sure that we get to be with the ones we love. Maybe we have to let them go and love them from a distance."

"I don't think I can do that." Simon shakes his head, his face pinched with sincerity and frustration that Roger is sleeping only next door.

I have the strangest notion that Roger is also troubled over his friendship with Simon and I get an image of him lying in bed staring at the ceiling.

"Here. This'll cheer you up," I say, passing Simon the gift wrapped present I have for him. He pretends to bite his nails then eagerly tears the paper off. He throws his head back and laughs raucously at the caricature portrait I had painted of him, Giselle and I.

"Now I'm getting in the birthday spirit!" he grins.

Simon's words about not inviting Shasta echo endlessly in my mind. Before I leave I phone him and it goes to voicemail but with my shaky breath, under control, I leave a message inviting him to the party. The rest is up to him.

22

"You've organized a DJ? Talk about going over the top, Simon!" snorts Giselle, red faced and harassed.

"Relax, it's nothing posh, more is the pity. It's just one of the guys who is a lifeguard at the spa who does a bit of DJ-ing in his spare time. He offered, and who am I to refuse," he replies, fanning his chin.

"Where do you think a DJ is going to go?"

"Oh, don't be such a killjoy. There's plenty of room in the lounge. I'll just rearrange the furniture."

"Sort it!" says Giselle raking her fingers through her hair. "I've still got to get changed." She runs off upstairs, rubbing black marks off her cheek which she got from lighting the fire pit for anyone who wanted to chill outdoors.

"For someone who got some last night you sure are grumpy!" Simon shouts after her. Giselle throws a shoe downstairs, missing Simon but making her point.

"Simon, you can give me a hand with these decorations," I say, holding tape in my mouth and hanging the crystal decorations from the windows.

"Oh, that's beautiful. I'll just light these candles...and if I dim these lights. There. It's pretty as a picture. Look I match." He twists to catch himself in the mirror, white shirt with a tiny silver pinstripe, diamante cufflinks and neat fitting black pants.

"Yeah. It's not over the top at all."

"Are you going like that?" he asks?

"Like what?"

"Well, it's not very glamorous is it?"

"It's my own house Simon, not Buckingham Palace!"

The short, loose black dress I'm in is smart enough. "Think yourself lucky I'm not wearing jeans."

"You're hysterical Tara!"

"I'm serious!"

The house is transformed from a cosy home to an ambient, sparkling party venue; although kitsch in places it's in keeping with his Diamonds and Divas theme. Simon theatrically grabs Giselle and I in a hug, then he skips off to greet the first of his guests, thriving on being the centre of attention.

"He sparkles more than you and I put together," says Giselle, looking down at her long white faux fur waistcoat

"You'll do. Is Cooper coming?" I ask nudging her in the ribs. She breaks into a grin that says it all.

Svetlana and James arrive at the same time as a group of Simon's friends from work. Svetlana has pushed the boat out with her outfit, looking like she stepped out off the red carpet in a silver sparkly dress, whilst James tones it down in black shirt and black jeans. They look so good together. I haven't spoken to James properly about Shasta. I want to hear about him but I don't want to put James on the spot either, plus I don't know if I'm ready.

Simon works the party like an old pro. Every time the door opens my heart lurches that it might be Shasta, but another guest arrives and before long the disappointment sets in when I realize that he isn't coming. The music is playing, the atmosphere is fun but it doesn't reach inside me..

"The punch is going down well," says Giselle, scooping a cupful out for Simon, which he gracefully swipes on the way past, singing "I Want to Break Free" doing his Freddie Mercury impression.

Cooper turns up, which livens Giselle up immensely, and they relocate to the corner, hardly speaking to anyone else because they're so enthralled with each other. The party is in full swing by the time Roger walks in. Simon's head shoots round in his direction, turning away from the conversation he is already in, enraptured by Roger's demure arrival. Simon brings him over and introduces him to his friends. When Simon dives for the dance floor and starts busting out moves, Roger looks mortified, and makes his way around the edge of the room. It's not a large gathering, but it's a noisy one.

"You look like you need a drink, Roger."

"I was expecting a quiet get together, not *Saturday Night Fever*," he nods in the direction of Simon who is in the middle of the floor, pulling some crazy shapes: elbows angled out, backside swaying to and fro with the odd pelvic thrust thrown in, he's taking up more space than anyone of his build and height could possibly need. He looks over and waves for us to join him.

"Go on," suggests Roger, hardly taking his eyes off Simon.

"I'm not feeling it to be honest. Besides it's not me he wants to dance with." I let the words linger and wait for an inclination. I can't find any words to tell Roger that Simon likes him as more than just a friend without upsetting the current status quo.

"I love that guy. If only he was straight, I'd snap him up," I say enthusiastically looking straight at Simon. Although that is not quite true, it's a start. I keep Roger in my peripheral vision, looking for a sign of his feelings.

"So you and Shasta have broken up, huh? I've got to say I didn't see that coming," says Roger.

At the mention of his name a cloud of butterflies swish in my stomach, but I maintain hold over my emotions. This isn't the time or place.

"Neither did I," is all that I can say.

"Sorry, I didn't mean to upset you," apologizes Roger.

"You didn't. I'm...I'm just still trying to accept it."

"He's a lucky guy. I thought Giselle and Simon would have made him see sense."

"Giselle and Simon?" I'm perplexed. "Why? What did they do?"

Roger looks anxiously around at Giselle who is in the corner with Cooper and he realizes he has said too much. His mouth twists and he draws back his lips. He glances over at Simon, who gestures for him to come and dance.

"Oh, nothing. It's just Giselle mentioned they bumped into Shasta and had a few words with him," says Roger, clearly not wanting to elaborate. I clap both hands over my ears wondering what they've said to him. Neither of them had breathed a word of the encounter. It couldn't have gone well.

"No! I should have known." Shasta had called me not long after they left the coffeehouse, perhaps they had something to do with that; it hadn't been of his own doing after all.

"They meant well," says Roger, trying to be reassuring.

A tidal wave of angst is building in me. "Well, seeing as how we're all interfering in each other's business you might as well know - Simon is in love with you!" As soon as I say it I'm thinking it's a step too far.

Roger's eyes flare open but he looks composed. If the words startled him it's not apparent. He must have known. He looks at me sideways then back to Simon on the dance floor.

"I'm not sure what to say."

"Aren't you curious to know how it would be for you guys?"

"Curious yes, but I've never been with a guy before."

"Before now?"

A small smile starts to crinkle his eyes, then changes to a melancholy expression of thoughtfulness.

"They say it's the person you fall for," I tell him.

"I just don't know if I'm...that way. I've been straight."

"You wouldn't be the first to flip."

"I felt there was something between us."

"But you two can carry on being friends regardless, no awkwardness, right?" Simon is going to kill me if this backfires. Roger shrugs, having no previous experience of a situation like this to draw on. The cluster of Simon's dancing friends trickle off and he sees them out until he is left with no one to dance with. His face is puce and he wafts his white shirt.

"I need to cool down," he says, walking past on his way to the front door.

"I'll join you," says Roger, avoiding my stare as he follows him onto the lantern lit porch overlooking the front garden.

Damn. I want someone to talk to. Giselle is still deep in conversation with Cooper, but I descend on them anyway.

"Were you ever going to tell me what you said to Shasta?" I ask perching myself on the edge of the seat and leaning over them.

Giselle looks up, about to deny it, then realizes there's no point.

"No. I was going to keep it to myself," she replies.

She explains that she just wanted to find out his story, but didn't glean anything more from him than I did. Apparently she went in all guns blazing, but he disarmed her by not getting riled by her feisty attitude. She says he seemed quiet and not very interactive. That I can believe. It's hard to argue with someone who doesn't give you anything to hold on to.

"He didn't look himself, Tara. He just seemed so distant. I actually felt a bit sorry for him. I don't know what to suggest to you guys, but this is affecting him as much as it is you."

"I don't understand it," I reply. A moment later I remember why I pounced on them. "I've a confession to make. I'm keeping out of the way because I've just spilled the beans to Roger about Simon."

"You did what!?"

"It just kind of came out. Don't go near the window!" I call after Giselle who is already dashing over. She hides partially behind a curtain and peeps out at the two men on the porch, standing together talking.

"Well, it looks peaceful so far," Giselle reports.

"Come away from there. They'll see you."

"They are looking fairly cosy actually...now they're moving to the swing. They're sitting down. They're talking. Oh my God, Simon has his hand over Roger's!"

The chair I was sitting on upends and clatters to the floor as I run to the window to see what is going on.

"He hasn't tried to take his hand away. That's a good start!" says Giselle her commentary is made in a loud whisper.

"Let me see."

"Oh my God! They're leaning in!" Giselle makes a high pitched noise of excitement and patters frantically on my arm with both hands. We fall silent and hold our breath in anticipation. Roger and Simon are about to kiss.

"I can hardly believe it." My eyes widen taking in the whole scene; it's better than watching the space shuttle take off. There's an unexpected movement on the steps up to the door as a short bulky figure wrapped in a pink patterned robe ambles up the steps wearing a frown that could sink a ship.

"Crap. It's Pandora! She hasn't seen them yet." I can't get the words out fast enough. If she sees her beloved son kissing Simon she will have an aneurysm.

"Do something!" Giselle's voice is so loud I'm surprised they can't hear it outside.

"What?"

"Let's go to the other window."

We dash quickly, tripping over each other and skidding on the rugs over the wooden polished floor to get to the window nearest to the swing seat. We tap on it, mouthing and pointing in the direction of Pandora, but Roger and Simon only have eyes for each other. It's too late. The sound of operatic wailing shatters the peace. A vicious tirade of expletives pours from Pandora, who is clutching her chest and her frantic distressed hand gestures are telling their own story.

"I came to ask politely for you to turn the music down and I see this!" Pandora shouts.

The music can only just be heard outside and I can't believe it would even be heard next door. I open the door to intervene before the neighbors call the police to the commotion.

“Pandora, please calm down. They aren’t doing any harm.”

“You filthy witch! I don’t know what debauched parties you’re used to, but I had no idea there was an orgy going on next door!”

“An orgy? Wow! Where’s my invite?” says Simon, doing little to assuage Pandora’s anger.

“Mom, it’s not what you think,” says Roger, already on his feet with his eyes darting from Simon to his mother. Although shocked and shaken he tries to calm the situation.

“You stay away from me! No boy of mine would kiss another man,” screams Pandora, turning and running down the steps, escaping the scene like she might catch plague. Roger runs after her, leaving Simon open mouthed and looking very pleased with himself. He puts his hand over his heart and looks wistfully after Roger, with Pandora arguing all the way back to their house.

“I’m here if you need me, Roger,” calls Simon, waving as they disappear into the house, continuing their bust up.

Spurred by the incident on the porch, the last guests leave with James and Svetlana, amid suppressed giggles. Simon is beside himself with happiness, but it fluctuates to concern for Roger like the ticking second hand of a clock. After a brief autopsy of the night Giselle and Cooper disappear, leaving Simon and I.

“Let’s go outside. It’s a clear night,” I suggest, bringing glasses of red for us both and wandering down through the lantern lit back garden as the golden yellow lights swing back and forth in the breeze. The fire pit is still glowing with the last few embers. I put another log on and the sparks catch the edges of the wood and rekindle the fire once more.

This is better than the party - sitting out here under the sequoia trees in the tranquillity of garden. Granted it's cool, but staring up at the dark indigo sky fringed by conifers is so calming. I can feel the gentle pulsing of the night around me, and the light moving through the limbs of the trees into the soil. Simon calms down and his flamboyant edge blurs as he speaks truthfully about how he feels about Roger. His eyes glitter and it's not just the firelight in them.

"Did you hear something?" I angle my head towards the direction I thought I heard a soft footstep and a twig snap.

"Don't start with the spooky stuff." Simon is on the edge of the seat. "Were you joking?"

I keep an eye on the shadows and listen hard.

"There. Didn't you hear that?" Now my heart is starting to race. In the dim light I can make out a black shape moving towards us, passing the bushes at the side of the house.

"Someone's here," whispers Simon, poised and ready to run. "Don't just sit there!" His voice is tainted with panic.

I stand up to face whoever is trespassing in the garden. Simon mistakes it for the cue to escape and sprints towards the house, making squeaky sounds which make him easy to trace. The lantern light falls on half the face of the man as he approaches, my heart kicks up a gear, flooding my blood with adrenaline but I can't run. It's a face I've missed.

"Shasta?" I swallow hard, not daring to believe it's true.

"Shasta!" shouts Simon, already at the back door. "Jeez, are you trying to give me a seizure?"

"Sorry, I missed your birthday, Simon," says Shasta, but he's looking at me.

"That's not all you should be sorry for!" he rebukes Shasta and closes the back door behind him, tactfully leaving us alone together.

"What...what are you doing here?" I ask, stuck for anything meaningful to say, void of anything more important than the fact he is here now and that I'm with him, breathing the same air. I want him more than ever. Every heart beat is making a treasured memory, a still photograph of each breathtaking moment together.

"You invited me," he says softly with a hint of trepidation.

I blink hard several times, to compensate for the staring and nod. Yes. Yes, I did invite him.

"I'd given up on you," I breathe, taking in everything about his shadowed face.

"I don't blame you," says Shasta, looking at me steadily as the firelight reflecting onto his high flat cheekbones brings his eyes to life.

"Why?"

"I would have given up too," he replies, focusing his gaze on my cheeks as he seems to have trouble meeting my eyes directly.

"You already did!" I snap. The longing doesn't go away despite the spike in my words keeping him at a distance. I'd like nothing better than to be in his arms, touching his olive skin and feeling the heat of his breath on me.

"You don't understand–"

"How could I, when you don't tell me anything?"

"You know how things are, Tara."

I shake my head. "No. No I don't. Tell me how they are, Shasta? I don't have your mind reading skills."

"People around me get hurt. Having something happen to you...it's more than I could bear. This way I could keep you safe."

"That is so selfish, Shasta." *But please don't take it the wrong way.*

"If something happened to you...if you were killed...I couldn't stand it. Please understand that. I didn't care what happened to me but I bequeathed you my spirit, that if something happened to me it would sustain you. Without you in my life I'm dead anyway. I've never known pain like this before. Although I was alone I never left you. I want something which is so selfish I can barely bring myself to ask."

We face each other and I see the pain he's been suffering matches mine.

"You know I never wanted to be parted from you, whatever the risks were. I'll take my chances. You don't get to decide that for me."

"I want you back, Tara. If you say no... I would understand but...I want us to begin again. I'm so sorry."

My body goes slack and the hurt I've been carrying begins to ebb slowly away. Shasta is facing me. We are close together - within touching distance. The silent story telling stare connects us together. The fizzing space is there again, pulling stronger than before. I can hear whispering in the woods all around me the words *I love you* as soft and caressing as a lover's touch. The message is kindled by Shasta and relayed by nature.

"I want you to say it. I need to believe it," I prompt.

"I love you. I always will," he replies.

"Do you want me?" I whisper, still seeking reassurance.

"In my heart I kissed you every night and woke with you

every morning, but it wasn't enough. I want you, and I know that will never change. Please forgive me."

"I already have," I reply, knowing not one cell in my body can resist; my fate lies with him, whatever happens.

We take a step closer into each other's arms. Our bodies touch and a spark jumps off me when his hand touches my cheek. He tilts his head towards mine and we kiss deeply. It dislodges me from rational thought as we fuse together. Our heart beats synchronize as he pushes against me, drawing me closer to him. He grasps my hand and pulls me away from the lantern light, to the dark moonlit edge of the forest. With hands ravaging each other's faces and bodies, borne from need, longing and starvation for one another, we fall to the ground, tugging at each other's clothes. We make love as though we had been separated for a lifetime.

23

I wake feeling as though all the puzzle pieces in the world have found their rightful place. I roll onto my side to watch him sleeping, but his arm moves and he skims his hand over my stomach as he pushes me firmly onto my back. He takes his weight on his arms and hovers over me, his jet black hair sweeping across my eyes.

"I can hardly dare to believe you are here with me," says Shasta keeping his face close to mine.

"Me neither. I virtually gave up on you. I virtually gave up on everything."

"It was the same for me. That's why I went away. I had to know what was real. I had to get back to the basics. You followed me because you were in my heart, but I wanted more. I needed to touch you."

"What did you find?"

"I found my shadows came too."

"Did you keep your beliefs?" I ask, knowing mine had been tested to breaking point and that even now I wasn't sure what I felt any more. How can it be right for someone to feel so much pain and live? If there was a loving force around us, how can that happen? And yes, I know it's all about staying steady and focused and being loving, regardless, but I hadn't been without anger and despair. "I know we're all connected but I wanted to be with you, here and now, in the physical world."

Shasta nods. "I got to the point where I didn't care what's ahead. I just wanted you now, regardless of anything else. I'm sorry."

I take in the amber flecks in his deep brown eyes, looking

to connect with the most infinite part of him at his very core.

"It made me think – about being Blanche's granddaughter – I thought about what a poison chalice that was. If I couldn't undergo a challenge and not lose myself to it then I haven't learned to use the energy. I toyed with burying the amulet somewhere and returning it to the ground where it came from."

"Why didn't you?" asks Shasta.

"I still might."

"That's crazy."

"I felt like I failed – at everything."

"You're human. I knew my soul was with you, but this me - this one touching you now, wanted something tangible, something real."

"Yet, you had control over us."

"No. I knew the last time I saw you that you might never want to see me again, but I felt it was the best way. You talk of failing, but I failed too, I failed to keep you safe and still I can't see it through."

"Don't ever do that again. Never make decisions for me. I'm tougher than you think."

"I love that about you. You're scared but you challenge it. You look the shadows in the eye and dare them to do their worst."

"Urgh. I hate that because you seem strong people think you can take any amount of crap."

"No. Not like that. It's why you grow so strong, so quickly. Your strength repels fear."

"Oh. I don't even want to think about light, raising vibes, energy medicine. I've had enough of hearing about it."

"Your inspiration has gone. I want to take you somewhere special," he says enthusiastically, looking ready for action.

"Now?" I glance at the clock on the nightstand.

"Not yet," he grins, kissing the end of my nose. "I have other plans for you right now."

White and grey clouds are rolling across the tree line of the mountains as we encroach on the open landscape of the foothills. We've been walking for a short while to get here, but it looks as though the weather is rolling in. A heavy snowfall won't be today, but it probably won't be far off. The icy air blasts against my waterproof jacket. Shasta doesn't seem to notice the cold; he seems so focused on where we are going. All I know is he's taking me somewhere he has recently been, but the rest is a mystery.

"Have you seen that weather coming in?"

Shasta nods then turns around with his hand outstretched to take mine.

"Come on. We'll be undercover shortly."

"Is there some kind of romantic hideaway out here?"

"Kind of. He strides onwards, effortlessly nimble, he steps over rocks and shrubs as we begin a gentle climb around the base of the mountain, between pine trees and craggy outcrops.

"Shasta, it's not a cave is it?" I lick my lips because my mouth is dry with the need to swallow. He faces me with a solemn expression.

"Heights, claustrophobia, anything else you're frightened of? Just in case I plan any more surprises."

"Surprises – but you know that."

"I'll be right beside you," he reassures." Where I'm taking

you, it's sacred. You did bring the journal with you, didn't you?"

I tap my rucksack and can feel the hard cover underneath. Before we left Shasta had looked at the pages that mentioned earth work and ceremonies. Two of the pages were stuck together. He passed it to me and when I prised them apart I discovered they were joined by a reddish-brown bloody thumb print with the swirls and whorls clearly visible. It's amazing to think it is likely to be my grandmother's finger print, perhaps from a paper cut. On these pages there was a very basic pencil sketch of what could be a hilly landscape and in tiny writing, which looked as though a butterfly had walked over the page, the words apex, golden key, entry point of golden ray. I don't know how I didn't see this before.

As we wind around the mountain, through shrubbery and trees, Shasta rounds a boulder, jumps, and disappears completely from view. Within a few strides I catch up with him, looking down at the hollow cavern between the rocks, sheltered by several pine trees.

"How did you get down there?"

"Jump. I'll catch you," he says, putting his arms in the air expectantly.

"Just like that huh?" I sit down on the rocky edge and jump forward, falling the last little bit into his arms.

"OK, stick close to me and walk where I walk. It's tight in places."

"Oh, no! Where are you taking me?" I ask, but he's already stepping ahead, ducking under overhead rock formations and narrow passages. "Shasta. Seriously! I try not to hate. I really do, but...I hate small spaces. I'm not kidding."

The rocky sides of the inside of the mountain feel like they are closing in from all angles, as though they have come to life. Against the oppressive sides I've not a hope of expanding my chest and getting a breath. My imagination is running wild and I can't wait to get out of here.

"Come on. It's just a few more steps then it opens out."

I edge forward two more steps and sure enough the tight entry way opens out into a cavern. Daylight spills from between boulders, but Shasta has lit a torch now and is making some kind of invocation or blessing. I feel like an intruder on this sacred site. I follow suit, not knowing which words to use I mentally give appreciation to the mountain for letting us be there. There is an underground stream fed from a gentle current which bubbles up nearby. From the torch light the cavern looks to go deeper into the mountain and I've increasing trepidation that Shasta will want to go further in. I stand beside him, making sure I don't lose him, but my heart is slowing down now, knowing I can easily get out.

"What is this place?"

"It's a sacred power spot."

"Should we even be in here?"

"With the right intention it's OK." Shasta shines the torch on the roof and walls of the cavern then points straight ahead at the direction the stream is coming from.

"You want to go in there, don't you?"

He nods and takes my hand, leading the way. Like a mantra in my head I keep reminding myself of the direction of the exit.

"No one can hurt you here. They're all dead," says Shasta.

"That's helping!"

"The ancestors' vibration is still here. Can you feel it?"

“Yeah, I feel something. It’s the urge to leave.” I push forward and we move through the cavern. A draft of pleasant cool air touches my face. I relax more and I can feel all sorts of effervescent tingling around me. The stream widens but slows the further in we go. We pass through an archway and the torch lights up beautiful glittering metallic flecks all over the walls.

“What is that?” I ask, feeling my back shiver with energy.

“That’s pyrite - fool’s gold.”

“That’s beautiful.” I’m in a trance for a few minutes, in awe of it. I bend down and pick up a piece of quartz, rubbing the dirt off so that I can get a better look. Shasta stands as still as a statue, looking around at the intricate shapes formed naturally in the cavern’s rocky formations. Unsure what he’s feeling I tune in to the surroundings, feeling braver the longer I spend inside the mountain. I start to sway on my feet, my weight shifting in a rhythmic pulsing movement, as though I’m moving to music. Then I hear it. The sound of light chiming chords, almost out of my hearing range, the cacophony of sounds grows louder, more delicate and more beautiful as though it were the angels own music. I close my eyes and tiny microscopic dots of light are appearing and disappearing as though falling into me and striking a note, before dissipating.

I open my eyes and realize I’ve dropped the quartz stone I was holding. I laugh and the ripple triggers more of the same. Shasta is standing watching me, not so much an infinitesimal movement or sound going unnoticed. His face softens and his deep languid lips curve into a wide smile.

“That was moving.”

“Maybe it’ll bring your inspiration back.”

I smile back at him.

"You know you're not supposed to remove anything from the mountain. If you do it must be returned."

"I wasn't. Oh-" I realize he thinks I was taking the quartz home. "What would happen?"

"It's a special place. It's protected here, that's why the old ones said it was cursed, to keep it from being exploited. The ancestors told people bad luck would fall on them but it was just a story," says Shasta.

He lights the cavern walls with the torch on the way back out. We talk about the sounds in the cave and he says the sound is the vibration of the mountain. He heard it for the first time when he came a few days ago. It surprises me that both he and James had been here; specifically that James had been using his remote viewing ability to divine if there was any gold in Big Spruce's hills. This place is what they came up with.

"Are we in Mount Nagual?" I ask sharply, suddenly realizing the implication of what he said about the sacred mountain. Shasta winks. I didn't recognize where we were because of the direction we came from. This is close to where we had seen Tray Buchanan and Shimlow with their associates on an expedition. We double back to the exit.

"There's more I want to show you," says Shasta, climbing out of the deep dry well of rock at the entrance to the cavern as my feet and hands follow the crevices he used for purchase. Now once more out in the day light it feels like we've stepped out from another world. We make our way through the trees, along the rugged pathways, strewn with pebbles and pine needles until we reach a plateau overlooking the foothills rolling into the distance. A stream carves around the landscape in a bow shape. We stop for a break partway up the ascent, devouring the food we brought to refuel before we carry on.

"Where's the journal? I want to check something," says Shasta.

I pass the blue leather book to him and he goes straight to the pages we looked at this morning.

"That," he says, pointing at the diagram of four lozenge shapes and a circle in the centre, "is up there."

"I thought no-one would go up there because it was sacred?"

"I've been there before and nothing terrible happened. If you only bring a clear heart it's fine. It amplifies everything. Fear draws in the darkness and that is what you get. This is a major power spot. If you resonate it'll give you a boost of energy. That's the real treasure. The real gold is up there."

He points to Blanche's journal at the diagram and description of the apex being the entry point. "The golden light comes in there."

"That's what your ancestors meant by there being gold here, but not everyone could find it."

"It would make sense. It was a metaphorical reference, taken literally."

"Maybe there's real gold too, but if they explore and try to mine it that would destroy this place and disrupt the whole network."

"It pays to believe in curses doesn't it? If only big business was thwarted in the same way," I reply.

We continue on upwards. Shasta strides on as through there is no gradient. We walk in silence for much of the time, saving oxygen for the exertion, but I'm also lost in the sense of being in a type of pilgrimage. I'm walking in the footsteps of my ancestors as much as Shasta is, despite our different backgrounds. Blanche and Shaman Lehman come to mind as I mull over what nature ceremonies they took part in.

I get the strongest image of walking on a golden pyramid, increasing in clarity as we climb. As though my grandmother has been listening to my thoughts I hear the words '*there's no shadow at the top of the hill.*' My hand drops to the ruby amulet with the Hermetic Seal of Light which is around my neck, and I realize I would have been out of my mind to get rid of it.

As the trees thin out near the top the ground levels off and the stone circle comes into view. The apex of the mountain is marked by four oval stones, carved with shapes and there is a hollowed out circle near the top where the wind passes through. The stones seem to mark the four directions and focus around a central stone. The wind carouses around us at the top of the mountain, but I feel no chill from it. Before we get close to the cairn we can feel the radiance from it, as though a power surge is shining down through the top of the mountain in a shaft of light which runs underground and passes to the earth.

Shasta and I look at each other without saying a word; speech feels crass and unnecessary when every other sense is heightened. The power through here is like nothing I've ever felt, the vibration through my feet is so strong I'm almost expecting the ground to disintegrate. I send a light pulse from myself and blend as much as I can with the golden rays. It also contains codes which are translated subliminally, much like the energy of the music in the cavern. The sense I'd had that it needs protecting wanes because knowing how strong it is, anything incompatible with it would be destroyed.

I remember Shasta's words - that anything taken from the mountain must be returned, and although the gold and ruby from the amulet are not likely to have been from here, I feel like they need to connect back to the energy network. I slip the necklace off and walk to the centre cairn stone. I place the amulet on it and stand back, letting nature do its thing. Through closed eye-lids I see a brilliant white and gold ray.

After a few moments the powerful feeling levels out. Shasta's eyes connect with mine and we know it's time to leave. I take the amulet from the centre stone cairn and place it back around my neck acknowledging the spirits around us and thanking them. On the way back down the mountain I look back up and the pinnacle is now obscured by the mist settling over the top.

The feeling of peace stays with us on the journey back to the car. Shasta looks more at ease than he did this morning and the dark hollows under his eyes have plumbed out. I feel tired from the walking, yet pleasantly revitalized.

When we return home, I discover the vibe is just what I needed to face the new drama which is unfolding. Simon and Roger are sat at the kitchen table looking serious. An awkward glance passes between them when Shasta and I walk in. Evidently something is on their mind, and that something has to do with me.

"Hey honey. Have you had a good day? Can I fix you a drink?" asks Simon cheerily.

"What's going on?" I ask, looking from Simon to Roger, who have the sheepish appearance of naughty school kids.

Simon bites his lip and looks to Roger for backup. Roger

squirms awkwardly in his seat and judging by the chalky drained color of his face he's upset about something.

"Tara, I'm sorry but after last night Pandora and Errol have kicked Roger out. I'm really sorry, but...can he stay here for a while?"

"Is that all?" I ask, relieved it's not much worse.

Roger and Simon look at each other and their faces relax into beaming smiles. This place feels like it's turning into Noah's Ark: Cooper is staying over with Giselle, now Roger and Simon. At least I can go to Shasta's for privacy: me and my portable toothbrush.

24

The main street in town is still busier than usual with the new gold-seeking tourists still showing up, though less so now. Much of the attention has died down while meetings, surveys and the powers that be investigate. As I cross the street and step onto the pavement I can feel him watching me. I turn and smile at Shasta who is sat in the car waiting for me while I go to the bank to deposit the takings from *The Book and Bean.* He looks from my backside to my face with a wry smile. Not watching where I'm going I walk into someone and immediately apologize – then I see who it is. I draw back from the smoothly benign face of Tray as his cool blue eyes appraise what he sees and he delivers a smooth, plastic smile.

"Tray!"

"Well. Look at you. This mountain air is agreeing with you," says Tray.

"I didn't think you were still in town."

"I was hoping I'd bump into you."

"What are you doing here? I thought business was finished."

"It won't be finished until I acquire that land we've been after. It's a point of principle now."

"It'll never happen."

Tray laughs and places a hand on my upper arm. "That's not the only thing that hasn't happened yet. How are you? Would you like to have dinner with me and we can talk? I think about you: some good, though some bad." He winks and his face hardens though it doesn't last.

"You're persistent Tray. I'll give you that but I'm not on the market."

"Well, I guess we'll be seeing more of each other. I'm just on my way for a business meeting now," says Tray, checking out his watch. Perhaps I should meet with him and foster relations to see what I can glean about their business, but the vague nausea I feel in his presence reminds me of the accident in New York and a time I'd like to forget.

"Is it about the gold rumors?" I ask.

"Meet up with me and you'll find out. I heard you and your Indian friend had broken up," he says tilting his head to the side, seeking clarification.

"You shouldn't believe all you hear, Tray. Who were you talking to?" I ask, my mind frantically wants to know how, being from out of town he heard such a thing. I feel an arm around my back as Shasta materializes beside me. In a brief glance I can see the flint-like features harden as he silently faces off Tray.

"Your bodyguard?" asks Tray, his presence is diminished by the taller man.

"Tray, this is Shasta." I can't help but smile broadly, but it slips a brief moment later when the raven-haired beauty appears beside Tray, smartly dressed and self-assured as she tosses her silky mane and greets him with a flutter of her eyelids. She looks up at us through heavy, dark eyelashes.

"Tara, this is Leonie. Have you two met?" asks Tray, seeing recognition on my face. He looks at Shasta. "I know you have," he says with a smug smile.

Leonie barely gives me a glance as she stands closer to Tray than you would expect for a business partner. Or perhaps it's her intention to portray this. She stands sideways to him, pressing her small bust into his arm with a low subtle look at Shasta.

"This is a surprise. Good to see you both, together," says Leonie, fixing a smile on her rosebud lips. Below my frozen features steam is building.

"Well, when it's meant to be it's meant to be," I reply, trying not to sound defensive, mimicking her tone, and smiling back.

"Shall we?" she nods to Tray, tucking her hand under his arm. They walk away and she turns away with a 'little old me wouldn't harm a fly' look. *My God, she is good.* She clearly wants the business meeting to look like a date. I know what his business meetings are like – the lines are definitely blurred. She's walking into his trap, but she thinks he is in hers. She's using the situation like lemon juice in a cut to see if it would sting Shasta.

Shasta looks steely, though he took on that appearance before Leonie turned up. So Leonie had met Tray through her radio broadcast and he was going to work his magic – another route to the Native American population and an ambitious, pliant one at that. He's a cunning operator, and becoming more so. When I first met Tray he had been a playboy and lothario, but something had changed. His carefree, anything goes in the name of all things fun, vibe had dimmed. He's got a cynical, sharper edge now. He still has the charm. He still has the smile, but a seam of grief turned putrid by anger is lurking below the exterior. If Tray is around, the chances are Daddy Warbucks i.e. Marshall Buchanan is around too. That realization drops with a heavy, sinking feeling and the need to be near to Shasta at all times.

"What do you think she's doing with Tray? He said it was business."

"She can do whatever she likes with him," replies Shasta

abruptly. "I'm going to see Dad. If you want a ride home let me know. Don't walk home. I know it's not far, but... call me."

We kiss goodbye on the street corner near the coffeehouse and I go back to work: re-running the scene with Tray and Leonie, thinking the squaring off of our relationships was an odd coincidence.

"Giselle the strangest thing just happened," I say, swinging down my bag behind the counter of the library counter, the blue leather journal of my grandmother's falls onto the floor.

"What?" asks Giselle wide eyed but diverted by the book, she picks it up and thumbs through it, then sets it on the counter top while I fill her in on seeing Tray and Leonie together and their apparent meeting.

"Well she didn't set it up. She couldn't have. Don't be paranoid about her and Shasta, just because they've got a past. You'll drive yourself crazy."

Perhaps I am being paranoid. It had all gone quiet on the Leonie front recently, so I'm probably being acutely suspicious, without good reason. Giselle was always one to smell a rat well before anyone else, she had a reliable intuition and I've always respected her opinion. I convince myself she must be right and ignore my own instincts.

"So, Cooper! What have you got for me?" I ask, ready to hear the latest installment in Giselle's romance. She leans in away from prying ears and gives me a brief but positive update before her eyebrows shoot up, signaling an interruption. I cross over from being engrossed in her tale to staring at the ghostly, thin, grey face of Cain Shimlow. He looks human but only marginally so. His face is so vacant it's like staring into an abyss. I haven't seen him since the night he was beaten, but Barnaby told me that apart from cuts and bruises he was fine.

"Hi Cain," I say expectantly, never sure how he's going to be with me, or how to be with him. His threats to me, a while ago, had never been aired between us, or confirmed; although I knew it was him. He's an old man and rapidly ageing by the minute, by the look of things. His unfocused gaze is aimed at the countertop initially but he lifts his head towards me, almost as an afterthought.

"I never got a chance to thank you."

"Thank me!" The shock of hearing pleasant words from him knocks me completely off guard. At first I think he's being sarcastic.

"That night I got hurt. You took care of me and I appreciate that," he holds his wobbling gaze on me until he finishes his sentence when it drops again. I suddenly feel desperately sorry for him, remembering him bleeding in the street and the confusion on his face.

"Aw, that's OK. No thanks needed. I'm glad you were alright. Do you know who did it?" I ask. A feral glimmer in his eyes, accompanies the slack focus of his face creating a deranged look as though he's not quite with us.

"No," he replies unconvincingly then laughs, though he's the only one in on the joke.

Giselle has busied herself reading Blanche's journal and Cain Shimlow's fuzzy gaze rests upon her.

"Can I get you a drink, Cain?" I offer, feeling awkward in the resounding silence and hoping he will pick up on the cue. He doesn't, and I feel uncomfortable for Giselle, interpreting his lingering look as one of appreciation for her.

"Cain...Tea? Coffee?"

He seemingly remembers where he is and shakes his head in refusal before pulling a tight smile and wandering out onto the street without having bought anything. Apparently he really had come in just to thank me. It's very weird, but the rest of the afternoon passes without any further strange incidents. Simon arrives after finishing work and when Sarah comes in he sits at the table with her for a while. It's good to see her again. She regales us with another one of her stories from her life and a gem of inspired wisdom, which sounds special at the time but rolls on past like a bumper sticker on the back of a car. His cheekiness knows no bounds, but he keeps her entertained and she stays longer than usual.

As Sarah shuffles out, looking flushed, Simon meanders behind the counter and whispers in a sing-song voice. "She will be missed when she goes, but when that is, no-one knows."

"Simon!" chastizes Giselle.

"Sorry, it was meant as a compliment," he replies, holding his hands up.

When it gets close to closing time the coffeehouse is empty so I suggest Giselle and Simon leave early, leaving me to close the store. I enjoy the ritual of closing up after the customers have left and the store becomes peaceful again. It reminds me how lucky I am to have escaped the perpetual stress of my previous life in New York. There's a certain satisfaction in closing up knowing we've brought simple pleasures into someone's life and tomorrow it will happen all over again.

As I roll down the blinds at the front door I hear a noise, but the place is empty of customers. I listen for another sound, but there isn't one.

“Shasta?” I call out, considering the obvious. I’m unable to tell where the noise came from and I make my way to the nook where the fire has dwindled to a few embers; I’ve already turned the lights off in there. I look in and my heart stops momentarily as I see the silhouette of a man sitting in the fireside chair, expectantly facing the doorway.

“There you are,” he says softly with an autocratic air. I can’t place the voice but a shudder runs through me. I know I’ve heard that voice before. My hand hits the light switch and illuminates Marshall Buchanan, his well-built physique fills the chair as though he had every right to be here.

“Now you’ve ruined the romantic atmosphere.”

“We’re closed! You have to leave!” I step forward to face him not acknowledging that I know who he is, or how edgy I feel. That would be admitting I know he is here meaning harm – and if I make a move to run it’ll force his hand. I need to be in a better position than this.

“Tara. Tell me, did you ever meet my son Vaughan, or was it just my other son Tray that you played with?”

I feel like he’s circling around me as he starts to reveal his hand. I have to get him out. I ignore the question and turn to walk out of the room without playing his game, expecting him to follow me. He jumps from the seat and blocks my way. I try to push past him, ignoring him as far as possible.

“Now don’t play hard to get with me. Once you’ve had the son the father is going to be even better – more experienced.”

“I have no interest in your son. I never have. Shasta is going to be here to pick me up shortly so you’d better leave." I stand defiantly and face him off, not letting the trickle of fear working its way down my spine show in my eyes as I narrow them at him.

"We're all alone Tara," he says soothingly. "Don't you think I know that? It's just you and me. Shasta is at home waiting for you. I know everything."

Nausea rises and a wave of icy prickles jag my face. He has been watching - him and his goons. I can't call for help. My phone is in the kitchen. I have to play it cool until I get near to the door, but it's locked and by the time I fumble with the keys it would be too late.

"Mr Buchanan. I don't know where you get your facts but-"

"Marshall. Call me Marshall. It's only right. Seeing as how we're going to be so close you and I." *So that's where this is heading.*

"Get out of my way, now!"

Marshall steps slightly to the side but keeps his eyes intently on me. I step forward to make my passage but he grabs my wrist and pulls me backwards, pushing me up against the wall. I bring my knee up when he pushes against me, only grazing his groin but it's enough to make an escape. Marshall grunts and bends forward as I run for the kitchen. I can hear him coming after me. I reach the doorway and run to the opposite side of the room, grabbing for one of the knives on the magnetic strip on the wall. Marshall grabs me from behind before I can reach it and he spins me round to face him.

"Stay away from me! You won't get away with this."

"Oh but I will. I always get away."

"Stop!" I push against him, but he is a powerful and immobile weight against me.

"It's not that I care for you, you understand? You're pretty, but you're nothing special. Girls like you are easy to find, but when your Indian lover wants to get close to you he'll know...that I've been there too. He'll know that I took you and he couldn't do anything about it."

"Bastard!" I seethe through my teeth unable to keep up the pressure against him, my arms weaken and he's all over me. He holds my hands together in his large grip. I lean closer to him as though I'm giving in. My face is closer to his now. The roughness of his evening stubble grazes my skin. I pull back my teeth, lean close to his ear and bite down hard, but his fleshy lobes move before I can get full contact. I know I've had some effect by the angry noise he makes. He turns me away and pushes my head over the counter top. *If I can just edge to the knives.* Suddenly one hand rubs over my backside and is swiftly inside my skirt, with his knee he knocks my legs apart and I can feel him fumbling with his zip.

"Do your worst," I breathe through bared teeth. My voice is ragged as he knocks the air out of me, but I want him to think I'm letting him. I want to take the pleasure out of him forcing himself on me. He weakens his grasp slightly and I move forward as though I'm making myself comfortable.

"It's better if you make it easy for me," he replies, his voice is a menacing whisper. Sensing a ripple in his concentration I lunge for a knife on the wall. I grasp it and whirl round to face him, but he is so close. He sees it and starts to wrestle it from my hand. He tries to turn the weapon on me. His face is red and angry, his teeth clench together with spit foaming around his teeth which he sprays with hissing breath. Fate is dealing me the inevitable now. He's too strong for me.

I'm the first to hear the front door close. I hold my breath, hoping it's not wishful thinking. Marshall is enraged, the red mist has come down and he's oblivious at first. Then I hear Giselle's lilting voice, talking to herself then she calls out my name.

"Giselle!" I scream.

"Did I leave my purse-" I hear her begin to say then I scream again. Marshall's eyes flash with frenzied anger.

"Two for one. The red head?" he leers.

"Get out Giselle! Run!" I yell, freeing myself at the distraction. I jab forward, pointing the knife at him.

"Party's over, for now," he spits as Giselle appears in the doorway. Her mouth falls open in shock.

"What the–" she stills for a moment processing what is going on as Marshall runs out the back door into the night as he escapes.

Giselle runs to the door after him and I stand shaking with adrenaline, having never been so glad to see her. It's a few moments before I can explain to her what happened and who he was, but by this time she is ready to call the police. I stop her.

"You have to report this. You're letting him get away!"

"I can't!"

"Why not?"

"Because if Shasta thinks he can't protect me, God knows what he'll do. There is one thing I do know – it'll be the end of Shasta and me if he thinks this was revenge against him. He's done it before Giselle. He broke it off with me to keep me safe. I can't risk him doing that again."

"That is ridiculous!"

"You were there. You know what happened!"

"Maybe Shasta is right. If he can't protect you then maybe you shouldn't be with him. This is some dark stuff he's got you involved in. Where is it going to end? With you lying dead at the bottom of a ditch?"

"You are not to say anything to him."

"What about Barnaby? Your dad is a Sheriff, Tara!"

"No-one! You are not to breathe a word of this to anyone. Do you understand?"

"What if he comes back? Please let Barnaby deal with it."

"No-one! It will have consequences. This is a small town: if Barnaby knows, Shasta will find out. I'm not risking it."

"You'd rather risk your life than risk losing a guy! You're crazy!"

"You are not to breathe a word of this, not even to Simon. Do you promise?"

Giselle shakes her head, her eyes piercing me with frustration and challenge. I'm thankful it's she who found me and not someone else; someone I couldn't trust.

"Answer me one thing then, Tara. If it was me who got hurt what would you do?"

I consider it levelly keeping eye contact with her. "I'd do the same as Shasta: I'd stay away from you then hunt down the person who hurt you."

"You two are a lost cause. You deserve each other!"

"You'll forget this happened?"

"No, dummy, but I won't tell a soul, only because you're asking. I still think it's a bad idea."

I put my arms around her, glad of something solid to hold onto while the shaking in my legs slowly gets under my control, but even though I'm somewhat reassured by Giselle's embrace I know this isn't over.

25

Outside Shasta's lake house the wind is howling mercilessly and torrential rain is driving sideways onto the glass wall. I'm wary that the window could blow in. Despite being surrounded by trees, and the risk of one falling during the growing storm outside, the house feels safe. The feel of having the outside on the inside remains, giving a sense of risk, beauty and power pounding, pummeling against us, yet we're protected.

"You're quiet," says Shasta, stroking the inside of my arm as I stare out across the lake.

"Am I?"

"What are you thinking?"

"I'm thinking I need to go home and get changed, but I don't fancy going out in this weather."

"Aren't you working?"

"Yeah, I'm in this morning. Giselle is taking over this afternoon," I reply, not telling him I'm reluctant to be at *The Book and Bean* after dark. I don't like keeping the reason to myself, and I'm trying really hard to be cheerful to keep him from tuning into my thoughts.

"I'll drive you home, then I'll take you to work," says Shasta, taking my hand and I pull myself onto my feet, bracing myself to go out in this weather. I know he's keeping me close, but it's the same for me. I'm torn, wanting to tell him about Marshall Buchanan and that I think they are closing in on him, but I can't risk it. I'd feel safe if I was with him 24/7 - for his sake and mine. Remembering Marshall's parting words - that he would return - makes my stomach churn and the bile rise in my throat. As we drive over to my house I keep the increasing anxiety to myself as my mind whirls with the knowledge that Marshall Buchanan knew our whereabouts. My home doesn't feel like the sanctuary it had been. The memory of the days I used to come to visit Rosa when I was a child feel so distant right now and I hold onto the image of her standing in the garden tending her plants.

When I walk in Roger is making breakfast in the kitchen, Simon is running around looking for clothes whilst playing with Hudson, and when I try to get in the bathroom I realize Giselle and Cooper are in the shower: together. While I'm changing Shasta comes bounding up the stairs; I can tell it's him because he's taking them two at a time.

"Simon and Roger are going to the hot springs later. They've asked if we want to join them?" he asks, pulling away the shirt I'm about to put on and gazing appreciatively. I yank it out of his hand, feeling dirty and soiled despite having had a shower last night and this morning, I can still feel Marshall's hands on me.

"What's up?" he asks. I need to try harder. I can't let him know anything is amiss.

"Nothing. It's just a bit crowded here at the moment." I nod in the direction of the voices coming from the bathroom. I reach up and kiss him, placing my hands on his chest over the smooth planed muscles. "Let's go with them to the hot springs after work."

"Is there something else?" he asks. I've a feeling that I'm about to be rumbled. I've been thinking about talking to him about staying at his more permanently, but it's feeling more imminent because of Buchanan's threats. That shouldn't be a consideration, but it is. I feel like I would have waited to jump off the cliff but I'm getting pushed.

"I was thinking it would be nice if I had all my things in one place," I look up at him seriously, the smile breaking through, feeling ridiculously bashful about even bringing it up.

"And?"

"And, how I would love to wake up with you every morning."

"Ah. I understand." His chiselled features soften and there is a slow uplift to his mouth.

"What do you think?"

"You want me to move in?" he asks with a tinge of laughter and steps towards the door. I suddenly hear myself laughing nervously at the joke, knowing he deliberately got it wrong.

"Well?"

"We can talk later," he replies as I follow him downstairs, feeling like I've walked out on a limb, though not sure how he's received it. He takes me to work and we don't mention it on the way over. I have the morning to think about it. For me it was a big step to broach it, loving someone unconditionally and nailing myself to an eternal cross were two different things, and I'm virtually feeling like a martyr. *Jeez, get over yourself, Tara.* I start the negative self-chatter. *It's only moving in. It's not life imprisonment.* I've worked through my stuff about keeping one eye on the door at all times. I'm ready for commitment, but if he says no to moving in...I'm not ready for that.

After work Shasta collects me and we head to the Hot Springs resort and meet Roger and Simon there. The steaming mineral pools are a stark contrast to the wet squally weather outside and are just the remedy to sooth the knots from aching shoulders. This is the first time Roger and Simon have been out publicly as a couple and Simon is grinning as though he's just won jackpot in the casino. His beaming face is lit with admiration for Roger. They are complete opposites but complimentary. Roger looks awkward though, unsure how to be around Simon, looking to him for cues yet checking out who is looking at him.

I sit in the jacuzzi with the two guys, while Shasta powers up and down the pool doing lengths. He has a swimmer's body and takes long powerful strokes with arms that have the wingspan of a small plane. Every languid muscle is visible as he propels himself through the water. The warmth in my chest spreads through my body in ripples as I watch him, thinking I can't wait to be alone with him. The boys are oblivious to anyone else. I'm guessing they only asked us along as a ruse to distract from their togetherness. It didn't work. They've only got eyes for each other, anyone can see that.

Roger and Simon are walking ahead of us as we leave the resort and when Simon sidles up close and lightly touches Roger's hand, Shasta and I acknowledge it with a look. From the corridor into the main reception a woman walks out in front of them.

"Mom," says Roger and he stares at Pandora.

Caught off guard, Pandora's face melts in horror when she realizes the two guys are out together. She turns and scornfully walks quickly away from him. Roger's hands fall to his sides and he dejectedly watches his mother leave. He forces a tight-lipped smile for Simon's benefit as they walk out into the car park where Pandora has already sped off. My heart goes out to him at being cut down and rejected like that, by his own mother.

"My place or yours?" asks Shasta as we climb into his car.

"Yours," I reply, wondering at what point we're going to talk about the issue. I wonder if he's reading my thoughts about this. When we get home I go to the lounge and stand in front of the fire, warming myself through as he fixes us a drink.

He puts it down and comes to stand in front of me. Taking my face in his hands he kisses me, as if I were made of glass, running his finger along the edge of my face. My heart squirms and cavorts in a different direction with every beat. I push further into him so that my chest is against him, as though I could somehow get under his skin.

"Tara, what does it mean to you to move in with someone?" he asks.

I ponder for a moment, reading the intricacies of his face, looking for the real meaning behind that question. He assumes that steady blank expression that gives nothing away.

"It means we get to be together more. It means we spend so much more time with each other. It makes sense. The way it is I'm between houses. You mentioned it a while back," I remind him.

"I just don't want this to be some whimsical notion. Moving in together doesn't mean much to some people. It means a lot to me. Don't take this the wrong way, but I don't want it to be a casual feature in your life. It has to be real, not just a practical excuse to cut down on hassle."

"You don't want to?" I ask trying to find my feet as

though the ground below me is crumbling away. He is saying no.

"The thing is, I love you, but-" he replies gently trying to make me feel better but having the reverse effect, knowing he is speaking truthfully and I've misinterpreted where we were at in our relationship.

"You don't need to explain-"

"If you'd let me finish." He takes both my hands in his, clasping them together in his long, nubile fingers, curling them around mine.

I swallow and look up at him, ignoring the sweeping disappointment pulling me down and I tilt my chin towards him.

"I don't just want you to move in, Tara. I'm not playing at this," his voice lowers to a soft urgent whisper.

"Then what?"

"I want us to live together as man and wife." His deep brown eyes have locked on mine.

My mouth trembles. I can't believe what I'm hearing. The world swims out of focus and the pressure of him squeezing my hands brings me back from the precipice I'm swaying on. I stare at him: checking the honesty in his eyes, making sure that I haven't misheard him. All I see there is sincerity. I need to say something but no words come. I close my mouth and lick my lips, aware of the firelight in his eyes and my reflection in them. My mouth moves but no sound comes out.

"Tara, will you marry me?" he asks softly.

The shaking which started in my knees gently convulses my whole body, consuming me whole. I twine my arms around his neck and kiss him.

"Yes! Yes, I'll marry you," I hear myself say from a place

far beyond reach of my mind in a place of pure truth and fearlessness.

In one swift graceful movement his arms wrap around me as both my hands reach for his face, grasping at him, kissing him fervently as we lock together. Our palms rise to each other and the whirling energies mingle. Sparks ignite and my blood catches fire. Our spirits entwine, our bodies seeking to fuse together. Bathed in the flickering, ochre tones of the firelight he pushes me gently away and undresses me very slowly. I have no inhibitions, only a sense of profound intimacy that goes way beyond sex. I do the same for him and we lie down by the fireside, baring souls and skin in blissful union, in the dim flickering light I realize this is the last lover I will ever have.

26

In the morning the diffuse, yellow sunlight is shrouded in a deep, moving mist as we load Penny and Sultan into the horsebox for a ride near Mount Nagual. It's fairly even terrain if we stay away from the foothills, which is crucially important as Penny is relying on me for her sight. The dazed feeling from the proposal the night before still hasn't left me and I'm drifting around grinning at nothing in particular.

"Does this mean we're engaged?" I ask, as much to myself as Shasta.

"You're not going to back out now?"

"No...not until I get the ring anyway," I laugh, looking at my left hand.

"I'll make you one. I've metal left over from used horse shoes that would do just the job."

"I've never had a ring on that finger," I say, widening my eyes and looking at my hand trying to imagine it, cynically wondering if it would burn.

He throws me a casually sexy, over-the-shoulder look and his eyes narrow when he smiles as we head out on the quiet highway. The early morning silence which is only broken by the whinnying horses behind us. Shasta parks up as we unload the horses and set off along the pasture where the river winds playfully along creeks which were carved long ago from the rolling landscape.

Penny is a joy to ride. There is nothing she won't do. It's me who holds her back as she chews at her bit to go faster, picking up scents on the drifting breeze her nostrils widen. I'd love to know just how much she sees. It's hard to believe she is virtually blind. I don't know many humans with her courage and indomitable spirit. Riding beside Shasta, feeling the cold wind nip my cheeks and tossing my hair around, the freedom of the wild is liberating. Scout is running up ahead, leading the pack, living up to her name as she protectively surveys the landscape. Our direction drifts and takes us magnetically towards Mount Nagual. Sultan is bouncing high on his powerful hind legs. He's edgy and bursting to gallop.

"You could let him run?" I nod in Sultan's direction.

Shasta shakes his head. "No, because Penny will try to follow."

"He wants to run and I can't blame him," I murmur, looking around at the freshly dawned wilderness.

"I'll push forward and give him his head once he's away from Penny," says Shasta, letting Sultan lengthen his stride.

I stop and reassuringly stroke Penny's neck. In the stillness I automatically tune to the surroundings some more. Once they are a good distance away Sultan breaks into a gallop and runs tirelessly until they are hardly visible. I get a sudden and unmistakably clear feeling of foreboding and a sharp twinge in my gut. There is nothing to fear out here and scanning the landscape gives no cause for concern either. *Turn back!* I hear the words spoken clearly in a woman's firm tone.

"Shasta!" I call and nudge Penny into movement heading back in the direction we came from as goose bumps rise on my arms. I have a feeling we aren't alone. Shasta catches up in seconds. With a perceptive look he knows something isn't right.

"We need to leave." I nod, in the direction of home.

I urge Penny into a trot and she responds without

question as we make our way back to the car. Half expecting someone to ambush us, or to be waiting, I'm relieved there is no-one there, but the snaking feeling up my spine doesn't go away. I try rationalizing that I'm psyching myself out because Marshall Buchanan has set me on edge permanently. Not giving fear the time of day I push away the feeling, and as we head for home I'm lost in thoughts of making it public that Shasta and I are engaged.

"Are we telling people?" I ask, still hardly able to believe it.

"Don't you want to?"

"Of course, but...it just sounds so weird...I need to practice." I pull down the mirror and soundlessly mouth the words 'we're engaged', 'getting married' and 'fiancé' in the mirror.

"You're crazy!" says Shasta. He's clearly more experienced at this than me, having been engaged once before. It's that sort of thing that makes me wonder what forever and happily ever after have to do with real life. I extinguish that thought.

"How do you want to tell people? It's a small town and if I tell my friends, foghorn Simon will broadcast it. What about your parents?"

"Why don't we get everyone in one place?" he replies without hesitation.

Rip-roaring heat surges to my cheeks. "I don't want any fuss. Maybe we should just pop out and see them?"

"It'll be just a casual open house thing," he waves away my doubts.

"I think I'd rather elope."

"We could do that too, but let's have a get together and you can get to know my family better."

"You're right."

Shasta grins and sniggers under his breath, trying to hide his laughter.

"What's so funny?"

"For someone so eye catching you don't like much of the limelight!"

I roll my eyes. "That was one of the thing I disliked most about being a lawyer. I don't like the spotlight."

"You weren't meant to be hidden away."

"Nope. I'm going to become a hermit."

He squeezes my leg as we pull up outside the lake house. "That suits me. Everything I want is right here."

When Giselle arrives into work I've already made a list of things I need for tonight's impromptu get together. Sophie is running around fussing over customers like a mother hen as usual, leaving little for anyone else to do. However that's the way she likes it and it works perfectly for me. That's why she's been working here as long as she has – because she's good at it.

"Giselle, Tara, I've got something to tell you," says Sophie, grouping us together with her quiet serious tone of voice.

"What, us?" I ask.

"It's old Sarah. You know she's gone into hospital?" she asks, though she clearly knows we hadn't a clue.

"No. We didn't."

"She's gone downhill very fast."

"Maybe we should visit her?" asks Giselle.

"I don't think she's up to it. I just thought you should

know why she hasn't been in," says Sophie. She goes back to her work, leaving Giselle and I standing.

"Well that's a leveler," says Giselle.

"That's sad. She did say she was ready though."

"Is anyone ever ready to die?" she asks.

I think about Sarah's instructions about the wooden box she gave me, that I put in the safe, and that we should pass it on to the recipient when she was gone. I'd thought of it a few times but now she's so ill I feel the weight of following her instructions as she had asked. I divert myself with work, plus there's plenty to organize.

Shasta is putting the word out to his family and close friends and I've already called my dad, James and Svetlana; apart from Giselle and Simon there isn't really anyone else I want to invite, but I'm likely to get rumbled when I tell Giselle.

"What's that?" asks Giselle looking over my shoulder and hanging her coat on the hook.

"Just a list."

"You and your lists."

"Can you come over to Shasta's tonight? It's just drinks and nibbles. It's very casual."

"Really? No occasion?" Giselle speculates thoughtfully.

I can feel the tremor of truth weakening my mouth when I try to say no, and I don't even try to restrain the involuntary smile flushing my cheeks. Giselle blinks and draws her head back. I glance over my shoulder then back at her, collusively moving away from Sophia and the customers.

"Shasta's asked me to marry him," I whisper, beckoning her to keep her voice low. She jumps back with her hands to her face, making a high pitched squeal and a muffled exclamation as I put my finger to my lips laughing. She places her hand over her mouth, smothering the noise.

"Congratulations," she whispers back as we briefly hug and then cut it off before Sophie twigs something is going on.

"Just keep it under your lid until later. We don't want it getting back to Shasta's family beforehand."

Giselle pulls an invisible zip over her mouth and excitedly stamps her feet, before adopting a passive face to greet the customers. I'd rather that Shasta would just mention it to his family casually and not make a big deal about it. I don't really know why I don't want a big fuss. It is a big deal, but it's also an intimate time between Shasta and I and the exposure feels harsh by comparison. However it's only a few of our closest friends, so it's no biggie.

When there's a lull in business Sophie comes over and stands pointedly beside me.

"Aren't you going to tell me?"

"Tell you?" I feign innocence.

Sophie puts her hands on her ample hips. "Whatever it was Giselle found so exciting," she says persistently.

The faint smile grows and bursts like bubblegum on my face; I'm unable to keep my feelings to myself.

"OK Sophie, but keep it to yourself, just until tomorrow," I reply and Sophie peers back at me. "Shasta asked me to marry him."

"And you're going to?"

"Yes."

"Oh. Very good. I didn't have you down for the marrying type."

"Don't get too overwhelmed there, Sophie."

"It's great news. It's just you young ones go in for long

engagements then it never happens. I've something to do. Hold the fort," she instructs as though I actually need telling, and she disappears into the kitchen, closing the door behind her. Somewhere deep within me her comment resonates uncomfortably. How did I get from bridging the commitment issue over moving in to suddenly agreeing to get married? *Because it felt right, that's why.* Anyway, he's not asking to get married straight away.

Sophie appears a while later, and with her finger she beckons me to the kitchen.

"It's all I could do in a short time," she says, looking down at the lavishly decorated chocolate cake with the words *Shasta and Tara* in a heart and *Congratulations* underneath. "I'm superstitious. You can't call it engaged until you've got a ring on your finger. That's why I didn't write it."

"Thanks Sophie," I grin at her thoughtful gesture, despite her pessimistic sentiment.

At the end of the day I load the cake into the car together with the supplies I've bought for the gathering, stopping at home to shower and change into jeans, a sleeveless turquoise top and high heeled boots. I arrive at Shasta's carrying Sophie's cake, feeling a little guilty that I hadn't invited her, although I had explained that it was just family and close friends meeting up.

"You look great in those jeans," says Shasta following behind me as I carry the cake into the kitchen; he touches my backside as I walk, which makes me giggle and I struggle not to drop the cake.

"Look at the cake. Isn't that sweet?"

"Yes. Yes, it sure is," he says standing behind me, not even glancing at the cake. He gathers my hair to one side and showers my neck and shoulder with kisses. A quiet night in together would have been a much better idea.

"I've missed you," I murmur against his cheek, feeling his arms wrapped around me, cupping my behind with both hands.

"Ooops! Put her down bro! Shall we knock and come back?" asks Seb, who is followed by Luna and Carson. I hurriedly put the cake in the cupboard, not letting them see the inscription just yet. Within minutes a couple of guys, who are friends of Shasta's, arrive with their girlfriends and I'm starting to wonder just how many people he has invited. Roger and Simon are making another public outing together and it makes me smile knowing how far they've come to be together. Giselle hasn't brought Cooper, which seems odd. I ask her about it, and apparently he had 'something else on', but it'll give her a chance to mingle. My dad shows up and Giselle sits alongside him, having privately adopted him as her own.

Shasta's friends are a good-natured and quick-witted bunch, who sprawl out on the sofas with tins of beer and plenty of banter. They tuck heartily into the food as though they haven't eaten for a week and start teasing Shasta over something which I can't hear.

Carson goes out onto the outside deck followed by Seb, while Luna comes up to me offering a hand to fix drinks at the dining room table.

"You look very at home in here, Tara," she comments drily. "Are you living here now?"

"I spend a lot of time here," I reply, looking through the huddle of friends at Shasta who is watching us closely. He takes the cue and wanders casually over, waving to Seb and Carson to come in. My heart falters and upsurges.

"Mom, Dad." Shasta takes my hand having the attention of his parents while the others continue to chatter; Simon is chattering persistently in the thick of it all with his voice carrying over everyone else's.

"Meet the future Mrs King. Last night Tara agreed to marry me." His handsome face turns to me smiling, but I'm already giddy.

"Wow! You two don't waste any time! Congratulations," says Luna, kissing me on both cheeks and giving me a hug, though I'm sure her reactions are automated with shock. Carson puts his arm around me and welcomes me to the family. He mutters to Shasta, "I knew she was the one," and casually picks up a piece of fried chicken and bites into it.

"You've done what?!" shouts Simon, only just catching up, having choked and spluttered on his wine as Giselle throws him a napkin for the spillage on his chin.

There follows a flurry of air kisses and congratulatory hugs and it's all over very quickly without too much of a fuss. Barnaby gives me one of his awkward bear hugs

"I've only just found you; now, do you expect me to give you away?" he asks shyly.

"You've got a while yet," I reply.

The atmosphere is light hearted and relaxed as two more of Shasta's friends turn up, and presumably another from the noise in the corridor. Suddenly I'm dumbstruck. Leonie appears behind them, and clearly they have come together. *Of all the nerve!* But then she didn't know about the engagement, and if she is an old friend of Shasta's why wouldn't she be here? Nevertheless it irritates me. I watch Shasta as he sets eyes on the new arrivals. He greets the two guys with a smile that becomes faintly pinched at the sight of Leonie. He shows complete ambivalence - whether for my benefit or not, I don't know. Actually it feels irrelevant now anyway. They stand around chatting while I bring out the cake.

"Hey, you missed the big news!" says Seb to the newcomers, singling out Leonie judging by the trajectory of his gaze. His cheeks bunch up, narrowing his eyes which twinkle with mischief. "Shasta and Tara just got engaged!" Seb pronounces with the widest smile.

Leonie's facial muscles perceptibly droop but she does her best not to let her face register her feelings. Her chest rises rapidly and her nostrils flare. Her eyes dart to Shasta and by the time they find me I'm standing right beside her holding the cake.

"Ah. Isn't that wonderful?" She lifts the fine arch of her eyebrow, but there is no delight in her chocolate brown eyes. "Cute," she says, looking down at the cake, digging like mad for something to say to cover up her discomfort. Seb fires me a look of quiet satisfaction.

There is a brief round of congratulations and slaps on the back for Shasta, before the others move away and Leonie approaches him. She extends one manicured hand, strokes his cheek and leans into him. Flames flash before my eyes and I'm about to spontaneously combust. Shasta is stalk still, and as her mouth is about to touch his skin she drifts from his cheek to his mouth, planting a slow kiss as he twists away. To me she says nothing; and with the poise of someone who knows they are being watched she sashays over to talk with Luna and Carson.

I know better than to bring it up with Shasta, who is in denial that she wants him, but he must see what just happened. Looking at Seb's amused face, he certainly did.

Simon dramatically flings his arms around me, looking misty eyed and unnecessarily overwrought.

"What do you think to a double wedding?" he asks with pleading insincerity and major tongue in cheek.

"I think you need to stay away from me, you lunatic."

"You wouldn't have to do a thing," he says, holding my arm as I move into the group. "You only have to show up." He sniggers loudly to himself.

Carson and Barnaby are deep in conversation about fishing while Luna bombards me with questions about when we're likely to set the date. I'm being hemmed in and, nearby, Shasta is definitely cornered - by Leonie. She is so tangibly feline, purring and brushing up against him. I can't get near him without being interrupted by someone. I make my excuses to get away from Luna - simultaneously Leonie breaks away from Shasta, passing her group of friends as Shasta and I finally get a few moments together.

"What did she want? I ask unable to restrain *all* of intensity of the scathing tone that slinks into my voice.

"Relax. She's just being friendly," he says dismissively, placing his hand on my back and glancing sideways at me. There isn't much warmth in his voice and I sense that his patience with my apparent insecurity won't last forever. I don't want him to think I don't trust him. It's her I don't trust.

Heady from the champagne, and flushed with excitement, I walk to the drinks table and reach for the pitcher of iced water. Leonie stands up and walks away from her friends, all teeth and smiles. She hugs Luna and Carson as though she's saying good night. As I tip the glass of water, holding back the ice with my teeth, she connects eyes with me then walks over to Shasta and Seb, hugging Seb first who looks like a wooden block. Then she hugs Shasta and looks over his shoulder at me with a cunning smile. In front of the others her demeanor with him is less sexual. A tornado of fury and frustration twists around inside me. I breathe out slowly.

My stare doesn't leave her while she walks towards me with a soft pout and drifty eyes smoldering with devious intent.

"Tara, thanks for having us," she says loudly, well within earshot of the others as she nears me.

"Going so soon?" I ask in the same decibel, my mouth pulled back straight hinting at a smile. She draws near until our shoulders are separated by a few inches. Without replying she looks down at my left hand and smirks.

"Sadly, no ring," she says, tilting her head to the side mockingly. "You know you're not engaged until there's a ring on your finger? Oh, like this one." She flicks up a finger on her right hand that wears a very average sized solitaire, she holds her hand out and pretends to bring it in and out of focus. "That's the one Shasta bought when he proposed to me."

"We all make our mistakes," I reply.

"You're going to lose the game Tara, because I'm so much better at it than you, and let's just be clear about this. I won't give up until Shasta is mine again."

"I know exactly what you're up to, Leonie."

"Do you? You are right about one thing. We all make mistakes: mine was leaving Shasta; his is whatever illusion he sees in you. He's always been a sucker for a sympathy case."

I close the gap between us, leaning in until my nose is

nearly touching her cheek, my mouth mimics a smile but my teeth are bared.

"Leonie. Let me be clear with you. There is nothing you can say or do that would change how Shasta and I feel about each other. But go ahead – knock yourself out."

"Watch me," she whispers back, sucking in her top lip leaving lipstick on her teeth.

"I'll show you out." I push the back of her arm as I move forward.

"No need. I'll be finding my way around this house soon enough," she says slyly, turning and flicking her hair with a loud, socially polite laugh to keep up the friendly pretense.

27

Moving out of my house to go and live at Shasta's feels like the end of an era; albeit symbolic. All my clothes and immediate personal possessions will come with me, the furniture and everything else will remain as Aunt Rosa had it: cheerful, lived in and special. It deserves one last day with Giselle and Simon before I go. Simon has offered to cook lunch while Giselle and I watch, goading him that it better be good with the array of military grade kitchen utensils he's using.

"Shut up. A professional needs good tools," says Simon, putting on a bizarre pair of funky pink and white onion chopping goggles.

"What is that anyway? Is that crab?" asks Giselle pointing into a mixing bowl as though she is about to sample it.

"Don't put your grubby fingers in there!" says Simon. Giselle pulls back screwing up her face at whatever delicacy she sees in there.

"You'll have to wait until you taste it. I'm not giving away my secrets," says Simon, wiping flour from his chin with his arm.

"Tara, did you get that box? Someone left a present on the doorstep for you," says Giselle, whirling round to see where she left it.

"What box? There are a few," I nod in the direction of a pile I'd packed to take to Shasta's, which are stacked beside the front door.

"No. This one is gift wrapped. It must be an engagement present. It's got your name on it."

"Really? I hadn't expected anything." It had all been so

low key and out of the blue that there was no time for cards or gifts. "But hey, a present is a present."

Giselle finds it and places the box, wrapped in red metallic paper, on the table. "I know what you're like Northy. If you'd known it was there you would have peeped. Maybe you should keep it so that you and Shasta can open it together?" Giselle suggests.

"Too right," says Simon.

I pick up the box, knowing there is no way I can resist opening it but I go through the motions: picking it up and shaking it. Something is loose inside, so that rules out crockery or glass which would have been bubble wrapped. Then there is another noise; like the sound of sand or stones shaking.

"Maracas?" I ask. "I wonder if it's from Shasta. Maybe he's hinting that we're going to Spain?"

"Or Mexico. Open it!" encourages Giselle, standing by my side staring at the box.

I slowly slide the red wrapping paper off and there's the shaking noise again; but I hadn't moved the box this time. As I lift back the lid I scream and jump backwards before I even understand why. A second later Giselle is also screaming.

"It's a snake!"

The agitated rattle snake inside the box strikes swiftly, catching Giselle on the hand and at mid lunge the box tips over. Giselle's panic-stricken scream drowns out the sound of the rattling as we stagger backwards, trying to get away from the animal slithering on the table and about to slide onto the floor. Simon's searing high pitched howling is deafening and my ears wobble to the point of bursting. His bolt to safety is completely blocked. The snake is between him and us. He clambers on the worktop a few feet away, yelling frantically, but it's Giselle who is really in trouble. She reels backwards clutching her hand, incomprehensible with shock. She shakes violently, but there is no time to play nurse. The snake is making its way across the floor towards us.

"This way!" I grab her by the arm, running and half dragging her towards the lounge, intending to pull her to safety, where we can close the door. Simon is reasonably safe in his position, as long as he stays there! While Giselle staggers beside me the front door opens and a different horror appears. It's Cain Shimlow. *What the hell is going on? Things between us have improved but a house visit…?* It's no time for questions.

"Cain! Help!"

Cain's acute peering eyes shift from me to Giselle.

"Thank you, God. I thought I was too late," he mutters, casting his eyes around the scene.

"What?" I shriek at his insane babbling.

Cain grabs Giselle's other arm and as we get into the lounge I kick the door closed with a bang before we get her onto the sofa.

"Call the paramedics, Cain!"

Cain is now standing there with his arms the same length. Frustrated by his inaction I fumble in my jeans pocket for my cell, using my other hand to lift Giselle's wrist which is smeared with blood. I rack my brains trying to remember what to do for a snake bite, knowing she urgently needs medical treatment, but considering sucking out the venom immediately. All the while I'm distracted by the panicky howls coming from Simon.

"Don't you dare bite me!" says Giselle, reading my mind, her face ghostly opaque with fear.

Cain is hovering, creepily motionless as though he's watching us from a distance, unable to help.

"Tara. You have to come with me," says Cain. "Now!"

"You're going to be OK Giselle. I'm calling 911," I say, trying to sound calm and faking a smile. "Just keep your hand below your heart."

"You don't understand," says Shimlow persistently. "I came to help you. They've got Shasta."

I shoot him a look, feeling my blood turn cold. The cell phone in my hand clatters to the floor. I reach to grab it, keeping my eyes on the crazed preacher the whole time. *Why would he care?*

"Who's got him? Where?"

"They're going to kill him. If you want to find him you'll have to come with me!"

Keeping my eyes on him I hit the emergency call button and rapidly blurt that there's been a snake bite and the address, stammering over the words, trying to reason why Cain is telling me this. This is Cain, who is intrinsically linked with the Buchanans - Shasta's inadvertent enemies. However Shasta felt there had been a separation between them after Cain went rogue. I need to act fast.

"Go!" says Giselle.

"She's got plenty of time," says Cain, pointing at Giselle, throwing the comment in without concern and she gives him a scathing look.

"The ambulance is on its way. Simon's here. You go!" Howling is still coming from the kitchen. Torn, I shake my head, unsure whether to believe what Cain is saying, but Shasta's life may depend on it. It doesn't make sense. Why would he tell me this?

"No. I'm calling the police!" I decide. My grip on the phone tightens. I know it's not what Shasta would want, but there is no choice now. The stakes are too high. Enough is enough! My finger moves to the screen of the phone then there is a clicking sound. I look up through the hair, which has fallen over my face, to see Cain pointing a gun at me.

"I hoped I wouldn't have to do this," he remarks jovially as though this is a joke. Every nerve responds by firing up - he can't be serious.

"What the hell are you doing? Put that away!" I snap, my voice doesn't reflect the ascending fear.

"You're insane," breathes Giselle, her eyes wide and staring at Cain.

"Maybe, but you could be dead soon! I know which I'd choose."

"Cain, why are you doing this?"

"Let's go." He motions to the door with his gun, then re-trains it on me.

I shake my head, not believing what is happening, but I stand up, discreetly dropping the phone into Giselle's lap without Cain seeing. That way she can call for help. Cain shunts the gun in my back, jabbing me forward as he opens the door, pushing me into the hallway. I trip reluctantly out, expecting the snake to be anywhere.

"Wait! The journal. Bring it with you!" directs Shimlow.

"What for?"

"Bring it!" he shouts. "You and it are more useful than your Indian buddy."

"I don't know where it is," I lie, knowing it's in my bag

at the foot of the stairs. He levels the tip of the gun at my head and I feel the cold steel against my temple. I walk slowly towards it, reaching for the journal, telling Cain what I'm doing just to stop him putting a bullet in my brain.

"Here!" I toss it to him, hoping he'll instinctively catch it, but it drops to the floor and with a sly knowing smile he makes me pick it up.

"Tara! What's going on?" yells Simon. "The snake! Where is it?"

I glimpse him standing on the worktop, using the island in the middle like a stepping stone and all the while Simon is making bizarre gurgling noises.

Cain pushes me forward and down the front steps of the house, putting the gun invisibly low to my side to avoid arousing suspicion from the neighbors. If only that was a possibility - there is no one outside.

"You drive!" he insists as he opens the passenger door, forcing me to climb over to the driver's side while he keeps the gun aimed in my direction.

"Where are we going?"

"Trust me. Drive. I came to help you didn't I?"

"So why are you pointing a gun at me?!"

He sighs and smirks. "This is for your sake."

"Liar!"

"And mine," he beams with a delusional gaze. "You know where the gold is. Your ancestors knew it and so must you. It's all in that book."

"No, it's not!"

"You were seen out there!"

"Cain, I have no clue what you're talking about," I reply.

"You're going to take me there. Marshall doubted it,

but I convinced him you were more use alive. Now drive! He may have changed his mind and your beloved may already be dead. I hope not though - two heads are better than one."

I shift the car into drive, succumbing to the fact that Shimlow has the upper hand. Accelerating hard down the street, I listen out for the sound of an ambulance, praying they get to Giselle quickly without being bitten themselves.

28

If only I could get hold of Barnaby. If I could drive past his house on the way, maybe he'd be outside. He'd think it strange that I would have Cain Shimlow in the car. Cain has the gun trained on me. Irrational thoughts of opening the door and bailing out of the vehicle flash into my mind, but Shimlow's finger only needs to move a few millimetres – it would take a split second - infinitely less time than it would take me to get out. He seemed so disconnected the last few times I saw him, but today, acting without regard for consequence, he has completely broken from reality.

"Cain, there is no need for the gun. If Shasta is in trouble I will willingly come with you," I say, lowering my voice to sound like his ally.

"That wouldn't do at all," he replies, as the corner of his mouth peels up revealing yellowing teeth.

"I have no idea what you want with me, but I can co-operate. I can't help you if I don't know how. If I do, will they release Shasta?"

"How sweet. A life for a life," he says sarcastically. "Keep driving!"

Under Cain's influence I have no option. I dip my foot on the gas pedal, and throw myself further into this. Whatever I can do is for Shasta. Blinkered, I will myself not to give way to morose fatalistic thoughts about what to expect when I get there. If they kill him - and I have no reason to think they won't - they might as well kill me too. At least this way we'll be together to face whatever happens.

Heading out on the highway we take several turns onto

quieter roads heading into deeply forested land with very few buildings. I know this area. I've been here with Shasta.

"Pull over here," says Shimlow, his voice brittle, as he signals with the gun to a grassy track where he wants me to pull off the road.

"There's nothing here?" Cold fear creeps up my spine and every nerve ending stands to attention. "Tell me what you want of me, Cain?"

"Shut up!"

I have no idea what I'm walking into, blindly being ordered into the unknown, thoughts race through my mind and images of Shasta beaten or tortured come unbidden to mind. *I won't think like this.* If only I had my phone, but I'd left it with Giselle. *That was stupid!*

"Cain, you and my mom went back a long way. Didn't you? You were her Pastor. Rosa really trusted you, and I know she cared a great deal for you. She wouldn't believe what is happening now. Would she?"

"Rosa was a good woman, but you inherited your genes from the Whitelaws – that is obvious. Generations of evil have been spawned in you. It just keeps on going! They say it takes seven generations to die out."

"Why do you say that?"

"You're bred from generations of blackhearts and pagans."

"Blanche had a good heart, she had a heart of gold."

"A good heart! My mother died after your grandmother bewitched her. She was too poor to see a real doctor. She was so poor she took the advice of a local charlatan. If my family hadn't lost their wealth in the gold rush, we wouldn't have known such poverty. I pledged to my grandmother that I would get back our gold and more.

My great grandfather hid what riches we had left, to hide it from the marauders, but later it was never found. Rumors abounded for years, borne by the Indians who your grandmother was in league with. They were in it together. They kept it secret. They kept it for themselves."

"Cain, it's not what you think-"

"Shut up!" he screams, both hands flying to his head. "I can't think. Stop it! Now walk!"

His agitation is heightening, so I quieten to counteract it. With mounting nervousness we press on through the trees. Breathing shallowly, my heart races at the thought of what may lie ahead. I need help, and fast, but the chances of anyone even seeing my car are remote.

An old, wooden, hunter's cabin lies in a small clearing. If Cain was telling the truth, this must be where they are keeping him. The thundering of blood in my ears is deafening as I try to imagine the scene in the cabin. Who is with him? A giveaway sob bubbles from my chest. *Don't you dare cry. Be strong. Be brave.* One glance at Cain tells me he's also fearful. His jaw is locked and flexing, thin skin over sinews strain for control over his pallid grey features.

"There! Through the door," snaps Shimlow.

"After you," I reply, fearing a trap.

Cain seizes my elbow and shoves me through the broken door, which grinds on its hinges as it gives way and I find myself in the middle of the room.

"Shasta!" He is bound to a chair with his chin defiantly jutting, and a trail of dried blood on his mouth. My heart splinters. He is guarded by two well-built, heavy-set men with cropped hair and wide, square faces. I lurch towards him, and get tripped by the bodyguard's foot.

"Tara!" His voice sounds shocked and bewildered. He

rocks hard on the chair in temper, but remains restrained – the bodyguards are indifferent. Beside the dirty, opaque window Marshall Buchanan sits on a chair facing the other three with a mocking look playing on his lips.

"Ah, good work Cain – but what kept you? Tara, I'm so pleased you could join us. Cain said you would be... useful. Let's hope he's right, for both your sakes." Marshall smirks at Shasta whose face draws taut as he narrows his eyes into piercing slits.

"Marshall. Shasta had nothing to do with Vaughan's death. You have to believe me! Did you tell him?" I turn to Shasta begging, as though this can easily be resolved.

"Oh, he told me. The thing is...I don't believe him. My son could have been saved. He saved your brother but he left my son to die in a burning building. He knew exactly what he was doing. And sadly...someone's got to pay. Sadly...today, that's you!" he flicks a finger in Shasta's direction, with finality.

Shasta's teeth are bared back, ready to bite. "Tara is not involved. Let her go!"

"Oh, but she is. You see we thought, or should I say Cain thought, seeing as he came up with the idea, that as you two seem to be in the know about the whereabouts of gold we could kill two birds with one stone. Pardon the pun. We'll be waiting a while longer for the experts to reach a conclusion but as we have local experts with a notable history, your job is to lead the way. You owe us that at least."

"We can't win. What you're looking for doesn't exist!" I shout.

"It exists. And you know it!" says Cain Shimlow, his voice shrill with a sharp cutting edge. "You know it. Your ancestors knew it. I won't rest until I know the truth. What were they keeping for themselves? You stole what belonged to my family," argues Cain.

"So you see Shasta, as a little insurance policy we've brought Tara along to help jog your memory. If you can't help us then...ah...it pains me to say this but...we'll have to kill her," says Marshall.

"Mr Buchanan, Sir," pipes up one of his henchmen, nodding to the window. Marshall looks and clasps his hands together as though preparing to give a speech. Through the window I can see movement through the trees.

"The next surprise has arrived. Let's go outside. It's getting crowded in here," says Marshall waving the air under his nose with distaste. The bodyguards pull Shasta up from the seat, giving me a brief chance to get near to him and I seize it - throwing my arms around his neck and grasping him before they pull me outside after Marshall and Cain. Of all the nightmares, I could never have dreamt of this.

Squinting in the sunlight as we step out from the dark, gloomy hut I blink to take in what is going on. Two people are entering the clearing and my spirits lift slightly when I recognize Tray, thinking he will somehow defuse this. He knows me, we've got history. He's our light at the end of the tunnel, but the light is brief. It's extinguished suddenly when the identity of his black haired companion is revealed. It's Leonie.

"Dad? What's going on?" Tray asks warily, quickly surveying the scene. "Why did you want to meet here?" he asks, but I suspect he already has the answer. Leonie's composure loosens and she looks suddenly perplexed.

"Isn't this fun! Look Shasta, another lover. I didn't

know which you would risk everything for, so I brought you both. Don't thank me!" Marshall clasps his hands. "Thanks, son. You played your part well. Leonie you're joining us, as insurance. Remember Shasta, one wrong move and one of them gets it; but which one? It'll be your choice."

Shasta shakes his head and faces off Marshall with steely determination, the contracting of his brow shades his unfathomably dark eyes and he looks battle-ready. My legs wobble beneath me and a brief wave of nausea mists my vision. I can see no way out. We can't give him what he wants.

"OK, I'll show you what I know," says Shasta, his voice low and raw.

I frown at him, not understanding but knowing he is probably stalling for time; stalling to find some sort of solution or a means of escape.

"I'm loving this game. Leonie, sorry to involve you but you've been more than helpful."

"Dad, is this necessary?" asks Tray, fidgeting and looking nervously at his father.

Marshall Buchanan's mocking face hardens when he glares at his son.

"You failed me, Tray. I thought you could take care of things here but once again it's proved to be beyond you. This is called using your initiative. This is for the real man who was your brother," says Marshall staring through his demeaned son as though he's transparent. "Get this expedition underway," says Marshall, dismissing Tray and tipping his head at the henchmen.

Tray looks like a lost child, without words or value.

"At least free my hands," says Shasta.

Marshall Buchanan sizes him up for a brief second and gives the nod. I breathe a sigh of relief when they remove the ropes from his wrist.

"Lead on. We're right behind you. Forget taking us on a wild goose chase," says Marshall, casting a look at one of the bodyguards who draws back his coat, revealing a pistol in the holster attached to him.

"We can't walk from here," says Shasta. He obstinately stops dead. Marshall turns around, his lips pursed together in a hard line and his nostrils flare with irritation when he looks at Shasta.

"Where are you taking us?" he asks.

"We'll need cars to get closer."

Marshall pauses then tips his chin in the air. "This had better be worth it," he replies, striding off towards a black Range Rover. "You two travel with them," he signals to his two bodyguards, pointing to us to get in.

"Boss." The taller henchman acknowledges the instruction, opening the door and shoving me roughly onto the back seat, then pushing Shasta into the front passenger's side. The thicker of the two men slides in beside me, removing his gun from his side, taking off the safety catch and leveling it at Shasta's head from behind the seat. The idea of wrestling the gun from him dies before it has a chance to mature.

"We'll follow behind. Do not let him out of your sight," Marshall snaps and struts off with Tray, Leonie and Cain Shimlow to the other vehicle.

There must be a way out of this. There just has to be. I'll try anything. I remember something about making friends with your captors, getting them to see you as a real person. I watch the meat-headed chumps, trying to think of what we may have in common.

"So, isn't this cosy? I didn't see this coming." I fake a smile at the man beside me, who doesn't acknowledge me at all. "I thought I'd be idling away the afternoon at home." I try again. "What are your names?" I persist, sounding socially inept at the connotations of the predicament. "Sorry, I guess you're not allowed to speak to us. I don't know if it was one of you two I met before, but if it was...sorry about the knife incident."

"You mean this?" says the driver with a strong New Jersey accent, one hand letting go of the steering wheel while he holds it up, revealing a laceration across the length of it.

"You were lucky it wasn't me," says Shasta, to the driver.

"Because you're such a mighty man, huh? Is that how come your here now? You punch like a girl," he raises a hand to his cheek and I notice the purple bruising to the side of his head - so much for creating a bond with the captors. He continues driving in silence, following Shasta's abrupt instructions. I'm hoping he has a plan up his sleeve, but he's weapon-less against the armed heavyweights. I silently ask for help, putting all the intention I can into a plea to the universe to get us out of this and to finally free Shasta from injustice.

29

"Where is this placc?" asks the driver when he turns off the Range Rover's engine, looking suspicious that he's been misled.

"It's the place you've been looking for," replies Shasta evenly, but there is no mistaking the challenging glare in his eyes.

As we get out of the vehicle Marshall, Cain, Tray and Leonie pull up behind.

"You wouldn't lie would you?" asks Marshall, sneering at Shasta.

"You have to go the rest of the way on foot," he replies.

Marshall looks angrily at Cain Shimlow, who has my grandmother's journal in one hand and a gun in the other; he distractedly leafs through the book. Marshall stares hard at him, as though he can move him with his eyes alone.

"Cain!" snaps Marshall.

Cain's head spins round to look at Marshall, his two eyes looking unconnected as he focuses on the pack leader.

"I followed them here before," says Cain nodding, his words trailing out of sync with the movements of his mouth. It strikes me he is on medication – and too much of it.

Marshall impatiently sends the group forward as we set off across the lush landscape of the foothills approaching the mountainous tree line, the closer we get the rocky, grey, uneven surface begins to rise up. It's Mount Nagual; that's where Shasta is taking them - the sacred Indian territory. The progress of the group falters when Leonie stops dead in her tracks

"Not there. We shouldn't go there, not without permission." Leonie's voice is fearful.

"You have it. From me!" counters Marshall, and he carries on walking.

I sidle up to Tray, who is walking behind his father, trying to foster my friendship with him.

"This isn't going to work out for anybody. Stop him before it's too late," I whisper, keeping my plea out of earshot of anyone else.

"I'm sorry. There's nothing I can do," he replies.

"Tray, you were with me in New York when I had the accident. Back then I thought it was the worst thing that had ever happened. But this-"

"You don't need to try to make me feel guilty, Tara. I know that your being knocked down was because of me. I'm not a totally heartless human being, but....what my father says goes. There is no changing it." Tray's softly structured face looks pinched and drawn. Leonie looks over and gives me a frosty glance, for once not hiding her true feelings.

There is no way of making a run for it out here, despite the increased density of the pine trees giving cover, the range of their guns and presumable fitness of Buchanan's men would make it a victorious man hunt for them. Perhaps when we get to the cave we could give them the slip? Perhaps that is part of Shasta's plan? He knows this place better than anyone. A ferocious icy blast of wind funnels between the mountainside and a craggy bluff opposite, reminding me how cold it is and how inadequately dressed Shasta and I are. He's wearing a black long sleeved sweater over a white t-shirt, as they had presumably taken him from home that morning. I'm thankful I have at least a bodywarmer over my thick sweater, but even that's not enough to block out the cold.

Heavy, bulbous, white clouds hover over the mountain top. A snowfall was forecast, but it wouldn't be the first time they'd got it wrong. We aren't equipped for being outdoors if the weather does deteriorate. I level up with Shasta as everyone walks in heavy silence. Marshall is breathless and less arrogant than he had been, but his henchmen are constantly watchful and Cain is brandishing the gun while he walks and every so often looks down at the book. *He can keep the damned journal. Shasta and I have to get out of here.*

"Tara, I haven't forgotten that we were interrupted from our cosy time together the other night. We should pick up where we left off," says Marshall.

Shasta wheels round to face him, keeping me behind him. Both bodyguards raise their firearms to protect Marshall. Shasta freezes and narrows one eye. It's clear to everyone that Shasta doesn't know what Marshall is talking about – and his fury is unmistakeable.

"Ah. She didn't tell you I paid her a visit. Naughty Tara. What will we do with you?" Marshall tells Shasta about the incident at the coffeehouse, taking obvious pleasure in goading him. I want to explain, but there is no point now. Shasta strides on, carrying himself proudly; but in his sideways glance at me I recognize his anger that I didn't tell him.

"I'm sorry," I whisper, but he looks away when he notices the bodyguard getting closer to my shoulder, about to stop us talking.

"Relax," says Marshall to the guard. "Let the lovers have their tiff." The man falls back by several steps, but I can still hear his heavy boots slide over the rocks. It leaves a few paces behind our backs where the others are following behind. Yet I'm uneasy with three loaded guns behind us.

"I don't know if we'll get out of here, but I love you more than anything and I want to be your wife, if not in this lifetime, then the next," I murmur, not caring who hears me. The bubble of frustrated fear lurking in my chest builds up and my eyes sting, but I won't let myself cry.

"Don't talk like that," Shasta replies tersely, using his eye he signals the rocks up ahead, as though there is something I should be looking at. He raises his brows and whispers, "Remember?"

I'm not sure I do. I think of the last time Shasta and I were here. We are nearing the cavern entrance now, I know that much. I remember Shasta going ahead of me then disappearing from sight as he dropped into the entrance to the rocky chamber. That is what he means. That is our escape route. I swallow hard and my heart hammers from adrenaline again.

"Down?" I mouth back with a miniscule nod, keeping facing forward. But is it wide enough for the both of us drop into together?

Shasta stops and looks at the mountain top, where the weather is changing fast as foreboding clouds gather. There's a noticeable temperature drop as the wind strengthens. The others slow up and follow his gaze.

"It's going to snow. We've not got much time," he speaks casually, like he actually cares about the welfare of the others. A small flurry of scattered snowflakes begin to fall in the pinkish-brown light.

Shimlow and the bodyguards look to Marshall for instruction. Shasta collects and holds my gaze with a knowing look which is unseen by the others. He holds his hand up level with his chest. He holds three fingers out while keeping one eye on the others, he counts down, from three, to two - I snatch a breath - one.

Together we lunge to a sprint. He grips my arm and we hurtle forward covering the seemingly long distance between ourselves and the rocky edge while expecting to hear gunfire. Before I have a chance to see where to jump it's upon us. Shasta propels me down, just marginally ahead of him before I have a chance to think about it. We drop down into the chamber and fall several feet to the stony hollow below. Shasta lands on his feet but I stagger forward and he is already pulling me into the entrance to the cavern, putting valuable space between us and Marshall's posse. He pulls me into the half light of the cavern, the odd, metallic smell mixed with fresh air brings a strange type of comfort – my claustrophobia is dwarfed by the sound of the others following in serious pursuit.

"There is nowhere to go from here! Shasta, we're trapped."

But he keeps looking ahead and moving forward as we travel deeper into the cavern, unable to see very far ahead but our eyes adjust quickly. Shasta pulls a Maglite torch from his pocket, and shines it around. The sparkles of the pyrite and quartz walls of the cavern reflect off the underground stream.

"There is a way out. If we carry on through the cave, it's narrow but it comes out higher up on the mountain."

Shasta pushes my back, directing me along the narrowing path and the archway to the next section of the cavern and then the next. The sound of the footsteps and shouts behind us echoes and reverberates off the cave walls. Leonie's whimper is the lowest tone and easily distinguishable. She sounds like she is overcome with fear at being inside the mountain she'd heard her ancestors speak of – and the apparent curse against anyone who trespassed. When Shasta and I had been here together we made an offering to the spirits of the mountain – this time we had barged on through. In retrospect I send a humble greeting to the spirit of Mount Nagual and ask for safe passage.

Shasta's hot breath on my neck would normally be welcome, but not now. He's pushing me faster through an archway on a narrow ledge beside the water. I hold onto the jutting sides of the wall, trying to grip while my feet edge along and Shasta is pressing me hard to go quicker. The sound of the others grows closer, with swearing and threats coming out from the darkness behind us. I can hear gravel and stones tumbling into water and grab hard against the crumbling wall for a grip as I find myself falling. I slip into the icy water below, submerging my head, before I bob up and gasp in reflex. My body warmer acts as a lifejacket. Shasta grabs hold and pulls me to a firm rock. Spluttering with shock I clamber out and get to my feet.

Then I realize our getaway was in vain. Marshall Buchanan, flanked by his sidekicks, is towering over us. Two guns are drawn on Shasta and I, preventing us from going anywhere. I screwed it up for both of us.

"That was a stupid thing to do!" shouts Marshall. "You've succeeded in really pissing me off! Now before I run out of patience, where is the gold?"

"You're looking at it!" I yell, exasperated and shaking.

"That's it! All around you. Go ahead. Take a good look. Was it worth all this?"

Marshall looks around the cavern, which glitters beautifully in the torchlight. Buchanan's two employees and Tray have their phones in their hands and shed their light onto the crystalline walls and ceiling of the cavern. They gaze around; apparently even they are mesmerized in the flickering sparkling light.

"There. I've given you what you wanted. No you can let her go," says Shasta, his voice level and controlled. Marshall looks around and starts to chuckle quietly but it gains volume and becomes eerie.

"You think we're fools!" shouts Cain Shimlow, breaking in on Marshall's victorious moment. "You think we don't know the difference between pyrite and the real thing? Its fool's gold!"

Marshall's upturned mouth contorts and twists into a monstrous, ugly shape.

"He's right. It's nothing more than pyrite," says Tray, piping up from the back of the party. *Found your voice at last have you?* "It was a wasted journey. Let's just wait for the reports to come back. Let's all go home," he encourages as Leonie clings to his arm looking shocked and fragile.

"You tried to make a fool of me! Where is it? Where is the real gold? Tell me!" shouts Cain. He's on the verge of losing control.

"This is it. This is all I know about," replies Shasta calmly, letting the ego and drama of the others drift over him as though he didn't care anymore.

"I should never have listened to you, Cain!" says Marshall. "You and your deceptive notions that they know something we don't."

"She does!" retorts Cain, pointing in my direction.

I shake my head, all the while racking my brains to think of another escape route. Shasta's time with Marshall is running out. He's lacking patience and hell-bent on twisted revenge to trade his grief. How can he possibly think killing Shasta would compensate for the loss of his son? In his world there is always someone else to shoulder blame. This is his way of getting closure for the death of his son – the son who was in fact a bully and an arsonist who sealed his own fate.

"Bring her!" Marshall strikes the air with his fist and points to Leonie. The short bull-like henchman takes Leonie by the arm and pulls her over to Marshall as he moves away from the ledge to a smooth area of solid earth within the cavern.

"This is your last chance, Shasta. Tell us what you know, or the only thing she'll have to remember you by is the bullet lodged in her heart," says Marshall.

Shimlow edges closer to me and I eye him warily. He moves ahead, slightly deeper into the narrowing cavern. The gun the squat bodyguard is holding rises slowly in his firm grasp and stops level with Leonie's chest at point blank range. Leonie screams and buckles slightly but he pulls her up by her lustrous jet black hair.

Shasta tangibly flinches.

"There is somewhere else we could try. We'd have to go back the way we came," suggests Shasta hopefully. He's playing for time and opportunity. Marshall eyes him suspiciously and throws his head back laughing raucously.

"You really have reached the end of the road haven't you?" says Marshall.

"Christ!" shrieks Tray's voice over the din as he grasps his short hair and pulls it outward and turns away from the scene.

"Let the girls go. They have done nothing to you!" instructs Shasta without making eye contact with me. But I can hear his thoughts in my mind. *I won't leave. I won't let him die alone.*

"That was the wrong one, wasn't it? Leonie, you weren't his favorite after all." Marshall signals to the other goon and within a split second he is aiming the pistol at me. Shasta lunges at the guy, who brings his hand up sharply, hitting Shasta in the face with the butt of the gun and realigning it on me.

A sob escapes and I reach out for Shasta. Both the henchman and Cain Shimlow close in, one on either side of me. Blood spurts from Shasta's nose as the other gunman trains his sight on him.

"No more ideas Shasta? Nothing else you want to tell us?" asks Marshall impatiently.

"I have done nothing to you. Why do you hate so much that you would kill the innocent to avenge the self deception and despair in your own soul? There is nothing I have to tell you that your conscience doesn't already know. I am not the man who killed your son! Your son died by his own hand. The people of the Reservation have never done anything to hurt you, yet you send your people to intimidate and annihilate their way of life, in the pursuit of something you already have. I don't believe in evil, but today I've seen in you something so dark it challenges that."

The gun aimed at me shakes slightly as the henchman's grip shifts on the weapon.

"Bravo, Mr King. A noble speech for your last words,"

says Marshall, turning his eyes to Tray and Leonie, who are slowly backing away from the group, discreetly trying to make their exit.

"Why won't you listen to the truth? Is it too painful to face the fact that *you* told your son to use whatever means to gain Reservation land? It's hard to live with your guilt for the role you played in your son's death, isn't it?"

"I've had enough," replies Marshall, steadily shifting his gaze to the ceiling of the cave with a wry appreciative smile. "Kill him!" he mutters casually and casts his arm down with the command keeping his eyes averted.

"No!"

My voice isn't the only one to reverberate – there are two - another female also. The bony hand on my arm tightens and pulls me away from Shasta and off my feet. Leonie screams and rushes forward to him, just as the shot rings out, then another. I hit the dirt while staring at the terrifying scene unfolding. Leonie falls to the ground clutching her shoulder, looking blank and mortified she folds to the ground. Shasta's face relaxes peacefully. He leans forward, tilts off balance and falls slowly into the water.

There is anguished howl of despair from me. Sobbing, I scramble along the ground towards him, as his limp body drifts slowly away in the stream. *This can't be happening! He can't be dead!* I try to dive in after him but Cain is holding both my arms tightly behind my back.

"Your turn," says Marshall to me, with a brief nod to his employee as he starts to make his exit. Tray is on the ground seeing to Leonie.

"Do it," I spit back at him, blinded by tears of rage and despair. "There is nothing more you can do to me."

Suddenly my body moves but not of its own doing. Cain's sinewy, gnarled fingers dig into my arms as he thrusts me into a narrowing corridor and out of view of the other men.

"Have it your way, Cain. Just finish her off when you're done," Marshall Buchanan calls out as Cain forces me into the darkness.

30

The wheezing and panting noises give away Cain's whereabouts behind me, but there is oddly some reassurance in the guttural noises coming from him. Alone in the darkness, surrounded by rock on every side we are entombed in stone, faced with the savage reality of a slow death from fear and lack.

If Cain hadn't taken me here I would already be dead. I'm angry for his intervention. I would already be with Shasta in spirit. The pain is too much to bear. I wrap my arms around myself and pull my knees up to my chest, cocooning myself from the bare rock, which feels like it's pressing in on me – gulping air as the wetness of my tears moistens my lips I touch and drink them with my tongue. The instinctive primal urge to stay alive counteracts what my soul wants.

"Move!" urges Cain.

But I can't move. There is nowhere to go. In panic my hands grasp around the rock face. I can't find an exit – my mind is insensible and illogical. I have lost it.

"You have to! I heard Shasta tell you there is a way out through here," shouts Cain.

He did say that, and although it was only a short time ago that space between then and now ticks painfully along, knowing with every grief stricken minute that time is moving on without him. The resurgence of claustrophobia propels me into action. If I am to die I don't want it to be here, my rational mind kicks in. I need to get out of here.

"How?"

"Push on forward. There will be a space somewhere."

Fighting against the urge to retreat from the solidity

of the rocks around me I crawl forward, feeling around, expecting to be blocked by the walls but meeting no resistance. Gulping and dry-sobbing with fear I inch forward, again no resistance, again I move forward until with my arms outstretched to either side I can feel nothing apart from the surface below me. *Oh, thank God!*

Feeling Cain Shimlow's eager body behind me makes me want to put space between us. I rise to my feet, and keep moving forward, then upwards: climbing and groping in the darkness, having to trust that this is progress and not taking me further into a stone coffin. The fear doesn't go away but I've changed my mindset: instead of seeing it as a dead end I choose to see it as a way out - one tentative step after another.

I don't know how long we've been going, perhaps not that long – it just feels like it. The tangy musty smell from earlier has gone as though the chimney of rock is being fed by fresh air. I take heart in that, but for every positive second it sheds light on the fact that Shasta has gone. Shaking with emotional and physical exhaustion I collapse onto the gritty floor of this apparently rounded section of the cave.

"Get up!" shouts Cain.

I shake my head, spent of all willpower. I can taste blood on my tongue, but I can't see from where, perhaps a scratch on my face. From the stinging of my hands and knees I suspect they are grazed. Weak and dizzy I close my eyes, feeling disorientated in the darkness. The fatigue and hunger are taking their toll.

"I can't," I reply.

Cain sighs irritably. "We can rest a while."

Of all the people I could be trapped inside a mountain with it had to be him. I snort at the irony and let my head fall back, for once glad of the cave wall for its support. Behind closed eyelids there is a glimmer of light that my eyes are not accustomed to. I blink them open to find we are in an oval space and the light is coming from Cain's cell phone. *He had that the whole time and didn't use it?*

Lost in his own world he is kneeling on the floor using the cell phone as a reading light, shining it on my grandmother's journal.

"Why Cain? Why is it so important? People have died."

He ignores me and continues to thumb through the book as I watch him through drooping eyelids with crazy tiresome fluctuating emotions. He brought me here; but he also just saved my life. I can't explain it, but I sense a bond with him and that somehow his life depends on mine, or vice versa.

"I hope you find it Cain, whatever you're looking for."

He looks over at me, curious but unsure. "You say that like its trivial."

"What if you don't find your gold?"

Cain's narrow lips peel back and his face contorts in the dim light; a ghoulish sight to behold.

"I must. I made a promise to find what is rightfully mine. To reclaim what belonged to my family. I've strived for the best, I've cleansed myself with the love of Christ, I've walked the way of God all these years, I'm pure enough to deserve the riches of heaven. I'm not a poor man, but I need the richness it would bring to my life. Gold contains God's shining light. It's the closest thing to heaven. The gold is the Lord's treasury. I'm a holy man. That is my next step. All my life I've been seeking, knowing if I can regain what belonged to us I'd have achieved the ultimate."

"Couldn't you just buy it?"

Cain looks at me as though he is bewildered by my question, as though I had completely missed the point.

"You have to find it," he replies, scrunching his face up. "Every man has to find his own."

"Not literally."

"Yes. Then it is special. That's what they said."

"Even if it was found in the earth, it still needs to be purified. The gold is just a metaphor. It's the gold ray of enlightenment. That's what I think we're here to find."

"To not acknowledge God is blasphemy."

"You transform yourself: find your own wisdom. You believe Jesus was special, did he have gold? I don't know. I'm just asking."

"He had the radiance–"

"The radiance of gold. A halo of inspiration."

"You twist things to make it work for yourself, so you can live your life without restrictions, disobeying rules-" says Cain.

"Pah! Don't talk to me about rules. You think it's OK to threaten, manipulate and control people. What are the real rules then Cain? You're right and everyone else wrong? Give me a break. The world is a big place and you think everyone should think like you: extreme, fundamental and separate from everything. We need to get away from that. Strip it back to the bare metal and acknowledge the truth that we are all the same, and get away from the 'them and us'. It hurts people. People die!"

"You will never convince me. You need to renounce the evil in you,"

"Ohhhhh. I don't even want to waste my breath talking to you about this. It will make no difference."

"I could save you now? Your soul needs cleansing by the spirit of Jesus Christ."

Jesus, are you having a joke with me right now? Trapping me in a cave with Cain Shimlow offering eternal salvation.

"Look Cain. Let's agree to differ."

"Your soul will be lost."

His words are whispered with searing intensity.

"Cain, in the journal it mentions the gold ray, there is a drawing of this place, Mount Nagual. This is where pure light comes in. It's powerful and protected here because no-one abuses it. That is a gift."

"No-one comes here because the Indians cursed it!"

"No that was just the rumor to prevent it being pillaged and abused while it was strengthening its power. There is a sacred site on top of it where those that really understood it used to hold ceremonies-"

"It was paganism, sacrifice and sexual deviation," he interrupts and reverts back to the journal.

"That is what my ancestors did. They knew it was a powerful and special place. They added to the pure energy with their peace. What you thought was witchcraft was a prayer for peace."

"You are deluded."

"I'll show you, but not now." My tongue is clumsy and I can no longer form my words clearly. While Cain looks for the meaning of life in the old journal I feel my seized muscles cramping and stretch my legs out, leaning on a stony outcrop. I put my head on the smooth boulder feeling like the ground is sinking. I drift to another dimension of sparkles of light, tinkling over my soul like beautiful soothing music as I slip into a world of peace, warmth and light where I become parted from the suffering in my heart. I can hear his voice in my mind, calling me away from the harder edges around me. *Shasta.* The name forms in my mind and I feel him as alive as he ever was.

I'm nudged from sleep by pressure on my legs and the sound of a man's harsh voice telling me to get up. Cain is standing over me, roughly jostling me awake with his foot.

"You've slept enough," he snaps. "It's at the top of the mountain, isn't it? You tried to give me a hint, and it's there in the journal." Cain holds the book close to his chest.

It takes only two seconds for the nightmare of the situation to come back to me. I get to my feet, forgetting that Cain has a gun in his pocket, but with the single minded thought that I must get out of here. Finding strength I didn't know I had, I begin the staggered climb, feeling for each fissure and crevice with renewed purpose. Cain lags behind, puffing and wheezing but there is a down draft. It gives me hope that life and air are within reach and I press on as Cain scrambles and loses his footing time and again.

The air gets colder; something floats into my eye, then more of the tiny feathery flakes caress my face. It's snow falling softly through the opening in the rocks. I move faster, thinking I may be able to get away from Cain. The light is dim as I near the mouth of the cave but the relief of seeing the moonlight behind the snow clouds lifts my spirits as I step into the open. I struggle over the last few tricky rocks and Cain catches up. I finally step out into a silent white world of softly whirling snowflakes and blue moonlight; a place where it joins another world. It's an auspicious junction where trials pay off and shadows vanish.

Cain's footsteps are hushed by a blanket of several inches of snow. My impulse is to find Shasta – to run down the mountain, and look for Shasta where I last saw him, although the stream's current may have taken him.

"Upward!" says Cain.

"No. Enough," I reply, breathing heavily and shaking my head.

"I don't want to have to use this." He shows me the gun protruding in his pocket. I hold up my palms in exasperation, wondering when this ordeal will end. Cain will have to kill me to cover his tracks. I have got to escape.

"Go!" Cain pushes me in the back.

Moving through trees on an upward gradient, the cold air and snowflakes clear my head. If I tell Cain I need to stop for the toilet I could go behind a tree and make a break for it. I could surely out run a man of his age. There is a chance his aim is impaired by fatigue. Then I remember when he shot and killed the bear who shared her den with a young toddler and his sharp eye for the target I saw back then. I'll try it anyway.

"Cain. I need to go."

His face puckers, not understanding. The wind whips snow from a drift in his face and he struggles with his footing. Then it dawns on him what I mean.

"Go there!" he says, pointing to where I'm standing.

"I need privacy. I'll go behind a tree," I reply, and start to walk towards a dark pine silhouetted in the lightening sky - dawn is not far away.

"Stop! You will go there or not at all!"

"I'm not some kind of animal." I abandon that idea and trudge upwards knowing it's not far now. After a few minutes I see the outline of the stones on the top of the mountain. The only thing left is for me to either overpower him or bolt. My heart races at the thought of initiating any action.

Cain is beside me on the few final steps at the crest of the mountain. The snow topped cairn stones come into view. The growing orange and pink streaks across the starry sky are a magical backdrop. My fear diminishes. If I'm to lose my body and become part of this majesty then so be it.

"This is it, Cain."

Cain rushes forward reminding me of an insect: hunched forward, narrow limbs ungainly and without smooth direction. I reverently hold back, feeling the essence of the place and the warmth and vibrancy of its golden energy flowing through me. Tiny hairs on my skin lift up to hold the feeling. I watch Cain as he brushes off the snow and fumbles under the rounded edges of the four stones in turn, moving in an anti-clockwise direction. The journal falls from his pocket. He makes grunting noises and talks to himself with escalating anxiety and desperation.

"Help me!" he shouts, as he turns to the final stone in the centre and the one on which all his hopes are pinned upon. I stand still and imagine myself becoming invisible to him, that I've absorbed enough light to be reflective of the surroundings, making me less physical and part of the energy descending through the early morning sky into the mountain.

His crazed primal shriek tells me he didn't find what he was looking for. He runs frantically around again, checking again, uttering expletives and swearing like I've never heard from him before.

"It's buried isn't it?" he yells, glancing at me then turning back to the stone monument. Even in his demented state he must know that these stones are immovable. He paces back and forward wildly, and loses focus on the sacred indigenous monument, looking for his answer elsewhere, going to undulations in the recent snowfall and clawing with his hands at the humps in the snow.

"Tell me!" he screams at me, saliva spitting from his mouth and hanging from his narrow pointed jaw.

"I'm sorry, Cain. The gold is here but it's not what you think."

"It has to be. It has to be." He removes his pistol from his pocket and aims it at me, but his eyes are askew and a bullet wouldn't hit me at that angle.

"What you're looking for is pure energy. White gold."

"Stop it! Stop with your lies!" he screams losing all remaining control. "It exists. It's mine. The point of my life has been to find it...it has to be here. It has to exist. If it doesn't exist..."

Cain steps backwards, looking skyward as the sun breaks the horizon and bathes the landscape in a brilliant glow. If only he knew he's receiving the purity and power right now, but he doesn't see or feel it and I can't help him. He collapses on the snowy ground, his head in his hands. A lank strand of grey hair falls over his face. He looks up with tears pouring down his face, looking around pleadingly. He continues to mutter to himself, and now seems unaware that I'm there.

"I can't live without a purpose," he says solemnly as though finding a solution and regaining composure. He rises to his feet, moving backwards away from the stone circle looking distant.

"Cain, there is always a way. Why don't we talk?"

"Tara, I'm sorry, for what I've done. No-one was supposed to get hurt. Forgive me," he says wistfully his words carried away on the breeze as he moves away from me.

Cain Shimlow brings the pistol to his head. He holds it there and seems to lose focus on everything around him, moving steadily backwards as though being drawn to the edge of the mountaintop.

"No! Don't do it, Cain!"

Hearing me his head spins round and his eyes meet mine. For a second I see real pain etched on his face; grey eyes catching light in the sunrise.

His face seems to change and become aware again. He looks like he has changed his mind. His foot slips on the frozen outcrop and he snatches handfuls of air. I watch helplessly as Cain vanishes from view. He falls silently into the ravine. I rush to the edge of the cliff side and look over. He is lying below, crumpled and motionless. Cain Shimlow is dead.

In a dazed stupor I pick up the journal from the snow and stumble off the mountain top, making my descent quickly. Several dark shapes come into view in the distance. I hear the buffeted sound of the whirring of rotor blades from a helicopter, just before I see the chopper rise up from the valley floor. My chest tightens. It could be Buchanan's men coming back for me. I hear my name being called out and a far-off recognition of the voice registers as the figures get closer. Cold and confused I carry on towards them, whether friend of foe.

The blurred faces get clearer and for a minute I think it's Shasta: tall, with black hair, except it's short. I'm wishing it's him with his hair tied back, but no. He calls my name again and I realize it's Seb at the front of the search party. He puts his arm out as I approach and I fall heavily into him as my legs give out. Over his shoulder several men, including Barnaby and Patrick, are making their way up through the trees. The warmth of another body and the relief of seeing their faces is overwhelming.

"Shasta," I splutter. It's all I can say looking at Seb, whose eyes are bloodshot. I can't bring myself to say the words. I can't say them if I don't believe them, and I won't believe he is dead until I see it. He had too much life in him not to be alive now.

"They shot him!" I restrain the sob in my throat. It would come hard to Seb too.

"I know," he replies. His voice is husky with suppressed emotion. "They've found him. He's in the air ambulance."

"He's alive?" A black veil is lifting. If he's in an ambulance then he may be OK - but maybe they lift dead bodies that way too.

"He's not looking good," says Barnaby tersely. "We found his tracks. He was trying to head up the mountain. Somehow he made it as far as he did. We found him half buried in snow."

I start to sob uncontrollably. "Will he live?"

Barnaby's face is grave, reluctant to give too much hope. "He's in good hands," he says, wrapping a silver foil blanket around me.

"Leonie? Did you find Leonie?"

Seb's mouth closes very tightly, clenching his teeth so

hard his jaw flexes in a way that reminds me of Shasta's. "Anyone else that was here is long gone," he replies.

I bite the inside of my cheek. They mustn't know yet.

"Except Cain Shimlow. He's dead."

31

The drive to the hospital takes too long. Many of the roads are thick with snow. Shasta will already be there, but in what condition?

"Is Giselle OK?" I ask, facing the debris of the ordeal.

"She'll be fine. They got her in plenty of time. What the hell has been going on, Tara?" asks Barnaby.

For the duration of the journey I make what explanations I can, tripping over myself to know the whereabouts of Leonie and the Buchanans but no-one knows. Leonie was shot. I saw it with my own eyes. I've no doubt her actions were to protect Shasta, which is shockingly honorable, but even if she were alive, which is possible if no body was found, would she come clean about what happened or would she be intimidated into protecting the Buchanans?

As we pull up outside the hospital, Barnaby talks about me getting checked over - I've no intention of wasting a doctor's time. I need to see Shasta. Followed by Barnaby I walk through the automatic doors. I wind my way through the corridors and I hear my name being called. Giselle and Simon are walking towards me, both of them looking pale, strained and surprisingly quiet. We throw our arms around each other.

"Thank God you're OK!"

Giselle's hand is dressed in a neatly wound bandage and she has been discharged. "What the hell's been going on?" she asks, her eyes round. "I still can't believe I got a snake bite!"

"Don't brag," says Simon.

"Shasta's been admitted. I've got to find him."

"What's happened?" Giselle shouts after me, but I've

spied a nurse and I set off to find out Shasta's whereabouts. The nurse doesn't know, but goes to find out. Barnaby fills Giselle and Simon in while they wait in the seating area. I pace back and forward watching every door for news. Eventually a nurse approaches and the hammering in my heart accelerates wildly.

"Is he OK? Just tell me." I can't bring myself to ask if he's alive.

"Are you family?" asks the nurse, checking out Simon, Giselle and Barnaby watching her closely.

"I'm his girlfriend," I reply, acutely feeling the casualness of the title.

"Come with me. Just you!" the nurse replies when the others stand up. Their glances at each other are wary and fearful. I follow her along a corridor, passing patients on trolleys and wheelchairs. I check every one of them in case it's him. The nurse keeps her distance just ahead of me. Either she is in a hurry, very busy or doesn't want to make eye contact.

"Can't you just tell me?" I plead.

"You can see for yourself," she stands at a window and nods into a room. I throw the door open without pausing. The doctor at the bedside steps back as his patient pushes himself stubbornly up to sit on the edge of the bed, and winces as he argues with the doctor that he is not staying in hospital.

"Shasta, you don't have my approval to be discharged!"

"I don't need it. I'm going," he replies, paying no heed to the doctor as he tries to stand up without moving his bandaged shoulder.

I stand watching, unable to speak at first, then step forward as Shasta looks up. Everything else in the room fades out in the narrow tunnel of perfect vision. I reach out to him, needing to touch him to know he is real. I press against him to make sure and he pulls me towards him.

"I thought you were dead," I whisper against his cheek.

"I thought you were," he replies. We lock arms around each other, cheek to cheek and heart to heart.

"If that bullet had been any lower you would have been," says the doctor, reminding us of his presence, before he leaves us alone in the hospital room, holding on to each other.

"I don't want to ever let you out of my sight again," says Shasta.

"Then don't."

"I want you to move in with me, tonight, no more waiting. I want to see you before I close my eyes at night and wake with my first sight of you. Then I know I'll never have wasted a precious moment without you," he says.

"I'll get my things," I reply, pressing my nose against his, eyes open staring deeply and listening to his ragged breathing. Giselle and Simon peer in the window from the corridor, tapping on the glass, mouthing indistinguishable words and pulling contorted faces then they pile into the room, both of them talking at the same time, followed by Barnaby.

"That snake had been fed steroids. It wasn't normal I tell you," says Simon, exaggerating the point.

"You scared it off with all that screaming!" says Giselle.

"I'll give you a lift home," says Barnaby.

"As long as it's definitely gone," says Simon, taking hold of Giselle's arm and making a fuss that the smell in the hospital is making him feel sick. Shasta grits his teeth from the pain of his gunshot wound and makes his way to the door then stops as the others go off down the corridor. He catches me with one arm, and I put my arm around his waist and we walk in silence.

Returning to the tranquillity of Shasta's lake house, I only once let my mind remember that this is where he had been taken from. According to Barnaby, Leonie had turned up at a hospital miles away with an apparent hunting injury - a gunshot wound to her arm. Buchanan's men were no marksmen. Apparently Marshall Buchanan was not in the country, and hadn't been for days. He was allegedly on a business trip to somewhere unknown on his private jet, for which no flight plan had been filed. There was more bad news for them. The results from the geology survey were back. There doesn't seem to be gold in Big Spruce.

"I'm happy they are at least far away. We can get back to normal, but I have a promise to keep," he kisses me on the head and walks away, without enlightening me.

Simon calls with some sad news - Old Sarah had passed away earlier today. It was time to carry out her wishes and give the box to its rightful owner. I'm choked with emotion when I drive over to the coffeehouse to meet Simon, so that we can fulfill her wish. I hug him on the doorstep and he's struggling to hold back tears. Considering we hadn't known Sarah that long she sure had made an impression on us.

We open the store's safe and remove the humble wooden box, wondering what it was that she wanted to make peace with. First Simon opens the envelope stuck to the top of the box and we sit down to read it together, as he holds the little padlock key.

To Cain Shimlow -

I hope this is what you were looking for. My husband unearthed them many years ago, and as he was a collector he kept and treasured them. He didn't try to find their owner, which I was always uncomfortable with, but he felt they were of national importance and didn't want to inform anyone and have to relinquish them.

I heard about your search to retrieve your family's lost treasures and suspect that is what Stanley found. It wasn't my place to return them, nor did I want the hassle they might generate after he died. Stanley was a passionate collector and no thief, but neither am I. If they are yours then please forgive us for not returning them sooner. If they aren't then I only ask that you hand them over to whoever you see fit. I'm sure you're an honest man and I'm sorry for any angst it may have caused you.

Yours sincerely,
Sarah Cunningham

Simon and I stare at each other thunderstruck. Who could have known that the benefactor was Cain Shimlow? But that did nothing to resurrect him now. Sarah presumed he would outlive her, little did she know he would die before she would. His treasure was real, but it was too late for him.

"Open the box, Simon!"

Through misty eyes he fumbles with the tiny padlock key. He opens the box and inside it are eleven gold coins which have been lovingly tucked into purple velvet compartments. There's also a gold pocket watch and a ladies broach.

"Now what do we do with them? Scatter them on his grave? Put them in his coffin?" asks Simon.

"We give them to his widow and then she can decide."

"It seems like a waste."

"I think that's what Sarah would have wanted."

Night has fallen and we close up the coffee shop and drive over to Cain Shimlow's house, where the lights are on and people are moving around inside. Sarah said we were to deliver the box anonymously. We park up at the corner of the street and Simon, who is already dressed in black, sneaks up to the front of the house, keeping low under the window frames.

He places the box on the mat in front of the door, rings the doorbell and races back to the car without being seen. We hunker down in the car as the door of the house opens and Cain Shimlow's widow looks around before picking up the box and going back inside. We watch from a distance through the window as family members gather around her. Our job is done and I hope in the circumstances we've done what Sarah would have wanted. Content that we'd carried out Sarah's wishes, I drop Simon at home before I head back to Shasta's.

Later that night I go to tend to the horses. As I groom Penny in the silence of her stable I hear noises from outside and strain my ears to work out what the sound is. Footsteps – they are light - but I can hear movement out there. I decide that my mind is working overtime and carry on grooming her regardless. Scout is sat outside the stable door, her soft blonde wavy fur moving gently in the breeze. She is wearing a piece of red ribbon tied loosely around her neck. I squat down to her, putting my hand out towards the ribbon, but she stands up and walks away from me treading softly in the fine covering of snow.

On the ground in front of me are two horseshoes like footsteps alongside each other.

"What is this?" I talk out loud to myself as Scout walks a few metres away and looks back at me. Then she stands still again. Enclosed in a clear glass holder is a votive candle, followed by another and another laid out in a line, then another pair of horse shoes. Scout looks encouraging. Her mouth is open and her tongue lolling as though she is smiling, but she won't let herself be caught. I giggle, intrigued by the surprise.

The white candle lights and horse shoes lead through the cedars, making a winding trail in the direction of the lakeshore. I grin at Scout as she again walks away from me when I get close. I break into laughter as the end of the treasure hunt is in sight. In front of me on the lakeshore the wooden jetty is lit with yet more lanterns and candlelight.

A small fire inside a metal pit is spitting and hissing as tiny snowflakes vaporize at the touch the flames. The tall figure in the shadows at the end of the jetty moves towards me as Scout goes to stand beside him. My heart stirs with the greatest happiness when Shasta takes my hand in his.

"What is this?" I beam, giggles breaking in my throat.

"I told you I had a promise to keep," he replies.

I pretend like I don't know where this is leading.

"Scout has something for you." He bends down to her and I follow suit reaching for the red ribbon in the bouncing firelight reflecting off her fur. Then I see it. Hanging from her neck, tied to the ribbon is a ring. Shasta unties it and holds it out to me questioningly. I look at him deeply, knowing the unspoken question he is asking. I reply silently and his lips part into a wide smile. I hold out my hand and watch the twinkling diamond in the firelight as it finds its home upon my finger.

www.ingramcontent.com/pod-product-compliance
Ingram Content Group UK Ltd.
Pitfield, Milton Keynes, MK11 3LW, UK
UKHW021036270726
13967UKWH00013B/2693